A GHOSTHUNTER'S JOURNAL

Tales of the Supernatural
and the
Strange in Upstate New York

by

MASON WINFIELD

Address all inquiries to:
Brian Meyer, Publisher
Western New York Wares Inc.
P.O. Box 733
Ellicott Station
Buffalo, NY   14205
e-mail: buffalobooks@att.net

This book was published and printed in Buffalo, NY
ISBN: 1-879201-29-1

Visit our Internet site:
www.buffalobooks.com

A GHOSTHUNTER'S JOURNAL

□ □ □ 3 □ □ □

PUBLISHER'S PONDERINGS

Everyone loves a gripping ghost story. The type of tale that makes you glance over your shoulder as you sit by a campfire while dancing flames perform a shadow show on the surrounding trees.

Ghost stories have been a fireside staple at my Rushford Lake cottage for years. With some friends, a camp fire without a strange tale or two would be as incomplete as a fire without marshmallows or Pink Floyd tapes.

But the characters in Mason Winfield's newest book are ghosts of a different color. Unlike our fiendish fireside yarns, the fictional tales contained in "A Ghosthunter's Journal" are not so fantastic that they are patently impossible.

Mason has married his knowledge of paranormal research with his wonderful storytelling abilities and has penned a book that causes the proverbial "suspension of disbelief."

The result is a delightfully diverse smorgasbord of supernatural and paranormal encounters, all of them set in Western New York.

Mason's first book, "Shadows of the Western Door: Haunted Sites and Ancient Mysteries of Upstate New York" is now in its third printing and is one of top 10 best-selling books since the company's inception in 1984.

Based on the continuing appeal of "Shadows," we have high hopes for "A Ghosthunter's Journal."

It is a genuine delight to work with Mason on a second literary venture. His passion and enthusiasm have colored every stage of this publishing mission. His attention to detail is a rare trait.

Running a small regional publishing company in this era of mega-mergers has never been more challenging. Our success is a testament to our team of dedicated authors as well as our behind-the-scenes staff. My thanks goes to Michele Ratzel who has been our chief number-cruncher since 1991 and to Matt Pitts, a valued marketing associate who joined us two years ago. Tom Connolly joined the company in 1999 and he has already been a valuable asset.

John Hardiman and the entire crew at Petit Printing and Type Plus in Buffalo have been instrumental in helping to make this book a reality.

On a personal note, I also thank Christian Williamson, one of my best friends who also happens to be my nephew. Christian's fascination for things that go bump in the night has been contagious.

Without further ado, sit back, read on and enjoy your journey down the supernatural footpaths of Western New York!

Brian Meyer
September 1999

A GHOSTHUNTER'S JOURNAL

Tales of the Supernatural and the Strange in Upstate New York

for Mason C. Winfield, Jr.   1920-1992
Long drives and rain set me to summing years,
And one poured half that talk we could have had.
Your life summed back. My debt, Sir, perseveres,
Each page that shines you. *Atque vale*, Dad.

PREFACE

[*Atque vale* : "...and farewell." From Catullus' Latin poem, "Ave Atque Vale" (*Ah-way aht-quay wah-lay*), "Hail and farewell."]

PREFACE

"Where the parapsychologist parts company with the magus lies in the treatment of the evidence."

John Beloff, *Parapsychology*

Late twentieth century attitudes to psychic phenomena and other paranormal subjects seem to coagulate into either indiscriminate credulity or lock-headed disbelief. Though in most of life's situations the real thing lies somewhere between the extremes, it should be safe to say that the outlook of whatever might be termed "the establishment" is solidly materialist: no God, no ghosts, no angels, no spirit. (No UFOs or "Earth Mysteries," either.) Except for a few token and politically-timed religious references, public variance from this position is fair game for ridicule. In the opinion of many, however, materialism has not won its argument to explain the world so much as the rhetorical battle on it. You see that when you start digging. I think neither psychic nor paranormal events are common; but reports of them pile up over time, and the average person doesn't have a clue what's beneath the surface of his or her community.

The house next door may have its drama of mysterious sound effects, moving objects, and troubling dreams. The Masonic lodge down the street could be the oldest building in the community, commemorative of mystical philosophies millennia old. The vagrant muttering to himself on the bus may be the devotee of a secret religion and possess talents that do not meet the eye. An object, artifact, or bone that would rock accepted belief might have been found beneath your own block by its first Euroamerican surveyors. A photograph from a family reunion may feature the pale image of an unexpected member. It's all around us.

In the fall of 1980 I moved back to Western New York to teach English at an independent boarding school. In many respects it was a good place for an independent learner; there were odd off-hours during the school week, and ample vacations in which it was possible to sustain private interests. My own included the paranormal.

My first book *Shadows of the Western Door* ("Haunted Sites and Ancient Mysteries of Upstate New York") was published in the fall of 1997. This "X-Files" survey of the western Empire State must have struck a public chord, because it's in its third printing. *Shadows*, though, was basically journalism, reporting on the tradition of paranormal subjects in my half of New York State. In that work (as well as my years of armchair interest) I came across captivating, powerful stories that were too "classified" to retell in any way that would allow the identification of concerned individuals. This book is a fictionalized account of some of them.

The millennium ends, and paranormal topics are hot in fiction and film, but I see very few realistic representations. It looks like people go from the idea stage straight to writing book or screenplay with few worries about the way things really happen or what the thinkers make of it. I came at this book from the other direction. Imagination has had some play in it, of course. I believe a book's readers should feel that they've been on a journey, and whatever artist is in me could not resist the temptation to make that of this; but there was no need to imagine much, and mostly I just moved the real stuff around. What I've encountered over the years is so much more gripping than books or movies because it's real.

There is probably confusion about someone who, in the last months of the twentieth century, titles his own book (however tongue-in-cheek) the journal of "a ghosthunter." Readers may think of a psychic, someone who "feels" influences; a Sherlock Holmes, arriving on the scene in a deerstalker hat; an exorcist or priest, maybe even a caped eccentric who fancies himself a modern wizard. The real business is nothing like any of that, and each of these tales contains passages intended to acquaint readers with current ideas about paranormal subjects, even taking them along the processes of my understanding. It may weaken the prose, but it might serve a needed purpose, and no one else seems to be doing it. If I were to add any other advice now for the would-be ghosthunter, I would say to be a generalist. Be the spider, with a bunch of lines out; camp at the center of the web, not in any corner; know what to make of it when any strand vibrates; know where they all connect.

Supernaturalism is alive and well on the reservations. The Seneca - the Native American nation historically associated with Western New York - are one of the original confederacy we call the Iroquois [also "the Six Nations," less familiarly *Hodenausaunee* (People of the Longhouse), though that's what they call themselves]. The influence of the Iroquois on the modern world may be greater than that of any other Native American group; some say that the outline of their union was the model of the representative democracy we Americans are so devoutly exporting. The Iroquois teachers have heavier gifts in store for the interior life, would more of us only realize it, and what I know of their spirituality is probably the heart of this book. I wonder why people in the Eastern parts of our nation go to Chaco or Shasta for their "vision-quest" when such a treasury is here in upstate New York.

If the world is going to the Devil on a drive-thru, I couldn't tell it during my research about Western New York. The people I encountered were helpful, unpretentious, and good-natured. Many of them devote great time and energy to a cause unlikely to gain them anything other than the feeling of putting a little more good in the world than it would have had without them. I read their obituaries sometimes, the scorecards of a life, and wonder about them. They go into the green graveyards with no other articulation behind them, no books, no speeches, and no record of what they felt or thought. I wouldn't "talk down" to anyone and I won't write that way; I wanted this book to have enough to chew on to accommodate second readings, but I've failed if it eludes the comfort level of the people who helped me write it. This book is for them.

East Aurora, NY
June, 1999

THE TWELFTH MEDALLION

Many literary critics seem to think that an hypothesis about obscure and remote questions of history can be refuted by a simple demand for the production of more evidence than in fact exists. But the true test of an hypothesis, if it cannot be shewn to conflict with known truths, is the number of facts that it correlates and explains"

Francis Cornford, *Origins of Attic Comedy,* and cited by Jessie L. Weston, *From Ritual to Romance*

THE TWELFTH MEDALLION

[If I were pressed for my general theory on ghosts, I'd have to say that I suspect every square foot of the earth could be as "haunted," for all we know, as any other. The spirits of the human dead - or whatever we take to be them - seem to manifest only in exceptional circumstances which may be related to energies where they are observed, either natural energies in the earth (maybe even geo-magnetic) or psychic ones related to human activity. If I were asked the chances of this being the whole story, I'd say probably ten percent, but it's the best I have. This is the one real "ghost" story in this book, and the only tale of any sort with a seemingly tidy ending.]

I

One March night in the early 80s I spoke to a historical society at an old train station-turned-pub near Lake Erie. At the end a handful of people came to the podium, which was not unusual. Psychic experiences can be intensely personal. Many people feel they have to hide them from a materialistic world, and it touches a chord when someone in a public set-ting gives them credence. Some even approach me as if I were a confessor. I always emphasize that I'm a quester just like they are, and that night one person was disappointed to hear it. Help was what she was after.

Lisa Warren was a pale, skinny woman with russet hair and owl-glasses. She was here with her fifteen-year-old son, a little bigger but oth-erwise just like her, and so shy he might have been mute. Her family lived on a little road by Lake Erie where a big house long said to be haunted seemed to be casting an influence over others near it. Her story sounded like a movie.

A year earlier Lisa's sister had come to live with her. Soon one of her little nieces began to talk about an occasional visitor, even referring to it as "here" sometimes as she was questioned. The adults sensed nothing but mild poltergeist phenomena which might or might not have been valid, but toddlers displayed odd, reflexive gestures mimicking a hanging: drap-ing belts, strings, clotheslines, and the like about their necks. The influence seemed to be getting stronger, and Lisa believed that the presence behind it was trying to kill the children in her house. She was hoping I could end it.

What they wanted was a wizard: some revivalist preacher to get Satan hence, some latter-day Solomon or Prospero, a Michael Scot, har-nesser of demons. What they had was a country English teacher, and I made no effort to conceal it. I comforted them as well as I could, using all the old platitudes: that there are no unquestioned reports from anywhere in the world of someone killed or even hurt by any force from the super-natural; that such influences probably don't know who or what they are if they truly do come back at all; that there may be nothing behind the whole subject of ghosts. Furthermore, I had never heard of a real situation in which a house sent out "evil" influences. The subject is virtually alien to serious research. Lisa was still convinced that something from the other side was trying to hurt the children, and that it might soon succeed.

THE TWELFTH MEDALLION

II

I hear a hundred ghost stories a year about my own region of Western New York. Not many of them are convincing, but I file them all. Those I go into deeper either interest me for my own reasons or involve someone asking for help. In cases of the latter, I ask for a little help back.

My approach to paranormal sites has always been "roots-up," and I deputized Lisa Warren to find out all she could about her house, about the house on the point, and about her own immediate area. This included anything dramatic in history and anything unusual in architecture. I looked her shy kid in the eye and got him to smile, suggesting he interview his schoolmates about local ghost lore. I also asked Lisa to get some help from whatever faith she had been raised in. There's no magic wand in psychic cases, few of which are sinister in any way, but the major faiths seem to have some power in such matters, sometimes even a decisive one. I won't speculate about why, but centuries of experience could help. My part of the homework was to talk to the historians.

As I look back on what I've written so far, I'm amazed at how much I remember of Lisa Warren's story. Something was familiar about it, and I'd only half-listened to her, searching my mind for what it was. As I drove the thin country roads to my campus apartment that night, I had it. During my high school and college years I'd spent plenty of time on the bay that footed Lisa's dreaded mansion, at the summer home of an old friend. Lisa's road was on the other side of it, but had she mentioned the bay by name, there would have been no need of all the figuring; and I'd heard something like her story before.

It was Kay Jacobson, the wife of that old lakeshore friend, who, ten years earlier, had told me a tale about a house on their bay that could only have been the one Lisa meant. A neighbor, a doctor's very Catholic wife, grew convinced of a psychic crisis centered around the house on the point. A prominent figure from the Church - Mother Theresa in the folklore - pronounced that house one of the most dangerous she had ever seen, and gave the doctor's wife some consecrated medals to bury around it. This was done in the early 70s, and, according to the story, the trouble stopped.

I remembered that mansion well, the most Gothic-looking on the point, but otherwise little different in size and importance from its handful of neighbors. On the point's landward approach was a large, flat, open meadow with a few trees and a shiny pond near a patch of woods. In my high school and college days, the whole area seemed spectacular and surreal to our lively little bay community. On our moonlit walks (in predictable states of consciousness) we sensed a thrilling quality about it, seemingly nothing between disarmingly still or turbulent.

In the weeks after my lecture the town and county historians gave me some background of the region around the point. Some of it was gloomy, and fit right into the unrestful pattern typical of paranormal "zones" where effects cluster. Some thought LaSalle's ill-fated *Griffon* - still rumored one of the ghost ships of the Great Lakes - went down hereabouts, and there were engagements nearby in all of the Colonial wars. A

British frigate in the War of 1812 chased some smaller American vessels into the mouth of the creek nearby and opened fire. An archaeological team reported ghost sightings as they worked on its banks, and odd sound effects: beautiful, melodic chanting carried on the still air of warm twilights. A burial mound near the creek was exposed by the water, and bones were carried into the lake. A remarkable artifact - a pipe in the shape of a mastodon - was found near here, dating from the last Ice Age.

The supernatural reputation of the house and point was new to the professionals, but I didn't make much of this. Historians uninterested in ghost lore tend not to notice it unless it has entered print, and it sounded like this tradition was new and very local. There had been a scandalous death in the suspect house in the first decade of the twentieth century. There was the suggestion of a little panky of the hanky variety between the lord of the manor, a manufacturer whose name I will not publish, and a Hispanic serving-girl, maybe a nanny. She picked a heck of a way to resign: she apparently hung herself at the threshold of the master bedroom. It was the talk of the county for decades.

Social behavior seemed odd about the point, too. People who did one irrational thing in their adult lives often did it here. A retired businessman from Buffalo returned with an axe to a summer party to renew an argument. (His intent was unclear since Todd Jacobson's father, the six-foot-six-inch former mayor of Amherst, confiscated the tool immediately.) An old woman who lived on the bay, supernaturally devoted to her passle of dogs, died or passed out in her home and was partly eaten by her own brood.

My Six Nations contacts felt that trauma was long associated with that area. The mid-seventeenth century war in which the Iroquois extinguished the Eries, the "Cat" Tribe, as a cultural group was a sprawling affair, one of whose climactic engagements was probably near the point. I suspected something else that my sources could not or would not recall for me.

III

Three weeks after our first meeting Lisa Warren and I met again at a lakeshore diner. She had done several interviews and taken excellent notes. Most valuable was her work on the twentieth-century history of the house on the point, including some follow-up on the girl who had died in it. The year was 1904, and Maria Sanchez was a twenty-year-old immigrant, but whether Mexican or Spanish was unclear. Most people who believed in the supernatural trouble presumed she was behind it.

The builder didn't long outlive the maid, which was no big surprise. He was in his late fifties at the time of their affair, and may have had a drinking problem. His children lived in the big house until the 1930s, when it was sold and underwent a pattern of short occupancies, absentee owners, and several periods of emptiness and neglect. The only steady modern occupancy was that of the current owners, a power couple who had been there for fifteen years. They were not inspired to warmth by Lisa's inquiry, denying anything paranormal, even unusual, about their house (as they wore heavy sweaters inside and a fireplace blazed on a summer day). Neighbors recalled a handful of murky old ghost tales about the point, which were useless for my purposes except as they revealed local tradition, the smoke beneath which there's often fire.

Lisa's triumph was a talk with some carpenters who had worked on the house in the early 70s for the current owners, about the time the fateful medals were allegedly buried. They detailed a list of oddities: never-opened basement doors, cold spots, sealed-off rooms, and false walls. Strange lights in the master bedroom had been reported from outside, and a very odd natural sound effect noted within it: one worker found that, from a certain spot, he could hear three people in a rowboat in the bay, hundreds of yards out and below, as clearly as if they were in the garden beneath the window.

One room upstairs - the presumed site of the illicit fin-de-siecle lovemaking - met with radical poltergeist effects whenever it was remodeled. Lisa's carpenters had found the work vandalized and their tools and materials thrown around the strange space whenever they returned in the morning. They had observed earlier attempts to rework the room, and, taking their own interest in the case, contacted others who had ventured an unsuccessful remodeling for another family in the 1960s. Similar effects were reported, and several times even vast, inexplicable quantities of bat droppings. So far as anyone knew, the room was still shut up and left alone.

The carpenters also reported odd behavior in children. One of them spotted the owners' little son wrapping the loose end of a clothesline about his neck, the gesture Lisa had recently observed in her nieces and nephews. They unwound the tot, who could have gibbeted himself by sitting down. Apparently outgrowing his metaphysical susceptibility, he was now a solid lad readying to play lacrosse at Middlebury. But the questions, as far as I could see, remained: what started the rumor-cycle up again, and did we really need to do anything about it?

IV

For the average believer, associating psychic phenomena at a site with a mournful death in its history is the instant tendency. It is not mine. I have no idea why psychic effects happen. Though I certainly keep many possibilities in mind as I review a case, I see no reason to indict the spirit of a departed human; even reported apparitions ("ghosts") are not often accompanied by sounds, moving objects, or other paranormal effects (at least verifiable ones). In short, blaming things at the troubled bay on a tormented serving-girl would be too neat a solution. Nevertheless, we had such a handy candidate for a haunting (even though her apparition was never reported) that this possibility could not be ignored.

As always, I had to question the validity of the case I was presented. I'd seen no psychic effects, but the researcher - disconnected from the site, visiting it rarely or briefly, viewing it almost like a pen at a zoo - almost never does. The evidence here was anecdotal, though it was good - a long and exceptionally consistent pattern - and combined with an enduring sense of oppression in many people who lived in the area. I considered that a sign of something, and it reminded me that there could be dangerous human crises with real consequences, whether or not the causes were paranormal. This was another reason to stay involved; but the house on the point was simply interesting. It fit the classic profile of a haunted site in almost every particular, and each venture at investigation turned up more in the same vein. I decided to keep digging.

On a warm May night Todd and Kay Jacobson joined me for an evening of brainstorming on the porch of my apartment at school. With us too was an old friend I call on in special cases, whom I wanted with this one from the beginning. This was Athena, a striking red-haired woman, an astrologer and non-professional medium with a near-genius level IQ. We'd conferred beforehand, and, with a few presumptions filling in the blanks, laid a likely chain of events before my married friends. What caused the recent outbreak of paranormal reports was the problem at hand.

"We need to track down as much as we can of the story you told me years ago," I said to Kay, a petite, dark-haired woman. "I at least want to be sure of the material details. Something makes me think the medals may be the X-factor."

Athena nodded. "I'm curious about them, too. A circle of medals around a house shouldn't quell supernatural influences. It might keep them out... or in."

"I'm sure of what Mrs. Czarnecki told me," said Kay. "Maybe a dozen of them are in a ring around the house, twenty or thirty feet out, just a little way down. She buried them herself one midnight with a garden spade."

"And they ended the 'evil,'" I said speculatively, actually emphasizing the last word. Since it's such a useless stereotype, I'm real careful about associating evil and the paranormal. Any force out to hurt children meets my definition.

"Mrs. Czarnecki thought that was the end of it when the medals were buried," said Kay. "Can't give you the exact year, but you didn't hear much talk around the bay about ghosts in the 70s. Till recently."

Todd Jacobson is one of my truest friends, but discussions like these most often fail to amuse him. A big, good-looking preppie who, I have to admit, answers to Fitzgerald's physical description of Tom Buchanan, Todd said (with about the same academic enthusiasm), "Great story. So why won't the owners even talk about spooks?"

"Maybe there aren't any," I said. "Maybe there were and the owners never saw any. Psychic phenomena aren't common, even where they do happen. Maybe the owners are diehard materialists who wouldn't admit anything until it was absolutely out of control - which it just about never is. I've seen all these scenarios before."

"Something set off the new cycle, at least the rumors," Athena said. "Maybe something changed. How do we find out if the medals are still there?" Todd offered to go around the point some night with his contractor-brother and a metal detector, and that part of a plan was set.

V

On the first Saturday in June a small party met at Todd's lakeshore home to launch our first psychic experiment. The original four were joined by Lisa Warren, Todd's brother and sister-in-law, and Father Holden, a venerable Franciscan Lisa had met through the Church. We started our evening with a late-afternoon tour of the bay, the cliffs, and the point. The current owners were touchier about their property than owners past, so we didn't get too close to the mansion in question. We sat on the cliffs and looked out on the sun over the lake as we compared notes.

In the week preceding, Todd and brother Rob had explored the troubled point and found a ring of eleven metal objects about fifty feet out from the suspicious house. He had shown me his diagram, a rough affair in Bic ball-point ink on a legal pad. The spacing of the eleven marks was fairly even except for an obvious gap on the landward side. It looked exactly as if there had once been twelve, and it was the last piece in the picture I was cautiously putting together. It ran completely counter to my observations about the paranormal, and I set it forth here with much abashment; basically, it made too much sense.

After the builder's family left that house there was a forty-year period of short stays, lasting until the current owners moved in. We didn't presume psychic influences were behind it, but it certainly matched the classic pattern of a ghost protesting changes in environment - like the departure of familiar tenants or the remodeling of new ones - either by withdrawing for good or by manifesting more vigorously. The fact that the present tenants at least claimed never to have been troubled could be explained by the burial of the medals about the time they moved in. The missing medal could account for the recent revival of bay gossip; the full ring had either quelled the psychic influences or kept them confined. If (as testimony maintained) the psychic effects only showed in small children, the recent outbreak would have been noticed only by local families that had them, and no longer at its suspected source.

I put no literal trust in folklore, but you'd have to be a fool to ignore it. I'm also used to foggy timing in psychic cases, but in this one the total pattern was consistent with what we observed of reality. Accustomed, however, to the incomprehensibility of anything pertaining to the paranormal, I can't tell you that I could seriously consider a word of the above theory. It was, as I say, too neat, too consistent with expectations, and leading to a picture that would have been very welcome to the leader of many a "ghost tour," dispensing quick and direct answers to paying groups of novices. Yet, as Jessie Weston points out in her gorgeous *From Ritual to Romance* (lifting its motto from Cornford's older book on Greek theater), when you're trying to make sense of situations in which evidence is nearly unobtainable, people can't reject your theory just by asking for more evidence. What counts is how many other things your theory explains. This is a very useful concept for dealing with the paranormal.

I laid all this out to my friends on the beach, as well as the only solution that made sense: that we had to get things back the way they were. We had to get a medal back in the ground and close the circle, optimally at a time when the questionable entity was in the mansion. This further complication was to make sure we weren't simply locking the spook out for good, which might only cause problems elsewhere.

"I doubt if it's that simple," said Athena, and she and Father Holden shared a smile. "But if it is, what are our chances of getting another medal from the Church?"

"I have the sense that these were very special, possibly even blessed by Father Baker," said Father Holden, a small, grey-haired, sixtiesh man. "Locating and returning the original medal could actually turn out to be easier than convincing anyone at the Basilica that there was a good supernatural reason to shorten their supply. At least get started looking for it and see how it goes."

"Who could have lifted a buried medal?" I said.

Todd made eye contact. "You know, there is an old guy out here a lot with a metal detector. He's the caretaker of the houses on the point. They call him 'Garden Ed.'" Eyebrows went up.

VI

The late twentieth-century "circle" is generally a much more free-form thing than the stagey classics of the nineteenth. Athena liked conditions that kept her from self-consciousness about producing results: soft acoustic and instrumental music in the background, and participants free to talk and write. Athena starts by talking about her impressions; then her eyes close and the session begins. Sometimes when she prepares she can shape the reading, much the way that what you read before you sleep can color your dreams. In this case she knew what she was looking for. Our idea was to let Athena range and try to open up to whatever harried spook might be in the region. At about ten we settled around a table on my friends' porch, readying for our reading. The waves sounded as they must have from the house that was our spiritual focus.

I've seen all kinds of readings. I've seen psychics as wide awake as anyone, looking into their patrons' faces and giving their impressions. I've seen the mediums appear bored, singing for their supper from the shallow reaches of their own minds. I've seen even Athena have an off night, stammering forth her associations from somewhere in her own unconscious, calling up phrases of little more originality and relevance than those on the bowling-ball-shaped toy, filled with murky water and a pale plastic octagon that floats its engraved platitudes into its window. ("Reply hazy. Ask again.") I've also had the feeling, very rarely, that other presences were at hand. The best of Athena's sittings are of this kind.

I've heard these tapes a couple of times. It's Thene's voice, from calm discursive beginning through spelled pause and then raptured resumption, but there's no accounting for the variety of the speech once she gets going. In her whispers, chuckles, statements, queries and non sequiturs, all different in tone and accent, you imagine a host of alternate personae: a nearsighted elderly couple looking for each other in a dim house; a crotchety lakeshore farmer scolding his mate; taunting schoolchildren; a confused mother looking for her daughter; faint, puzzled voices you hear once and not again. She may have been plugging into the early days of the house and the point. I could swear I caught a few words of Huron-Iroquoian, and I only know a few. No voices spoke directly to us, though, and none sounded vigorous enough to be an indignant haunter. The only one that approached clarity was a querulous voice that seemed, not angry, but abstracted. To this we tried to speak. I would compare the experience to trying to hold a phone conversation with a four-year old wandering in and out of the room in which the receiver dangled.

We asked it its name and interests here, but it never answered us directly. It left us and came back. It seemed in a state of urgency, fretting about this and that, muttering to itself, responding to some hidden summons as if there was a bell ringing far off. Whatever psychic shallows Athena could troll was surely a chaotic place.

The spook seemed to have forgotten its name. We had to get it to tell us what other people called it. "Nenn-ni... Everybody looking for Nenn-ni..." it said once through Athena. Its replies were generally so lacking in substance that the experience became tiresome, and it must have registered, because Athena stopped talking and came to, almost like waking up from a light sleep. We gave her a running summary of the voices and played back parts of the tapes. "Doesn't look like we hit this time," I said. "No 'Maria Sanchez.'"

Father Holden just sat quietly and smiled. He would become one of my most valued friends, and I would learn that his favorite means of teaching was guiding others to their own realizations, sensing that the process was part of what could be learned. The young aren't so patient. Athena looked at us like were were a little slow. She is fearfully bright. "Nenn-ni?" she said, arching an eyebrow. "Nanny?"

We listened again to the last few minutes of the tapes. "She's not vengeful," said Father Holden. "She's confused. She couldn't even remember her name."

"I go back to my original plan," I said. "We need to get the spook back in the house and a medal back in the ground. In short order."

"What does it mean to get a ghost back in a house?" said Todd. "Do these things even have a place?"

"Our ideas of place and time are almost certainly irrelevant," said Father Holden. "But they may not be useless. Psychic essences do seem to be site-specific. This one is apparently branching out, assuming that there ever was any real trouble ten years ago, and that the medals settled it. There's a danger in these cases when we cling to our first impressions, and people can be very impressionable. But I agree that your plan makes the best sense so far, and it doesn't seem as if it could do any harm. If it comforts a troubled neighborhood, even psychologically, it will do good."

VII

It was late summer before things fell into place, and the surprising thing is that they ever did. We caught quick breaks on two fronts.

Todd and Rob Jacobson had dropped in on the old caretaker suspected of lifting the medal. He was too shifty at first to answer questions, but he was clearly a packrat, and they had the feeling that anything he'd ever acquired was still with him. One mention of a curse brought it all out.

On a late-night metal-detecting venture "Garden Ed" and one of his fishing buddies had turned up something on the landward side of the special mansion. They were hoping it would be an old pistol or the like that they could sell. It turned out to be a medal that they could suspect was made of gold. Most of the delay in getting the object back was spent in a frenzied search of the groundskeeper's curio den of a home. The object was gold-plated, and with some Latin and ornamentation on it, but it was otherwise unimpressive. Obviously something invisible that had been done to it was the key to its effect.

We'd been beating the bush for contacts with the mansion's owners for weeks, and one turned up. Tom and Lee Davis were a Buffalo couple I'd interviewed on another case years before. We'd since become good friends, and it turned out that Lee had graduated nursing school with the woman of the house on the point. Lee called her in July just as the couple planned a vacation. They didn't trust their seventeen-year-old to mansion-sit, and asked Lee and Tom if they were interested. I heard about it the same day.

The seance was next. Our plan was to hold it in the house on the point, reach the spook we thought was behind the trouble - which we felt had been the most vigorous voice at Athena's last sitting - and signal someone outside to bury the medal near its original spot. All we needed was for the second sitting to go right.

On a late-July night that Athena had declared an astrological high point we started our hopefully final seance. We were happy to include Tom and Lee Davis, the couple that put us here in the first place, though they were not otherwise involved in the case. People provide energy, and it's the more the merrier at seances - as long as there aren't any jokers. All it takes is one, and it was probably good that the two most likely candidates - the brothers Jacobson - were outside with beeper, medal, and shovels. They'd already dug their spot, and it wouldn't take a minute to rebury the medal.

We thought the owners might object to so many strangers in their home, so we held our sitting in a screened porch. That was just as well, for it was perfectly atmospheric, more in touch with the warm, still night, and in constant earshot of the nurturing waves. This space was almost an arboretum, furling leafy plants all around us as if they sprouted from wall and ceiling, beaming dusty candlelight back to us. Even humble fixtures - tables, lamps, and chairs - took an occult glow.

Maybe the impressive house had some influence as well, because Athena took surprisingly little time to find her voices, and she was as deep in as I've ever seen her. To hear her speak for these presences is, in a dignified fashion, what it would be to station a fine human impressionist, a Bobby McFerrin, in a dark rain forest with a live satellite hookup, and hear his renditions of random, faraway sounds - shrieks, whistles, calls, roars, songs - that no one can give sure species. You feel that person serving as your eyes and ears in some tangled realm a long way away. There are so many questions you want to ask, but the first direct response to you might imperil her, certainly her capacities as an observer. You just have to listen to what the hearer gives you and hope the forest doesn't swallow her up for good. You find yourself far away into the best of Athena's speaking.

At one point around ten o'clock Athena seemed totally taken over by a single voice, which we could only assume was that of the impulsive Maria. She spoke haltingly, as if her spirit-control were out of practice. It took awhile to figure out what she was getting at; she seemed to be cooing to children; she fretted about some damn curtains for the longest time. She had an accent.

Once Athena even opened her eyes as she talked. I'd never seen her do that at a sitting, and it was a sign to me of the influence's strength. She looked about the room in front of her, right through us, even when she made eye contact. It was as if she watched a troubling film play itself out on a screen around her; we were all behind it; we could observe her through it, but only she could see the images.

Thene delivered up a languid, preoccupied ramble, as if whoever spoke through her was hurrying from room to room putting out little emergencies, not wanting to face any, daring to neglect none. I could see why the children were copying her mortal gestures: it was a sympatico. She'd been so solicitous in life that her discarnate personality was still tending tots; she didn't know what she was sending them, which was another part of her dying obsession. She would never be more "here" than she was at the moment. I hit the button on the beeper. I was sure that the medal was in place within seconds.

"Maria-Nanny" went on for another few minutes but a change seemed to come over her. Without moving, Athena in her chair was doing a great job of conveying the impression of a complete about face, of a person looking at something behind her in an environment in which physical direction had no meaning. It was a young girl losing concentration for a few moments, trying to ignore herself being called.

"Maria, child," said Father Holden, who must have seen all this before. He called her several times more. "*Maria, niño.*"

"*Padre?*" Athena said for her, but she was listening over her shoulder, not to the good old man in front of her. The confusion that came over her had to be seen to be imagined. I honestly think there was not a one of us in that room who did not believe she had been taken over. It was as if we were so engrossed in a movie or play that we believed the lead actress was the character she portrayed. We felt sorry for her; we wanted to comfort her instantly; we wanted to help her be at home.

"*Maria, mi hija,*" said Father Holden. "My daughter, my girl. *Tienes que marcharte.* You have to leave us now."

Athena searched inside her mind before she answered. Her eyes darted. "*Me tengo que ir?*" ("Where should I go?") Most Americans have some Spanish lines floating around in our minds, but I had not known that Athena was fluent.

"There is a house for you, my child," Father Holden said, with the gentlest voice I have ever heard. "*Una casa para usted.*"

"*A donde?* Where?"

"*Sigue la luz, mi hija.* The light. Follow the light. Yes, the light."

"*La luz?*" Athena said, then looked about. Her eyes shot from one to another of us as if hoping one among a roomful of strangers might intercede for her against a ruffian. We said nothing, none of us. The change came.

Athena shrugged her shoulders as she sat and literally took on the impression of shouldering a burden for a journey. She looked like someone realizing that no solution was easy to a problem that was worse, that she had to trust herself to a leap into a cloud over a chasm, hoping to land on the other side; to a swim between air holes under the ice. Tears came.

"The light, my daughter," said Father Holden.

If it hadn't been on tape, I doubt any of us would have believed it. The last utterances were abstracted, waifish, halting, and dimming. I think we all got the impression of someone wandering away from us down a long dark corridor - one forbidding but so familiar that it had even become comforting - then recognizing something that caught her attention, following it out of hearing. And then she brightened, and murmured what I could swear was "*Padre?*"

Athena's eyes fogged over and she blinked, as if she had fallen asleep in her bed at home and, without closing her eyes, come out of a dream to find us around it. She wiped her cheeks, astonished to find them wet. She cried a bit longer, unaware what there was to cry about.

"*A Dios,*" said Father Holden thoughtfully. "To God... Maria."

VIII

We walked on the half-mile horseshoe beach, Father Holden, Athena and I. A high wind soared above us, whipping smoky clouds past the moon, making the diamond sky a mobile of disparate elements, lucent, beautiful. It was adventurous; it was every sky from poetry or folklore I'd ever imagined or loved. I wondered if it held a new star, a small one drawing away from us.

Near the bay's northern point we looked back to the one holding the houses. The once-troubled mansion was lit up as if it hosted a party, and I thought I could still hear its music. Our friends had been a little spooked by the night's doings, and seemed to be cutting loose; but I could hardly believe what we had all seen, not because it was apparently paranormal, but because it had gone according to design. I was astonished, almost guilty, that this plan of mine appeared to have fallen in place. I wondered what I had done. It could have been a sense of power, but I felt nothing but responsibility. It's easier to let fate take its course; then you don't feel to blame if things go wrong. "Did we just see what I think we did?" I said.

"The pattern points that way," said Father Holden.

"Do you think she's on her way... to 'Heaven'?"

"It is my faith," he said.

"Yeah, but do you really think it?" I looked at him.

"I can't prove it to you."

"I don't expect to see it proved," I said. "I just have to wonder what we may have sent her to. I'd feel like I'd killed her again if some plan of mine had banished her into nothingness... undreaming sleep. Darkness. She fought so hard to stay."

They sat at a table. I stood at the edge of the water, gazing into the dark Erie. The Great Lakes are huge, but this part of this one, this honey-eyed bay, had always seemed domesticated to me, tender; at that moment it was vast and enveloping. I could have seen wonder, mystery, and infinity in a cup of water, in a woodland pool. That must have been a true moment, because it is there.

I shot a stone into a silver wave. It skipped a few times, looped up once and caught moon, shining like a coin, and then vanished into the thinning white wakes.

"Is that what it is?" I said. "Is the living world like us on this beach? When someone dies and shoots into the beyond, is it like that rock I just skipped into the water? Some of them glimmer a minute in the sight, in the memory of those who loved them, and then they go under. Most of them never surface again or make it back to the shore. That last skip into the light we just saw could have been Maria's flicker. But all they knew is gone.

"I never thought it would come to this. I guess I never thought about anything. It was enough work to get everything arranged right; it was a project, and it kept falling into place, so I went with it. I guess I wanted to see what would happen. It was like that time I shot a robin with my BB gun when I was ten. It was a long way off and a hard shot, and I just popped from the shoulder to see if I could do it. It was sickening to see the bird drop. I still think about that. What did we send her to?"

"Someone was calling to her," said Athena, who had heard the tapes.

"She fought so hard to stay," I said. I looked back to the trees on the cliffs behind us, then out over the bright waves and the bow-moon above them. I imagined that it launched that tender, tiny new star. "She was so afraid. She was clinging to the light."

Father Holden waited. "There was another light," he said.

THE LITTLE PEOPLE

...But Lewis and Clark, in their *Travels to the Source of the Mississippi River*, found among the Sioux a tradition that a hill near the Whitestone River, which the Red Men called the 'Mountain of Little People' or 'Little Spirits,' was inhabited by pygmy demons in human form, about eighteen inches tall, armed with sharp arrows, and ever on the alert to kill mortals who should dare to invade their domain.

W. Y. Evans Wentz, *The Fairy Faith in Celtic Countries*

THE LITTLE PEOPLE

No part of their territory lacked its presence; but to the old Seneca the stretch of hills along the Allegany River near Salamanca was a zone of psychic wildlife and indigenous witchery, "dragon-ridden," as Yeats would say. For me, to drive the roads, admiring the vistas and woody slopes, is to envision the metaphysical fauna of Iroquois lore: the old witches huffing their fiery breath on the midnight trails, the little forest people, the bipedal deer, the giant cannibal High Hat... the spirits seem to steam from the very ground. To actually be part of the landscape - to run, ride, or ski the hilly paths - is to breathe and feel them.

The other world must have been too much with me that hot early June afternoon as I rode the State Park trails. At that spot on "Snowsnake" where the course falls away, the trees part, and you get a shot of landscape about eighty degrees wide, something spun my wheel and yanked the bars, and over the both of them I went. I hit and rolled, the bike bounced on its tires, and we came to rest as if I'd set it beside me to admire the view. Usually I come up cursing from a spill like no other time in my life - the occasions are therapeutic in that respect - and hop right back on; but that day I just sat where I was. It was the first time I'd stopped and really thought in weeks.

The school year had ended in mid-May and I'd been running non-stop since. I'd already squeezed in a Vermont trip and a pair of doubles tournaments, one of which I'd won. Even that day had held about all I was asking out of life at that stage. I'd read history over breakfast, played a couple great sets, given a pair of hitting lessons, and spun down to the park for a ride. I would write in the early evening, and was looking forward to that late-night assignation with the new woman. Everything was new and fresh between us, everything about her was magic to me.

But the past weeks as I reviewed them, contented as they were, seemed compressed into days. Even as I read and wrote, supposedly intellectual activities, it had been with purpose; it was a computer function, moving words around or taking them in. There had been no down time for growth or understanding; I realized again that packing day or life too full was not the best route to either. What counted was to know life as well as have it. I resumed the ride; but the time-out had been needed. I renewed my vow to be more reflective than life usually inclines us, not to let its meaning get ahead of me, not to lose its savoring as it passed.

I showered (with biodegradable soap) in the State Park lake, engulfed a burrito, and wrote on my laptop in the Ellicottville coffee house. Looking forward to the fifty-minute sunset drive to East Aurora, I checked my answering machine, hoping to hear the musical voice of the flame of the day, accepting my invitation to a midnight tryst; but an earlier one of a different sort was proposed, and by my Seneca friend Eric Reynard. He must have known I was nearby and would accept, because he left good directions to the house near Salamanca, ten minutes back toward the park.

I entered the maze of hilly old roads, some of them once timeless Native American paths, and climbed and plunged among the green that had seemed so impenetrable from Route 219. Now I was invisible to those still on it. I peered into the trees, the pastoral scenes, the dirt-sideroads.

On a bench behind their house I joined Rick, a ponytailed young man of middle height whom I'd never seen in anything but jeans and a casual shirt. With him was his cousin Alvin Green, a dark-skinned young Seneca with black hair cut away in front and long down his back. Alvin was six-three and very lean, but wide-shouldered and really put together. He looked like such an athlete - or a warrior. I wondered if the old braves had been like this. Like most of the Iroquois I knew, Alvin was a plain-spoken fellow who cut to the chase with whatever he said.

We sipped beers, starting a fire, watching day dim. The lawn sloped to the treeline where the hill fell away and gave us a fetching vista, each succeeding ridge thinner green and realler blue. It's remarkable to study a natural landscape in these northern woods, observing its transition from full day to night and meditating with it on its changes. "This was my grandfather's cabin," said Alvin, breaking a silence. "This patch of land goes pretty far back in our family. Our Uncle Peter lives here now."

"Peter... Arvidson?" I said.

"Yeah, the historian," said Rick. "He gives talks at the museum in Salamanca."

"Uncle Peter lives in town most of the year," said Alvin. "He moves out here when it warms up. Says it's the only part of the year he really likes anymore. He goes for a walk every night. That's where he is right now. Somewhere out there," he said, gesturing with his Molson toward the trees.

"If anybody talks to the Little People, it's him on these walks," Alvin continued, smiling. I knew what he was talking about - the *Djogau*, the Iroquois fairies.

"He says he's never seen them," said Rick. "But he still looks for them."

"He thinks we're crowding them out," said Alvin. "They keep moving farther away."

I was fascinated. I knew that some Iroquois claim that their Little People are or once were real, and that actual tokens of these tiny humans - tools, weapons, pipes, even scalps and bones - are still on the reservations, handed down in families, never shown to Whites. I thought of the diminutive tunnels and artifacts found beneath some Central American cities, and the ancient mini-mummy from a cave in our own Wyoming. I wondered if there could be any real story behind the Little People.

A small old gentleman in a wide-brimmed hat came out of the trees and climbed slowly toward us, leaning on a long stick that he held a foot from its top. Though flanked by a big short-haired fellow of about fifty who gestured and talked constantly, he smiled and seemed alone with his thoughts. It was easy for us to get rid of our beers and move the cooler before he should have noticed. The Iroquois teachers know what alcohol has done to indigenous peoples around the world, and most of them disapprove so strongly of drinking that it's a gesture of respect to forbear in their presence. The man beside him walked with a beer, it was true, but I would learn that 'Ol' Ed' was the one Iroquois Uncle Peter suffered to drink around him - possibly because it was useless to discourage him, possibly because it was safer for him to be in sight when he did it. By the time the old fellow neared us, he was fully socialized. He sat in a green wood patio chair and seemed happy to see me. Ol' Ed fell silent, looking around and blinking.

"This is Mason," said Rick. "That writer-guy I told you about."

"The writer-guy?" said Uncle Peter brightly. "Well, hello, Writer-guy. That's a fancy title."

"A jock of the mind," I said, tapping my temple auspiciously.

Uncle Peter beamed and clapped himself on both knees. "What brings you out here, Mason Writer-guy?"

"He likes to write about folklore," said Rick. "And religion. I know he's into that Celtic stuff pretty good. I thought it might be fun for him to meet you, Uncle. I figured maybe he could ask you a few things."

"Maybe he could," said Uncle Peter in his melodic, wobbly voice, eyeing me over so deadpan that we all laughed. By the time the fire prospered, a handful of young Iroquois men had brought chairs down from the house and joined us. They were pretty reserved. Rick and Alvin introduced me to them, but I don't remember names.

"You meet any Little People, tonight, Uncle?" said Alvin when everybody was settled.

"Aah," he said as if he disliked the answer. "Too much gas and bustle around here. They like their own music. Maybe I'm just not ready yet, too. I keep thinking I'll see them once at least before I go on from here. I think I'm getting closer."

He pointed at a space in the treeline. "Right down there is where my uncle - Uncle David Green - used to meet his friends, the Little People. Whenever he wanted to talk to them about anything, Uncle David left a bit of tobacco there at sunset. Next evening they'd be waiting for him, and they'd talk till it was dark. He was special friends with one of them. Used to tell me his old age would have been miserable without his good friend among the Little People.

"This little fellow was a chief, I think. Uncle David didn't put on any act, but we're descended from Red Jacket, so I guess the little chief considered him worth talking to." There were a few chuckles.

"I think there was a good friendship there, because the night after Uncle David died folks could hear drums and a mourning-song going on in the woods. Before long they turned to songs of celebration and praise, and people could hear my uncle's voice among them. We thought maybe Uncle David stopped off to say his goodbyes to his other friends before he left the earth for good. There was certainly a batch of laughing and singing in the woods every night for a few weeks after Uncle David left us."

I savored the beautiful tale, gazing into the blue space above the fire where thin fumes twisted trees and horizon. Bright sparks flew into it when somebody kicked a log. One of the newcomers, a tall longhair, cleared his throat and spoke. "My grandfather saw the Little People when he was a boy, down on the reservation in Salamanca.

"It was a bright sunny morning, and he was playing near the garden at the back of the house. He looked up to see a couple of small folk near him in the grass. One of them asked if his baby sister could come play with them in the woods. She was walking up the pathway, and he saw one of them take her by the hand. He didn't know what to do, but his mother came running and picked her up, and the Little People were gone. He said he never saw them again, but he remembered that day. It was the only story he ever told like that, but he told it all his life."

I'd read a tale like this somewhere, and wondered what was going on. Either this guy's grandfather was the source of the motif, the event was common, or I was getting my leg pulled. One of the oldest jokes around the Long House has been to string along gullible Whites who'd done something to deserve it - with impossibly straight faces. "Were the Little People red-skinned or White?" I said. "What were their clothes like?"

"I never asked him those questions," said the fellow. "Just little people, I guess. They seemed at home in the trees and flowers - like they belonged, more than we do." A couple others shook their heads as if to say, "Go figure," or some other phrase of affable wonder.

"Aaah, heck," said Ol' Ed in his dusty voice. "I had a meeting with them little folks that made me swear off the malt liquor, and you can talk to me right now if you want." He looked around, blinking.

"You swore off the malt liquor?" said the fellow who'd just told his story, and a few guffawed.

Ol' Ed had a beer in his hand, which he raised to eye level and studied so peculiarly that everybody laughed. "I did swear it off, though," he said in his high halting voice. "You laugh if you want to. But one night back in the sixties I was walking home up the railroad tracks after a little too much evening. You know that bit of tracks right down by the river?"

"'Witches' Walk?'" I said, referring to the legendary flats of the Allegany near Salamanca. A couple of them looked at me as if surprised.

"That's the place," said Ol' Ed, "and if something was going to happen around here, that'd be where you'd figure it. Well, it was a cool November night, and I musta slipped or something and got a knock on the noggin from the rail that woulda left me there till dawn. And dead I woulda been if I'd laid there all the night. But I came to a coupla hours later, cold to the bone, with flurries of them little people pulling me awake. They tugged on my hair till they had me up, and pulled my pants' legs till they had me moving. They didn't give up until the blood was flowing around back in me, and the lights of my own warm cabin in my eyes. I wasn't better from that for a good long time, but I woulda slept my way right into the next life if not for them little folks." Ol' Ed looked around like he dared anybody to tell him his story was unlikely. I wasn't sure what I thought; I'd read something close to this story, before, too.

"My grandmother used to tell me about something in her family when she was little," said Rick, "back in the days when disputes over land weren't always peaceable, don't you know."

"At the end of April my great-grandfather Isaac Jamison was having trouble making the rent on his piece of land. After a useless talk with the agent of the Holland Land Company, he was wandering around the banks of the river, wondering how to break things to his family, when he heard a voice asking him what was wrong. My grandfather saw a little man right near him.

"When grandfather Ike got to the part about the rent-collector always foreclosing on people so he could buy their land himself, the little man shook his head. 'Not too long ago, a word or two to The Cornplanter would have settled for a rascal like that, and it wouldn't have been pretty. Give him his money, though, right on time. I'll see that it won't do him any good.' The little man pointed beneath a bush. There was a sack of silver dollars.

"Grandpa Isaac started thanking him, but when he looked up, the little man was gone. A few hours after Grandpa Isaac paid, the rent-collector noticed that the satchel didn't look the same. He opened it up, and the silver coins had become maple-sugar patties the same size and shape, even with George Washington's head on them. He hollered out loud, but Grandpa Ike already had the receipt. The money'd have to come out of the rent-collector's pay or his boss would think he was crazy.

"From then on good luck followed Grandpa Isaac. When he died he left plenty of grandchildren and money for them all. They said until the end of his life every now and then when he was at a party he'd slip off to the woods at the back of the house with an extra glass of whatever he was drinking. When he came back both glasses would be empty, and he'd look like he'd just heard a joke."

Uncle Peter squinted with happiness and made a little triumphant stroke as if delivering a hook to a shadowy opponent, and laughter went around the fire. Into its aftertones Uncle Peter said, "Sometimes life teaches us lessons we need to learn."

"The Celtic Little People will do that for you, too," I said. "That reminds me of an Irish tale I told last month at a gathering. On May Eve."

"Oh?" said Uncle Peter.

"It's called 'A Night on Knock-Grafton' - a tale that shows you the fairies can be tricky and powerful, but also sometimes a bit silly." Uncle Peter looked at me with interest, so I went on.

"There was a good little man named Lusmore with such a big hump on his back that he could hardly walk. He made his way in the world by weaving and selling baskets. One night on his way home from the market he stopped and rested by the ancient fort of Knock-Grafton."

"What was that like?" said Uncle Peter.

"Never seen it," I said. "But probably a big green earth-mound, maybe with a ring-ditch, maybe a standing stone at the top, maybe a circle of them. The fairies were thought to live in such places."

"We had things like that around here," said Uncle Peter. "Our historians didn't know who made them."

"At least yours admit it," I said. "But Lusmore picked a bad night to rest beside an old earthwork: Halloween, the Celtic New Years' Eve, when natural and supernatural realms overlapped.

"Lusmore heard angelic fiddles and pipes from inside the mound, and hundreds of beautiful little voices, but like a broken record singing, 'It's Monday, it's Tuesday...' (I sang this ridiculously.) Then they'd stop, as if waiting for they didn't know what. Then they'd do it all over again. Figuring they needed some help, at the pause in the music Lusmore piped out into the night, 'And Wednesday, too!'

"They went quiet, but then the voices took up the song delightedly with Lusmore's addition. A door opened in the side of the hill, golden light streamed out, and a wind blew Lusmore like a leaf into it. It was a magic palace, brightly lit and decorated in the center of the prehistoric earthwork. 'Aren't you the grand fellow,' the fairies cried, 'to give us a fine new ending for our song!'

"A little man came from the crowd and said, 'Lusmore, Lusmore, your hump is no more!' He clapped, and Lusmore's hump slid off his shoulders to the floor. Cautiously, Lusmore raised his head and stood up so straight he was afraid he'd hit his head on the ceiling. The fairies sang even more merrily than before, and he danced with them all night.

"Next morning he woke up in the green enclosure with the birds singing around him. After praying that it wasn't a dream to every saint he could remember, Lusmore reached behind him. The hump was gone. He jumped up from the ground as spry as a dancer, and went skipping home in a fine new suit. Since the hump was gone, his old clothes wouldn't fit him, and the fairy tailors had decked him out while he slept. People hardly recognized him.

"The story did the rounds. Next Halloween Jack Madden, another humpback, came to the moat of Knock-Grafton, hoping for a spot of the same medicine and a new suit to boot. But Jack Madden had always been a peevish lout, keener about what he could get than what he could give. The music started, but, because of Lusmore's improvement, with no natural pause. The fairies were chanting their 'Monday, Tuesday, and Wednesday, too!' to their hearts' content. Jack Madden couldn't wait for his goodies, and spouted out, 'And Thursday, too!' against all time and tune. 'And I'll be a 38 regular,' he added, 'when you straighten me out.'

"The mound opened, light streamed, and the wind blew Jack Madden into the hall, but this time the fairies were mad. 'Who spoiled our tune?' they yelled. The leader stepped up, said, 'Jack Madden! Jack Madden! Your life we will sadden!' and clapped his hands. Lusmore's old hump came out of nowhere, flew under Jack Madden's collar, and zap! stuck to his back as if it had grown there. The fairies kicked him out into the moat, where he was found double-humped and groaning in the morning."

The others chuckled politely, but Peter Arvidson seemed delighted with the story. He reached his stick into the fire, and turned a red log as he spoke. "Like I said before, sometimes life teaches us lessons we need to learn. When we think we're through learning is when we need to learn the most. I remember a story about an old chief on the Tonawanda

Reservation. He thought he knew most of what he needed, so he needed his encounter with the Little People, too.

"The old chief was a farmer and merchant, and doing well after the British got kicked up north to Canada. There'd been a batch of Mohawk around here under Joseph Brant, and when the war ended they weren't coming back for their land. This was how Chief George Ben had gotten his head start.

"He gave himself a White name, calling himself after two men the Six Nations still praise - George Washington and Ben Franklin. He almost named himself Washington Franklin, but that was the name of a big former slave who was living up here, and someone gave the chief the feeling he wasn't supposed to like the Blacks too much. So George Benjamin it was. Everyone called him George Ben.

"Chief George Ben had great hopes for brave sons carrying on his name. But his wife had nothing but daughters, and he stewed about it all the time. Whenever they had another girl he was madder and madder. You can tell he needed some help from somewhere. Longhouse People don't think that way. He'd given up hope of a son and, when the seventh kid was born, he was out in the fields watching some guys dig a ditch.

"Word came that it was a boy. He just 'bout went crazy, dancing in the fields, ordering up whiskey for everyone. But when the naming-ceremony came, Chief George Ben couldn't think of anybody in these parts special enough to be the godfather to his son. Oh, no! He was going to Geneseo where there were some real aristocrats.

"Round the end of the day Chief George Ben wasn't too sure where he was. He met up with a very small man at rest on a pony, who told him that he'd missed the sign at the crossroads, back the way he'd been. The Chief couldn't remember any crossroads, but he turned around, and ran into the little man again. 'How'd you end up here?' he said.

"Chief George Ben got some new directions and rode off, but he was lost again when it got dark. 'You don't listen too good,' somebody called out. It was the little man, who invited him to spend the night. They came to a cabin in the woods, but it was a big, fine place inside, with family, servants, and a feast waiting. Their liquor made him so happy that George Ben wanted to stay up all night; but it was so strong that, after dinner, he fell into a deep sleep.

"Time passes fast with the Little People," said Uncle Peter. "Well, Chief George Ben had himself a good long sleep - about six weeks. The little man had taken George Ben's clothes off him and hung them on his horse. When the horse got home everyone thought old George Ben was dead. After all the speeches and services, everybody was just settling down again when the real George Ben woke up in the house of the Little People, bare naked.

"'Up and out of here, you lazy beer-head!' hollered the little man, holding three big snarling dogs. Grabbing the sheet he'd slept in to cover himself, Chief George Ben ran to the road.

"He asked for rides from people passing him on horse and cart, but they thought old George Ben in his sheet was a ghost. They ran off and warned the village. Every door was locked and the priest sent for by the time George Ben made it home around nightfall.

"The priest threw holy water on George Ben, and, when that didn't keep him away, beat him on the head and shoulders with the cross he carried. Only when George Ben got it away from the priest and gave him a couple knocks back did things straighten out; but George Ben was a changed man after that, you better believe."

A couple of the young fellows whooped and clapped at the end. "And now that I've got my piece in," Uncle Peter said, getting up, "I might as well get some sleep and let you young guys do your thing. It was nice meeting you, Mason Writer-guy."

"I better get up there," said Alvin Green in a minute. "Sometimes he has trouble with the stairs."

"He's got Ol' Ed with him," said one of the others.

"Ol' Ed has trouble with the stairs," said Rick and Alvin pointing at each other, and we all laughed. The others went up to the house, leaving me and Rick looking at the nearby trees, the fading distance, and the bright afterglow in the horizon. I didn't know what he was thinking, but I was positively giddy. For a writer, a White guy, a folklorist, to have been part of this evening's story-telling was inspiring. It was dizzying. It was an auspice, a blessing on the season. It would have to be a summer of growth.

"All this book-work you're doing," said Rick. "All this teaching, writing, studying. What's the point of it?"

"I want to get somewhere," I started, a little disarmed. "It takes work. I want to get published, get out there, get a voice."

"I know that," said Rick. "But what for?"

"You can't help the world if it can't hear you," I said.

"Well, that's my point," said Rick. "Are you ready to catch what you're chasing? Once they do listen, what are you going to say to them?"

"To love the earth, to love the truth, to love animals, to love thought..." I stammered. "To love each other... To try to find spirit... It's hard to put it into one sentence. I don't have only one thing I want to say. I think I'd try to show them, not just flat out tell them. You have to illustrate what you're saying, you have to grab them. This is hard to summarize."

He thought a bit, looking off to the sunset behind me. His dark eyes carried flecks of the rose-gold sky, slurred into a tiny, gorgeous, almost glyphic pattern that I thought might be some old symbol. It vanished when he blinked and turned to me. "Well, that sounds pretty good. I hope you get your chance."

Alvin Green came down from the house now brightly lit inside. He said something to Rick, then turned to me. "The guys have some business to discuss with me and Eric. It's private like - just for the members of the Nation."

I shrugged. "I gotta get going."

"I didn't say that right," said Alvin.

"Get Uncle Peter up," said Rick. "He says who stays or goes."

"Don't worry about it," I said, heading for my car. "Thanks."

THE LITTLE PEOPLE

"Wait up for me, OK?" said Rick.

"Why?"

"I want to talk to you about something. Just wait, OK?"

I stood in the driveway, looking again at the sky, studying the salmon afterglow through the spaces in the black-pine branches, marvelling at the almost liquid scene, wondering suddenly if I belonged anywhere. Not many people guess anymore how introverted I am. Even into my twenties, tiny slights of the sort that other people at least appear to take as part of the rough and tumble of life could hit a nerve and send me into a funk from which I doubted myself almost completely. I see that my least successful adult gestures - bluster, bravado, whatever - have been attempts to blind others to that vulnerability, succeeding only, perhaps, in blinding them to my essential care for them. I'd respected the Native American experience - and disliked White presumption - too much ever to presume it was my place out here; but the storytelling had swept me up completely, and I'd come crashing down at the end.

Rick came up. "I talked with Uncle Peter," he said. "Those guys can go someplace else if they got something to discuss."

"No problem," I said. "It's been a great evening."

But even as I answered, Rick brought his hand around from the other side of his body and showed me something cupped in the palm. The milky light was still strong enough for me to see that it was a human skull, perfectly articulated, about the size of a ping-pong ball. It was tawny, tarnished bone as far as I could tell. A few of its tiny teeth were missing.

I was dazzled. This I had never anticipated. My credibility had been stretched long before, but it had never yawned wide enough to admit something like what this seemed to mean. I didn't want to dishonor the moment or this relic by staring at it too long, but it had to be real - and it couldn't be. I looked away, so dazed that I listened absently to what Rick, a leader and a teacher in the Six Nations, was saying. Only later did I realize how affirming it was.

"You know, it's all the same," said Rick. "What you're doing, what I'm doing... Celtic, Iroquois, Hindu, Spiritualism... Christianity, Judaism... We're all trying to pull the world in the same direction. Some bad people think that only their exact take on things can be right; but sometimes some pretty good people get wrapped up into thinking that way, too. Maybe the difference is that the good people can't bring themselves to hurt others too bad in the process, and most of them eventually get it by the end, anyway. May take them a bit of time, that's all, and you need to have a little understanding for it. But it's all the same, and you're doing your part in it the best you can."

When he was sure I'd looked my fill, Rick cradled the relic into his side. "See you later this summer," he said as I stumbled off. "You OK to drive?"

MEDICATED GOO
(THE SALVE OF KNOWING)

And one day towards the end of the year, as Caridwen was culling plants and making incantations, it chanced that three drops of the charmed liquor flew out of the cauldron and fell upon the finger of Gwion Bach.

Lady Charlotte Guest, the *Mabinogion*

MEDICATED GOO

I

From a vacant wheelchair - the only seat outside the nursing station - I worked on my laptop, waiting for my interview. The nurses and I ignored each other, but from time to time a big old man in pajamas and a sort of punitive desk - a combination of high-chair, stocks, and, seemingly, commode - entered my notice. Man and desk-thing edged an inch or two at a time down the hall, attempting to be furtive when passing the nurses. Every time he seemed about to get out of sight, a nurse came up behind him, flipped a switch on the back of his chair, and drew him back the twenty feet he'd taken fifteen minutes to cover. One time he just had the door to the stairs open, and when the nurse came up to close it he swatted at her tricep with his thick-wristed hand. "No slapping, Bob," she sang.

She set him directly facing me three feet away, and double-clicked the latch at the back of the appliance. The fellow rocked a bit fruitlessly, then sat still. This was quietly amusing the nurses, and I was resolute not to ruffle. I worked a few more minutes, feeling the old fellow eyeballing me. He had glasses, slick thinning russet hair, and ruby cheeks and nose. His tiny hazel eyes had the gift of remaining expressionless behind their bottle-lenses.

"Hey, buddy." I eyed him above the screen. "Get this... offa here," he said confidentially, knuckling the tabletop that flared around his waist like a timber tutu and kept man and contraption one. "Yeah, just... get this offa here."

I kept working. "Well... Tell you what," he said. "Have you got a butcher knife, or a... hacksaw?"

"Now Bob, don't annoy the nice man," said one of the nurses, wheeling him away. "Remember what we told you about annoying. Come help me with the paperwork." The noncommital hazel peas regarded me as they withdrew.

A khaki-suited young doctor of Asian, likely Filipino, ancestry walked up with his hand out and introduced himself as Rob Notaro. "You must be Mr. Winfield," he said amiably. "Man with a laptop."

We walked through a few doors and came into a glassed-in space for observing people they were hoping to give society-practice. All around it were others: living quarters, rec spaces, kitchens, laundromats, et cetera. We sat where we could focus on a kitchen in which a fellow was making from utter scratch what I could have sworn were pastry turnovers but for the fact that the filling of choice was a single bay leaf apiece. As we watched he took one sheet of the manic delicacies from the oven and put another precisely in.

"That keeps Andre busy all day," said Rob nodding to him. "We were hoping you could give us some ideas."

"You mean besides substituting a little jam for the bay leaves?" I said. The man was about thirty-five, neither tall nor broad. He had olive skin and short curly black hair.

"He was a graduate humanities student at UB. He was also a poet and performance artist, pretty involved at CEPA galleries. You might even have heard his name. He was a little on the edge to begin with, but he was bright and very functional. He seems to have encountered something that literally blew his mind. Through interviews with his friends and professors, we were able to establish that he was involved with a strange group of people in the city, and he hasn't been the same since. We think he was exposed to a new drug."

"Ever think of the cops?" I said.

"We didn't find them easy to interest from any angle. Andre didn't have a trace of anything illegal in him. Whatever befell him was surely self-administered, and he shows no signs of hurting himself or others. He's a simple, sweet-tempered sort who has lost his ability to function.

"Usually people that damaged show other signs of trauma. Drug use, head wounds, past psychological problems, mood swings, hormonal levels, chemicals, brain waves... Nothing. This guy just doesn't fit any of those patterns. It sounds like there may be a cult involved, possibly religious. We thought this situation might cross more into your domain than ours. We certainly wouldn't know where to begin."

"A Buffalo group?" I said. "I'll poke around a little. Where do I start?"

"He keeps ranting about someone named 'Taurus.' Taurus this and Taurus that - seemingly the person who gave him the drug. 'The Salve of Knowing,' he calls it."

I repeated it. "A handy phrase."

II

Truly secretive groups are rare, I think for several reasons. One of them is that truly secretive people are rare. All it takes is one member of a group to babble once and the key to understanding is out. Another reason might be the simple vanity of individuals. Many people captivated by the mystery of occultism would like to be widely regarded as mysterious themselves. The paradox comes in that this takes publicity, which they often crave. Also, many groups actively seek converts. It's not unusual for modern societies to solicit members through flyers pinned to telephone poles, and this is not to refute their legitimacy. Their interests may be so compelling that they're compelled to share them. Maybe there's even a financial incentive at the top; that's not a good sign, but, again, no automatic denial of the group's mystical sincerity, merely the proof of a material goal added to it. Would you think a doctor was illegitimate because he charged for his services?

So. I was looking for a group I'd never heard of, led by a man I didn't know. I tapped my professional contacts - religious, academic, literary, occult - to the last drop and got nowhere. I sent word out through the informal "New Age" network. Still no go. When I started asking people in the community, though - a last step that would have seemed foolish had experience not taught me better - it turned out that the name "Taurus" was all I needed. The man behind it was a familiar figure on the Allentown streets, a frequent visitor at many shops, and a fixture at the grungier clubs.

Mystics often stand out from the general population in respect to their sex drive, either the conspicuous lack of one or (like some politicians) the proverbial "motor always running." For years Taurus - of the latter category - had salivated over my friend Kerry, the younger sister of one of my doubles partners, and dropped into her Allentown dress shop to make a pass about once a week. She had always rebuffed him, but so blithely that his feelings - if he truly had anything besides appetites - were never hurt. It was effortless for Kerry to get us invited to a meeting of his group. I met her at an Allen Street cafe and we walked two blocks to a small party in a second-floor apartment right out of the 70s - fragrant music, tie-dyed incense, and blaring shawls. I was astonished when Kerry introduced me to the mage himself, a shaggy, wide-faced bohemian of forty. This was the mysterious Taurus?

He certainly stood out in my visual memory, despite the recent haircut. I'd marked him years before on the streets of Allentown, thrashing around outside Topics coffee house, studiedly projecting hippie dialogue. *Man,* for instance, was a personal pronoun; everything noteworthy was "far out"; and *Oh, wow!* was a standard interjection. This was a quarter-century after Woodstock One. His image as the paragon of a loser had been sealed by another spectacle at a Buffalo vegetarian restaurant (the late, lamented Preservation Hall).

Evidently the tame, twentiesh hippie couple at Taurus' own table shined not brightly enough, because an unseemly measure of his banter tossed the way of another and a big dreadlocked Black man. Refined, well-spoken, and with a linebacker's build, the Black could handle himself in any arena; but, resenting the intrusions on his behalf, I almost said something. In our day some Whites try very hard to befriend Blacks because it's cool to have Black friends. It infuriates some Blacks who sense it, and this one seemingly did. Furthermore, he could hardly talk to his friends under the incessant jive. It was an effort of humanity not to snarl, but his everwearying rejoinders clipped such agreeable poise that the longhair could pretend they were whimsical and continue his flow into the neighboring conversation. After what seemed half an hour the Black delivered a line and a look so direct that not even Taurus could mistake either.

The longhair made eye contact, stunned, all pretense at whimsy failing. For the first time he understood the knife-edge he'd danced upon. The big man stood, laughed scornfully - a pounding seemed possible rounded the table, and sped outside, leaving Taurus blinking in relief. This was the elusive mystic? Tell me next that Wavy Gravy is the Anti-Christ. Yet Gurdjieff and A. E. would have seemed wackos, maybe even John of the Cross, had you met them before you knew who they were supposed to be and fame made you accede to their eccentricity. Life had taught me to make no final judgments on appearances, and I decided to settle in for the ride with Taurus.

The reverse at first didn't seem true. Host and guru Taurus wasn't thrilled to share the spotlight, but his group was actually pleased to see a writer. Maybe they sensed a convert, even one who could provide them

the covert notoriety they might have craved. I was here only to observe, and
for a solid hour observed nothing more mystical than wine, grass, and
stoogery. This had been typical party merriment among the "soft" drug set
for decades; maybe these things really should be illegal, if for no other reason than the needless fools they make us mortals be. I was glad Kerry and
I had arrived late; the point of the evening might be coming sooner in my
visit.

The pipe they passed throughout the evening was undoubtedly
laced with something, probably opium. I had no difficulty refraining, nor
did Kerry. I needed to keep my faculties, and didn't want whatever happened from their drug, if I was offered any, to be confused with some
other I could get every day if I cared. One time that I allowed the pipe to
circulate past me Taurus made some quip I couldn't hear over the Deep
Purple, but I'm utterly immune to that sort of pressure. Kerry just told him
to get on with things in the tone I could imagine her using to decline his
fortieth pass.

Their theme music was a 70s compilation tape, and, though some
of it I liked, virtually none of it met my definition of psychedelic. Just
because the musician did drugs and the disc is decked with Op art doesn't
mean the music has that hypnotic capacity, and for me most of this was
having the reverse effect. About midnight the first funky strokes of what I
immediately recognized as the old Traffic song "Medicated Goo" seemed
to perk everyone up. Taurus commenced broad gestures like a cartoon
character readying for a delightful dish, making eye contact with some
favored associates sure to take the cue. He went rummaging around in his
wooden chest and came up with a thumb-sized tub used for the tacky resin
I knew as "baseball grip." He passed it, never leaving his hand, from the
middle of the small room, hovering over the Ouija-board table so that each
of us might dip in a fingertip. ("You put it on right here," said one to
another newcomer, gesturing to her forehead. "When we all do it.")

Bearing in mind that this was a potentially dangerous contact drug
that had already ruined one good mind, I had to be careful. I also wanted
a sample. Noticing that the drug seemed to effect nobody yet, I judged that
the skin of the fingers - with few pores - was impermeable to it. I dug a
wallop of a dollop - probably double the usual dose - with my middle finger, the pad most tennis-callused. Taurus and some others 'Oh-ho'd'
admiringly, as if this alone was the mother of all feats.

Cool to the touch, "the Salve of Knowing" was a waxy, tawny,
translucent substance with a smell piny like retsina, the Greek wine. With
a joking gesture I transferred almost all of my sample from one hand to a
dollar bill in the palm of the other, which I folded and transferred to my
back pocket. It was effortless to distract my fellows; these folks were really looped. Only Kerry was on to me.

As we all waited with our fingers poised, I realized that the
sprightly song had been the signal for the expected delight, and that its
position on the tape may not have been coincidental. Its opening tones
provided a moment of anticipation as the group could look around at each
other and realize that the moment was here, like children suddenly remind-

ed that a contraband treat was waiting ("Here it comes again!" "Are you ready for a mind-ride?"). As the song readied for its first vocals, Taurus could rise and shimmy about the room in his best impersonation of rhythm; the song entertained while he passed the ointment and made sure everyone was served; and at its finale, a repeat of its introduction before the last chorus and its long fadeout, was a single, sonorous Winwood soul-grunt at which everyone could apply the knowing rub. In concert, every-body raised their indexes and spun the daub into a fingertip-sized space just below the middle of their foreheads. I'd like to think Taurus knew this was "the third eye."

I did likewise, but with just the residue on my finger. It was enough. I sat waiting, for a few seconds wondering if anything would hap-pen, for a few seconds more wondering what it was, hearing different music, a distracting crest of steady, almost liquid sound effects - rustling and tinkling like bubbling brooks and winds through trees - that kept me from hearing any outer sounds. Then patches of faint azure light - which I envisioned like neon-turquoise starfish sequentially climbing up to coat an egg that was the world - seemed to creep up and around the perception-areas of my mind, so that I was no longer seeing anything around me but tame, bright, milky blue-green light. All other thoughts fell away as I clung to the only vivid one in my mind. It became all-consuming.

For some reason, the thought was "Scheherazade" - yes, the woman who told the 1,001 tales of *The Arabian Nights* - perhaps inspired by the imagery of the hanging shawl before me, perhaps by the Renaissance album of the same name I had recently played, perhaps from having read the word in the last week. Tracking every image and implication associat-ed with this thought in my mind, I lost touch with all outside it.

I saw images forgotten but so familiar - from films and paintings I couldn't remember seeing but knew I had, even images formed within my own mind from strips of literature I had read over the years back to my earliest days, even inspired by songs and smells, sense impressions of all types, all wondrous and beautiful and heart-inspiring. I saw the sublimity of the Near East, the majesty of Islam, the wonder of fiction, and the intrigue of love - all symbolized in the images of fascination and grace that my mind was reviving, whipping up from its own depths. I smelled the champak and the jonquil, I plotted with viziers, I duelled with scimitars, heard the sitar and tabla, felt silk and skin and amorous allure... I saw the honey-skinned dancers, wedded Parvati's vestals, ancient women so sens-ual no one of my century knew them...

In probably thirty seconds it was subsiding, and I was ever more part of myself. If nothing else, it was a wonder to feel these images from the deep ranges of my own mind, but they were absolutely possessing. I felt like I had nearly passed out. My admiration - and pity - for these hearty souls doing the full dose increased. No wonder it was but one a night. They must have been absolutely obliterated. I would be lucky to walk in fifteen minutes.

III

On the following afternoon I brought in enough of my smuggled sample for Rob Notaro to test, and this time there was no waiting period at the clinic. I described what I'd seen.

As if he guessed that I had tried it, Rob's expression said, "And?..." I told him everything of my experience, down even to an analysis and absurd conjecture of the focal image "Scheherazade."

"It's a mind drug," I said, "a contact hallucinogen like a brain-cocaine, though from my dose I couldn't give you its limits. It was over quickly, I would say within a minute. It seemed like an hour, and the after-effects were longer. Right as it crested I forgot about everything except the thought I held in my last moment of detachment, my last moment in the world. That was the one the drug homed in on. I could feel the other thoughts falling away around it. Fascinating."

"Where do you think your images were from?"

"I think from within my own mind, but from such hidden corners that it was a marvel to watch it bring them up. It was the most comprehensive churning of the deep ocean of my mind I've ever experienced. You know how you occasionally get a random image from your childhood-mind that's so fascinating and has so much impact, associated as it is with all the other moods and emotions of the moment in which you had it? This thing brought up a harvest of them. It was heavy. And I had a tiny dose. It tapped so deeply into hidden corners of my mind, but it was focused around a central image. This thing may have real potential."

"Did it give you any idea what happened to our friend Andre?"

"The quick observation is that he OD'd. From the tendency of the 'Medicated Goo' to make a single thought spellbinding, and the observation that he seems to be fulfilled doing a simple repetitive action, I'd say that Andre's having flashbacks, and focusing on a coincidental concept that may seem simple to us, but for him, it's all his world. That's my best guess. He's stuck in Goo-gear."

"Interesting," said Rob. I could see the wheels turning. "Be real careful about this, OK? If you decide to do any experimenting, it's against my advice, OK? But if you're going to do it anyway, you can do it here. It would be safest."

"Sure, Rob," I said smiling insincerely. He knew it. I wasn't doing a potentially psychic experiment in any laboratory, let me tell you.

IV

The drugs in vogue when I was a kid were all soft - nothing addicting, nothing potentially lethal, nothing (like they have now) that could quickly make itself more important than any of the other life-drives. For me they were just like toys, preludes to real adulthood, and I didn't bother with them a year or two out of college. Now I'm too busy. I always thought that if I was ever to take up any drug again, it would be like Doyle's Sherlock Holmes does his dope: rarely, on special nights, when everything else is done, in the privacy of home. Lock the doors, turn off the phone, stoke up a fire, and observe the drug's effects on your mind.

Learn from it; do something with it; write, paint, muse. Use it like a fine wine, not candy. I'd arranged a March night like that in my cottage.

Rob Notaro had appealed to me to stay in touch with him about my experiment. Out of respect, I called him just after dinner, and, as he'd requested, right before the experience. "I'll call you back in an hour," he said. "If you don't answer, I'm coming over with an ambulance."

I locked the door, put on a stack of CD's, set pen and journal before me, and set out to see what this drug could really do. I still had an ample dab, at least as much as I'd seen any of Taurus' crew do at a pop. I fingered it, still on the bill in the baggie, wondering if it had kept its power.

The more I thought about what I was about to do, the more I realized I was taking a risk. I was mighty happy I'd done a weak dosage at Taurus' place. I wondered how those folk could do the shots they did. They were also stoned and drunk every time, and that had to block some of the drug's effect. I suspected that my more moderate dose had been what enabled me to step just enough back from the experience to measure it. For me it might have been a discrete walk in a garden, from which I could still describe flowers; for them it was a day at Disneyworld and too many rides to remember.

I rubbed a little dab an inch above the space between my eyebrows. I looked into the fire, fascinated as always by its deep citrus colors, reds and yellows and oranges, in the cinders and gilt black of the bricks around them. One of my favorite songs from the Relativity album *Gathering Pace* came on, and I dwelt into its medieval feel, into the strings and harmonies. I watched a spark fly from the red logs against the sooty gold-licked bricks. I thought of one of Taliessin's riddles about fire. I was gone.

I saw the spark soar up and out the chimney, wondering at its course in the untimed night. I saw it pick its course above the cottages, the trees, the campus, the hills and woods beyond, through time, across continents, to other fires. I looked in on the old bards at their hearthside chanting, with the ages of taletellers, blind Homer to the unknown Beowulf-poet, strumming their lyres with bronze strings that firespark hue, spinning their worlds of melody and verse, their other-worlds of magic and purety found nowhere but in the mind of the imaginer. I heard their astonishingly captivating tones, music and poetry in one, and realized I could have listened all night without understanding a word. They spoke to a part of me that had never been addressed in my life, and it was a treasury to hear it.

Even as I tripped into my own imagination, I was struck and spellbound the more by the seeming truth of what I saw: the mead-horns, the sooty beams, the hounds, the darkness of the old halls. It was all as I knew it would have been, had I been thinking of it. I never pictured the old Gaels in those clothes; had the Greeks worn their hair like that?... but I realized it was all probably true. These images came from no book or movie, and I wondered if I had seen Merlin from some memory in my ancestral past that this substance was able to get me back, as if it were a peephole into the collective unconscious. As soon as I thought about the effect of the drug, I was drifting out of it.

Something serious came to me. I had never seen these images before. There was such historical authenticity to them, totally without the ring of familiarity such as we always have with memory. I wondered if they were my own images. Some of them were unlike any that I would have expected. I actually began to consider that they came from some source that was more profound than my own human mind.

Taurus' people were invariably fried when they did this drug. It occurred to me that they had a treasure they didn't appreciate. I wondered if, since the last strong thought seemed to be the one the wondrous drug allowed me to follow, I could have focused this visionary experience by guiding the thought, by choosing it.

I felt like such an idiot. I felt like Sabu in *The Thief of Baghdad* when he realizes that he blew one of the genie's three wishes on a sausage. I had a job to do, and very little of this substance; it might have been good for a joyride to Mars or Atlantis and (despite the poetry of my coincidental vision) I'd just done a swingset in the town park. Ah well. I guess I had to know the ticket was valid.

I rested awhile with these thoughts, deciding where to guide the revelations of "the Salve of Knowing." In a few moments, I was ready. I would track this drug. As I took it, and from my first seconds of consciousness, I would focus upon the question of its origin. I rubbed most of the remaining ointment on my forehead.

V

I tried hard to cling to that stroke of thought, to focus upon that twig or leaf in the stream of verbal and imagist flotsam that goes through each of our minds. I tried not to repeat any phrase lest I be distracted by some word or rhythm in it; I tried to hold to the root concept, the idea of knowing about the drug, this mysterious "Medicated Goo." I did not have to hold on long.

As the effect of the drug came upon me I felt the germ of that idea rising like a balloon from beneath the sargasso, breaking the ocean surface and soaring into the air with all reeds or entanglement falling from it; labor rising, effortless once aloft. It was like that with hanging on to this idea, tightly just long enough - then the ride was on.

I sensed, better than I saw, webs of shadowy operatives, maintaining this contraband illumination along generations beneath the pages of history. I saw scenes of revolutions, what had to be the Terror and the streets of Paris, what had to be the halls of the Vatican, inner sanctums in Tibet, rain forest shamans and high Andean civilizations, Popocapetl and Pachamama. At last, I saw the dark tangle of trees and vines, the gleam of a fire and the sound of drums, and the paint-smeared face of a Yanomamo doctor looking up from his work like a bloody-jowled predator. He even saw me. This may have been the most secret drug in the world. As I drifted out of its embrace, I asked myself how an apparent fool like Taurus came up with a supply. I hoped there was enough left for the answer.

VI

I recovered myself, breathing very deeply and focusing on my perceptions. I felt sure there were no immediate side effects to either of the hits I'd done. I reflected again that they were tiny relative to those I'd seen others take, and the third venture couldn't be that much worse. I wondered whether to undertake it.

I'd been sloppy when I'd last applied "the Salve of Knowing." There was still a fine residue in a dime-sized space on the rolled dollar bill, and even a bit more in a fold around it. I got as much as I could together on the end of my index, a dose only slightly smaller than my former two. Convinced that there was a question I had to have answered, I looked at it for just a second, then swirled it into a penny-sized spot on my brow. This was the last. Who was Taurus?

I was much more with myself than in the past experiences with this substance, and mildly astonished to find myself drifting into this problem as well. This was a harder question than the others to keep in focus, or else there was a fundamentally dodgy quality about the subject that even dodged the drug that was his claim to attention. It was not hard to sense his anxieties, his clutching at certain gestures or life-style guises that seemed to promise him social success (which, apparently, had been at its height in the late-60s and the need of readjustment had not yet become apparent). How had such a sad sack gotten this far into a serious game? Who hired Howdy Doody as a gunslinger? The answer was not illustrated so much as sensed.

The poor fool Taurus had merely blundered into some situation or scene from which he could smuggle something he would never see again. He had abused his welcome, let it be said. "The Salve of Knowing" was doubtless kept nowhere in large quantities; it may even have been volatile in measures larger than the tub I had seen, no deeper than five or six stacked quarters. That was part of the reason he was being so precious with it. It was why Taurus didn't know how to use the drug, and why he had started employing it to form a cult of adoration around him. He was a newcomer to the mystical business, which was one reason he was so hard to trace through my usual channels. But why was he being so secretive? What was really behind it? And then I saw it.

An old figure started to form into my view, as old as granite. It gradually faded in behind a stony veil, behind the obsidian sheen I remembered of Montezuma's mirror, and never came fully clear. I was not sad of that.

I saw it, the slow resolution of an arch-demon, of a god, except that it was real, superhuman, and totally inhuman - not the image into which Man was made. I even saw the name of it - *Yodhe* - and heard it, something close to "Yo-thee" (though the consonants at the middle make a deep th-sound rare in English, and both syllables seemed equally stressed). It throve in some realm and fashion that perhaps would always transcend human physics. I saw it: *Yodhe*, "the Unhealed" - a quartzy, scabrous mass of hooks, claws, black arachnid eyes, tufts of bristle; Yodhe, the Unhealed, a huge iceberg of living matter, deathless and nearly unkillable, but in constant agony and anger, scorched and suppurating from its most recent battle with the flame of its enemy, millennia of millennia back. This was an old name, and from some other language. What was its connection to anything? I recoiled, my own revulsion serving as a stroke that brought me out, more suddenly than I had come out of the other trips. This was enough of "the Salve of Knowing."

But as a flash at the end, it came to me how Taurus and the creature were connected. Taurus too had learned to focus the drug, and through successive uses of it had come in contact with this hideous being in its faraway realm. He realized that its goal was again to be at work in the world, to be fully incarnated in the body of a human - and that that way it could be killed. Taurus - already so tormented that his life was useless to him - was planning nothing less than to get it inside of him as it wished to be inside some human, and blow the two of them to Heaven. It would feel safe inside him; it would never suspect such suicidal altruism out of Taurus; in that, it and I were joined. I snapped back into myself, sitting in a comfortable chair before my fire. The same song, Relativity's fey "Siun Ni Duibhir" (*Shoo-ann nee giver*), was in its fadeout; my visions had taken seconds.

VII

I was shocked, sensing that it had to be a dream; but for me my visions were vivid enough to be coming from somewhere else. There was no doubt in me about them, or that they were the same ones Taurus had received. The inflexible hostility of the being that was out there filled me with absolute horror. I was livid at just the thought, just the aftertaint, with a sense as outre as any nightmare I've ever had. I had the sense of horror as if the Gestapo were pounding at the door for me, and I was weaponless.

The phone squealed. It was Dr. Rob, at ten sharp. I had forgotten all about him. "You hanging in there?"

It took me a few seconds to regroup, but I was exhilarated to hear another human voice, and this a very logical, capable one, as sternly sane as any that exists. I know I sounded like a stoner. "Amazing. That stuff is amazing. It's all gone now."

"Really."

"The little ritual I observed on the night I was there was just play. They were using the drug for head-candy. I think it's much more strange and serious than it was made out to be. I didn't think any of them got it at first, and I think Taurus is the only one that gets it now.

"I think this is an ESP drug, Rob, or it can be used that way. I think it can plug into the information areas of your mind and draw something buried out of it. It seemed to help me range the mental corners for every little detail that might pertain to the thought I started the drug with. It focused me, helped me sort the random perceptions that come up and keep them on line. That might be its gift. It's like a laser-effect upon your thought.

"I think it says a few things about existence and cognition, maybe at least about the brain, that we were never sure of. It seemed almost a 'collective unconscious' drug, as though it took you on a quick tour of one complete file in your mind, a file of associations and maybe even buried knowledge about the image or concept in focus. I got things I didn't know were in my mind. It's one of the heaviest experiences I've ever had. I'm still not ready to sum it up. It was amazing."

"Any idea where your hippie friend got it?"

"A few," I said. "I thought of it as having a South American origin, maybe circulated among Native American cultures since the beginning, maybe circulated to European and Asian ones long before officially accepted contact between the continents. I bet that drug is a perishable, natural substance. I get the feeling it could have been an extract of some rare plant from the rain forests, just one more mystery we'll lose when we burn them all. There are a lot of imports around Taurus' apartment, and he's surely got some underground connections.

"But don't suggest that Taurus made it. He's more than he looks like he is, but he's no chemist or herbalist. I doubt he has any pipeline to the source. I bet someone gave it to him, or that he smuggled his stash away like I did. Probably at one point in our lives all of us have attended a party that had a rock star or celebrity. I was at one in college that included Grace Slick and Paul Kantner. Kantner was talking with my girlfriend and Grace swatted her on the ass. In a mystical sense, that had been Taurus' one brush with the jet set."

"Any ideas about the folks that control the drug?"

"That was almost completely blocked from me. It was everyone and no one. I was getting images of generic mystics throughout the last millennia of human life that I could have retained from any of a hundred books on mysticism and occult conspiracy. I thought the stuff was originally developed and preserved by a priesthood and monarchy of Native American cultures. I saw Maya and Inca buildings, Andean and Mesoamerican landscapes.

"I did get a horrible feeling, so strong that I believe it was true. It can't be, but I believe it. There was a horrible, gigantic, demonic being in another realm, seeking to manifest into our world in the being of a human, almost like a reverse-incarnation of God into Jesus. That would be the end, for meaningful human life, if it ever did. Its complaint with Hitler, Stalin or Mao would be that they were too soft. Taurus - from whatever source, probably through repeated use of the drug - has come in contact with this being, and realized it as it is. I even saw its name: *Yodhe*, the Unhealed. What a moniker. He's trying to get it to possess him and then kill himself."

"What?"

"Sounds pretty noble, doesn't it? Didn't look to me like he had that in him. He thinks it's that sort of a menace to the whole world, and that close to its goal - maybe there's other desperados willing to be its avatar, against which it's weighing Taurus. He's willing to do anything he can to end it, even if it means taking himself with it."

"Are you all right?"

"Yes, Rob, I'm perfectly all right. I'm describing for you my perceptions while under the effects of the drug, followed by my assessments of them and the convictions they left in me. Any further questions about that?"

"OK."

"It was a very heavy, surreal experience, and I'm doing my best to explain it to you. I hope you can handle that."

"OK."

"Well, I've given it to you. That is Taurus' goal, I was told during that experience. And I believe it. It is a conviction."

"We've analyzed your sample and come up with nothing," Rob said. "Residues of this and that. Stabilizers, lubricants, fragrance, nothing too out of the ordinary for a New Age potion. It looks like a 'feel-good' ointment, like a semisolid version of a massage oil. You're sure that's what they used?" I let my silence answer. "Just asking," he said.

"Is it possible that the vital agents were perishable?" I said. "Are there things that do that?"

"That's what we figured. Some that metastasize - break down - into simple elements, some that sublimate - evaporate - completely. From your description of the way they handle that stuff, it does look like they want to keep it out of the air. It sounds like you weren't able to do that with all of your sample, at least the part of it you gave us."

"Did you guys try any of it?" I said. It was Rob's turn to let silence - or just a muted chuckle - do the talking. "I wonder if it's not psychosomatic, anyway. I feel like I just had the first telepathic experience of my life."

"We need to have a talk about this."

"We can have it," I said. "So. You guys all out of your sample?"

"Unfortunately, yes. It was useless, anyway."

"Right," I said. I didn't believe him. "Guess we go back to Taurus, don't we?"

"Right," he said. I doubt he believed me.

VIII

You might think I would have followed up on Taurus and gotten to the bottom of his goo as quickly as possible, but welcome to life. Worldly issues took precedence. The end-of-the-year sprint at school has always been a madhouse, but that spring the cycle of coaching - the tennis team, though undefeated, was a smorgasbord of spazzable commodities - wrapping up my course, grading final exams, writing reports, and administering to my duties as department chairman were all I had on my mind. Furthermore, I had no real sense of urgency.

I can't remember all the fantasy literature I read as a kid, but surely I sensed that images from that source kicking around in my unconscious were responsible for my last vision under Taurus' "Medicated Goo." I lost accordingly my drug-inspired faith in its dispenser, and all ability to take anything about him seriously (like the prospects of a volcanic suicide). I was again sure I could reel in the vain fish Taurus whenever I wanted and put what I got out of him into a picture, just for the willingness to listen to him and the ability to sift false leads from true. He would be more than he had seemed, this Taurus. Be that a lesson to me, about overestimating my own judgment and underestimating people and situations. How long do I have to keep re-learning it?

In the first week of June at two in the morning I'd just come in from a date and was brushing my teeth to the late local news when I saw the video of the post-explosion fire at a familiar-looking Allentown building. When I heard the address it sealed the matter, and I gave Rob Notaro a call. It had happened only hours before, but it was all over by the time we arrived outside Taurus's second-floor apartment. We stood in the early daylight hoping we might be able to put something together from interviews with the onlookers. We could see from outside the yellow police line that there was no point in crossing it.

As I looked ahead to the cycle I knew was coming, it was outwardly the beginning of a cheerful day. The birds were in song, even the dawn was warm, and the high leaves of the oaks and elms were already touched by the faint optimism. The fire-plundered porch yawned, though, like the mouth of a corpse.

On the steamy night that would follow, it would be the buzz of Allentown, the shops, the bars, the cafes: the explosion that had blackened the quarters and taken the life of Rocco Romulus Rostelli, the inimitable and peripatetic Taurus. No tears fell, but consensus held that the poor rogue had been too private with nothing but his own demons; and that he'd not deserved his fate. But that morning, I looked above at the first peachy tingle past the eastern leaves and wondered at the ranges of dim universe beyond it, the hurtling eons of time and matter and constellations, the gleaming trinkets that single spirits of awareness must represent in them. I wondered if Taurus had joined his unhealed god or stood them both to the judgment of a wholler One.

THE VOICE
FROM THE WOODS

Zehre mit geisterglut meinen Leib, daß ich luftig mit dir inniger mich mische und dann ewig die Brautnacht währt.

Novalis, *Hymns to the Night*

"Tear my body with spirit fire, so I can mix with you more inwardly, airily, and then the wedding night will last forever."

THE VOICE FROM THE WOODS

[I knew how this case ended before I knew even ostensibly why. The understanding I have of it was pieced from many sources like a puzzle rather than built from a foundation like a tower, and it seems to retell best as a single fable.]

I

Of course no human being is a 'type'; but from all I could tell, this Rochester businessman had been a true American gentleman, a little plainer-spoken than the Continental variety and less given to literary allusions in his daily speech, but no finer man could be found. And he was proper; I never felt like I knew him, no matter how much I talked to his friends, colleagues, and neighbors. Even his diaries and recorded interviews seemed incomplete. This was consistent with his life: he was friendly, but never familiar.

The old fellow had earned his success. He'd come to Rochester after World War Two to work in the smoky factory in a plain of train tracks. He rose high, but kept the trust of all. Even during the strikes he was treated with respect as he passed through the lines to his office. He was a model of manners and discretion with, so far as I could see, one indulgence.

His great release seems to have been to walk the grounds of his Genesee Valley home all the nights of the snowless seasons. Though during the days his poised, dark-haired wife took the gardens as her single charge, in the nights they were his, to stalk the moon-shadows, look into his pond, or pace among the flowers and trees, always with the sense of joy and detachment that might, in a lighter man, be called rapture. The nights were his "magic casements."

In the spring of 1980 something disturbed him on one of his evening walks, a strange sound formed of natural noises. He hardly noticed it until it was over, and then caught himself, wondering if he'd truly heard it; but it seemed, at the moment of a rise in the breeze, as if a word had formed. He could imagine a high wind, swirling all the leaves and debris from a lawny grove into a chance spiral below the lone high maple in its middle, making a vague pyramid of whirling forms; as the spiral rises, becoming the base of a cone of leafy atoms with the top of the shadowy tree, and begins to gyre up from the peak of it, then like a throb comes a single, definite, spoken syllable, like a question: *Which?* He imagined it in a woman's tone.

He stopped where he stood, and looked out across his broad lawn to the jagged grove. Beyond it wound a narrow old road that met his driveway, and below, within a mile, the bridge above the river. He could see the streetlights, each in its own dusty drop of brightness, and, across the far ridge he liked to imagine in his evening jaunts, the sloping farms and estates. He wondered if he could have heard this sound.

II

He made nothing of the experience, which he could surely have imagined. One day the following week, though, he came home and found his wife unconscious in their warm garden. He revived her; she was merely exhausted, she said. The doctors narrowed her condition to three possibilities, one of which was that nothing was wrong. Her husband and grown children told themselves this as long as they could. Before long the spells of fainting and unconsciousness came often, and her memory frayed.

During the first winter of her decline her husband's devotion was remarkable. He was, in the words of an old nurse, "a peach of a guy." He sat by her in the clinic every week night, hours at a time. He talked about his day and their children, and all they could do together when she recovered. She smiled and nodded as if she believed.

The garden had been her joy, and landscapers worked for days before each of his wife's Sundays home. Each time nearly redone, it beamed with new themes: in April it might be cool hues and pastels, the whites, yellows and lavenders of tulips, daffodils and hyacinths; in June it could be pirate hues, brassy rhododendrons and brave roses, gaudy purple, red, and salamander; in August, the heated tones of carnations, geraniums, and mums. The neighbors found it touching, the chief executive conducting her wheelchair tours through the skirting color-choir, the nodding carillon of blossom-bells.

III

He had last heard the voice on a November night as he walked, by then, for relief rather than joy. His winter had held so many trials that he'd almost forgotten it, and thus he was shocked to hear the natural voice again on the first warm evening of April. As before, it had come to him in a single syllable, at the peak of a rise in the normal night-noise. He'd stopped and considered, unsure of what it may have said, and wondered for the first time if this was something that would need his attention.

During the second summer of his wife's collapse hardly a week went by that he did not receive some call. He never doubted his own faculties, since only in this regard did they seem to be slipping. The situation set him to unaccustomed speculations. He analyzed the voice.

Its tone was murky, but the manner of its appearance never varied: always at the apex of one of the night's tapering sound effects. It was not always completely natural, though. Once he could swear that the voice came to him in a slow-belling-strum as the wind soared over the rumbling of a truck on the fast road below his home. Another time, it seemed to be as the train went through town a mile to the east. The voice was always, however, accompanied by wind and rustling branches.

He was continually surprised by the voice's once-nightly appearance, and it was hard ever to catch any of its words. Few if any of these articulations were of more than one syllable, yet the old gentleman - who had had a fine education - realized how many of the most suggestive concepts are embodied in the simplest terms. Indeed, there was that archetypal cast to the words he could discern, doubtless terms that existed in any

Copper Age human tongue. It was almost as if he was not hearing the true English sounds of the words so much as receiving their meaning, directly into the back of his mind. He could never decide if this was a repeating theme whose every utterance was a clarification still unclear, or an unfolding message that would be lost if he could not catch enough of it as it passed. One of the few times he could be fairly sure what the voice had said, the word was *Say*.

Except for its slightly musical nature, no syllable he heard was particularly sweet. When he set to analyze its precise tone, he came up with impressions of sounds: a human voice; the hiss of wind through trees; and sometimes a muffled rubber-on-metal clang, almost like the stroke of key upon string, or the strum of an ethereal lyre. This was what gave ring to that leaf-and-wind-formed syllable that suggested a voice.

As he analyzed it in his recollection, he realized that the voice was not clearly gendered by pitch or attitude, yet his image of the being behind it was female, a grand woman, greater and wiser and more powerful than all humanity, like one of the imperious goddesses of old. He could think of it no other way.

The idea of a nocturnal voice coming through the effects of nature was strange, but not for that reason terrifying. He had never expected human thought to explain everything; and he'd always had such a faith in nature that he considered nothing earthly truly sinister. This experience, though, was troubling. Something else not entirely pleasant occurred at the exact moment of each word's reception: a tiny shock against the very back inside of his skull. It reminded him of static electricity.

He might have taken these messages personally, timed with his sadness, but he did not yet have the sense that the voice was directed to him. He thought of it as a tone that a human mind had picked up as language, probably by standing in just the right place and time, like a lineman tapping the phones of speakers states apart.

IV

Over the following winter his wife's condition grew worse. By the second spring it was an expression of pathos rather than faith to wheel her around the garden. He could endure the nurses who waited on the porch and spoke to her as others would speak to toddlers. He could imagine their muttering when the van pulled away from his driveway or prepared to leave the clinic for it again. There came a climactic moment when even he no longer believed that anything he did could reach her. Within the bounds of her mind she might well range galaxies, a queen of infinite space, but there were no signs of it from without.

Whoever could have been there on his nightly walks would have seen that the husband's expression was no longer rapturous. As if they gave the occasion for a challenge, he paced with new questions. Was this the sum of his life, to be left an old man, with money, home, and position, but lacking his only key to content, the woman he'd loved since his youth? He'd always figured for a different reward. For the first time in his life he searched for something beyond the tangible to explain it. He talked with his minister.

On an ivied bench in the garden one evening in May, heavy with his sorrow, he thought back on the episodes of their long marriage. Not all had been blissful. He had served in the war; their daughter had been gravely ill; several times their fortune had hung on one of his decisions. Yet until this recent grief they had all come out smoothly, sweet in memory like the ending of an adventure or romance whose middle scenes were grim.

One image stayed with him, of his wife-to-be soon after they had met. How clearly he saw her, alive in that form of her first womanhood, half-girl still, that he had met her and she had first become his. He remembered one of their early evenings and thought of some young debate, finishing one of his replies to her and sharing the laugh across the years. It gave him an odd comfort, and he continued it, speaking to the night like a hearer, to the image of his vanished wife. He so nearly saw her in the space beside him that he thought of asking her guidance to lead him through this final stage of their life together, and carried on his monologue so heartfully that he almost felt her talking back. Yet his grief amplified his fancy, and he could imagine her beside him, a girl to him as he was. What he would have said to her.

He thought of another incident later in their lives, and yet another of her former selves, the young mother, would have her say, appearing in another space of the piny grotto around him. That set loose a slow cascade of erstwhile hers, in his mind, in his garden, in former gardens or episodes from their full marriage. He spoke to his wife as if she were with him then, in all the guises he saw. They came to him, each with a speck of advice or joyful sharing or concern. He envisioned all these earlier beings of her - woman, girl, mother, matron, lover, friend - and addressed feelings and episodes from specific moments of their time together, each of which he could remember by the appearance of the woman before him. Almost an interpreter between the varied selves, he interrupted some impatient response from a maid to let another, perhaps a grandmother, have her say. They settled and resettled problems from the past decades of their lives; they discussed the good times and savored old laughs; they were proud together again of their children; he summarized old business conflicts, reminding each shadowy her how they had been resolved; he told her how many times she had come to him like this when the weapon-fire neared. Absorbed in this, he almost forgot that he was alone. As he guided or consoled or laughed, taking joy and company from her varied selves, reliving them all again, inside himself he knew that he had known a great love, one that had been worth all the sorrow of its fade. His words ran out, but he looked into the silver pool awhile longer.

Then he went in to his ample home, and passing through the moonlit panels thrown by the tall windows, settled into his bed like he was uneasy on it and pulled the sheet across his creaking body. He could only guess how long it was before he woke in the middle of a dream to a syllable from the voice.

It was an odd sensation, half-waking to the tapering windy sound that would peak in the single word, but without which he might never have remembered the dream: the vision of a vast, towering green woman imposed upon a night-scene, upon the tall pyramidal maple he'd sometimes envisioned when he heard the evening voice before. Her image was made of dense lucent green, like a hologram reduced to lines and splotches of an emerald glow.

She lay like a natural monument, half-reclining on an invisible throne in a gauzy robe, long hair flowing over her shoulders so that she filled the pyramidal shape of the upper half of the tree. And her word had more tone to it than any others he could remember from any other time before. It was almost as if all the others had been black and white, and this one was finally colored; the word was *So.*

He sat up, the sheet falling from him, more startled than he had been by any of the other voices. They did not follow him into his home! A new tone seemed to have entered the summer, and he was oddly averse to his nightly walks. The admission crept on him slowly, though, and it took him at least a week to realize that, for the first time in his life, the country night for him was something to dread. Two of his greatest joys, his wife and his walks, were taken from him almost in a stroke.

V

He took to walking in the clear mornings when he would fear no voice. One dawn halfway into July he passed the square formed by a hedge and backed by a rock garden and a row of slim trees, a shrinelike space in which, his daughter had once told him, "the pixies dance." In its center, he noticed the small form of a chipmunk, crouched facing the altar-like rocks and pillaring trees, calmly motionless, as if frozen in the act of worshipfully approaching. He expected it to spring up and streak away as he neared. Not a hair of it was mussed; he thought it was sleeping. He nudged it with a toe; it was gently dead, but it lay symmetrically placed, both by its spot in the enclosed space and its own pose, crouched upon its haunches with its forepaws beneath its little cheeks, its tail straight behind it, its tiny eyes squinted shut like a child feigning sleep. It was the oddest natural corpse he had ever seen. He had always presumed life a puppet-master with no interests once the strings were cut; he had always thought death a random artist.

Weeks later, a pair of woodchucks of identical size and pose, fur mussed by the evening's short rain, seemed to have fallen dead in full symmetrical wriggle two feet apart, facing the back windows of his churchy manse. He studied them curiously in the emerald blades and dewy beads. Their attitudes were supplicating; their last gazes would have been of the broad windows of his house that sheened like Merlin's prison on nights that the moon ranged the northern sky. He had noticed the effect himself; he could fancy that they did it homage. More came.

During the day nothing would touch these offerings, which were always gone by the next dewy, misty, or rainy morning. The businessman was not used to thinking this way, but it would have taken little to convince him that a supernatural force was at work, demanding a response and escalating the gestures until it came; but he was filled with anguish from his own causes. He hoped that the day of reckoning would never come, that he would die a peaceful death or join his wife where she wandered before it.

Soon there could be no doubt that a strange hand was at work. He studied one of the corpses in his yard, a squirrel, crouching serenely, but deftly wrapped at neck, shoulder, and tail-base with fine stems which were just beginning to dry and unravel. The green threads were delicate, and spun - a dozen to a score of strands - rather than tied about the tiny creature. They clung to their position about its body as if they were molded, had grown, or were wind-curled into pose, rather than woven. They could not have served as bonds, even if their tender strands could have held; they were as likely to appear wreathing neck or torso as hampering the limbs of the little mammal. They could have been nothing other than decorations, and the offerings constructions of art, but what grim Bacchanal was leaving them?

In number, frequency, and artifice they grew. No animals were bigger than the badger or woodchuck, but the weavings continued to deck them, still flimsy weeds, grasses, and vines (sometimes flowered); but there was the sense of increasing urgency. One morning he found a circle of thirteen dark mice, their dew-tousled heads to the center like the stars of a macabre colonial flag, each identically wreathed at neck and waist with tiny violet-budded vines.

VI

Like a playmate it taunted him, the night outside, mild and breezy and one of those he used to love. He could hear it play as he tried to sleep and could see its reaches in the silver moonlight that fell across the bed. It joyed and rushed and covered unknown lands, but he lay stiffly and warred with his thoughts. Something had to be answered.

He could not understand why his wife who had done nothing had been punished. It had to be a stroke at him, the cruelest of all. The old businessman wondered what he had done to deserve it. Could it be for the sin of his contentment when so much of the world was grieving? Was it all for the love of his evening walks? Was it too much to ask even one simple happiness for a whole life through?

He had always been, he thought, a good man: fair to those he employed, kind to friends and family, never asking anything of the world past what he had earned for himself. It did not seem to him evil to work hard, to succeed, to be civic-minded, to wish to put his family beyond financial worry for as many generations as he could. Not a regular churchgoer, he had a belief in a God like that of the Christians - in Whom, though, it seemed curious to abide this torment of His creatures from, seemingly, another past-human force.

The wind peaked and spiraled as he reasoned, nothing surprising in this county by the lake; but when once the hiss rose to its long-developing crest, the old businessman was sure he heard the voice. He didn't flinch, though his heart froze. To hear it as he thought about it was terrifying. It could have been no mistake, and yet as often, its word was just beneath hearing. It was certainly a call; and almost at the apex of the next breeze, he heard it again. The word was *Bid.*

At least four more times he heard it. Its tone had never been more surely female. He dressed in the static chill of his room. He went into his garden, intent to challenge this force that was calling to him, to walk into its embrace. He had started to think that this incomprehensible cry was connected to the malady of his wife. If he could triumph, maybe she would return; if he were blasted, well, nothing mattered anymore; her loss he had endured already, and of his she would never know. And if he came to confront it, and it dared not reveal itself, then he would never fear it again, and at least that weight would be lifted.

He had always felt that the voice came from the north, and he followed his impressions, ambling off in that direction into the grounds of his neighbor across the road, keenly looking and listening for whatever impressions the night might give. These were broad lawns, fields, farms, and groves, with horse-paths leading through woods to more fields and groves. He had never really been curious what it might be like to walk here, knowing that it was developed land in a civilized country; but night's witching made it all wonder and dread.

In three quarters of a mile he was in a second tract of open fields and clumps of trees. At another time he might be afraid to be caught trespassing; were that his only worry then! When, in another few minutes, he emerged from the boughs above him, he came to a grassy field perhaps a half mile square, roughly circular and ringed by pines that loomed like far-off mountains. In the center of this pastoral amphitheater was a wide, high tree by itself, the very one he had often envisioned as he heard the voice from the woods. It was this setting he had seen in his dream, superimposed on the goddess-woman in her laser-green. He saw this with no sense of shock, since within himself he realized he had expected it all along. Something within him and something outside of him had been in contact for all this time, with the conscious self unaware. He felt curiously left out.

He stalked the southern verges of this large space, letting the tree-shadows cloak him. It was almost comfort to blend with darkness, to be as obscure to any observer as that observer would be to him. He was strangely at one with the night and with his own mood, as if his very aura had turned to colors that had never been his, to those of something blue, green, and cool. He savored these impressions and waited for his mind to be right, filled with little fear. He had nothing to lose. He had been purified by his trials, and he was worthy. He asked it, with the questions in his mind, what it wanted to say to him. He waited.

He knew something was there that was not normally visible, and that it was his capacity of seeing, as much as its absolute presence, that would give him sight of it. He stalked and stood, as if by standing in just the right spot (and he would know it), he would envision what had called him. There were times and places that he thought he could see within the image of the tree the green woman of his dream; but gradually the impressions grew fainter, and soon he was in his own world completely again. If he had been given his answer, he did not know it; but he had asked the question, whatever it was. With some relief, he turned to go, an hour after he had come into this space.

Within a week his wife passed over, at least from this world, and so smoothly that no one was sure when it had occurred. She had simply slept and forgotten to wake.

The old businessman heard no more voices in the night, but a slow change came over him during the day. At times he seemed to be listening to something other than the meeting or conversation at hand, as if to an inner chorus or melody so captivating that he dropped everything to hear it. Each material voice around him had to wait for the far-off message.

It was recognized at the business he had once directed. His son was sent for, and he stayed for a few weeks to see to things. Measures were taken so that the father need not trouble himself with anything he did not choose. If he woke in the morning and seemed to hear music in his head, he could walk about his grounds or sit in the garden. If he dressed for work, he was taken. People were understanding, and he could seem to himself to be assisting. When greeted by old friends and colleagues unaware of his condition, he smiled discreetly like his former self; but soon he could not listen to them because of the priority of the other sounds only he could hear. These spells became frequent and lasting, as if the border between the medley of his inner voices and the single one of consciousness had perpetually blurred.

It was not long before he passed over, much in the manner of his wife. A nurse said that his last expression was one of intent listening, of open-hearted concern, but perpetual curiosity, an inability to hear something that he left this world still trying to understand.

PICKLE-WORMS

Little Lamb, who made thee?
Dost thou know who made thee?
    William Blake, "The Lamb," *Songs of Innocence*

PICKLE-WORMS

In her voice I could see that April day - mild, breezy, and bright - and I ran up hilly Emery Road thinking about it. I'd first heard it minutes before on a message I almost didn't play. Bent on a run in the inspiring day, I'd come in from an afternoon of tennis coaching and was lacing my Nike Daybreaks when I noticed the machine flashing. I actually considered saving the message for later. Time was a factor, sometimes down to the minute, as one weighed what to undertake between duties of a schoolday, and potential surprises were best put off till it was over; but that day my curiosity got the better of me. I played the message several times.

P. J. Anderson had left work and home numbers but no idea what the call was about. Her voice was wonderful, a breezy skylark tone that I associated with the soaring day, and as I ran I was replaying the ring of it, wondering what she looked like, what she wanted. You can tell that the winter had been romantically thin and that now "April with his showers sweet" was making the sap rise, but that was a special voice by all accounts.

It had so much good in it, so much real self-assurance. I'd been let down by voices, even photographs, before, but I'd be astonished if this P. J. Anderson wasn't good - and pretty. She believed in herself too much. Grasping for the nature of that voice as I ran reminded me of *Gatsby*'s Nick Carraway wrestling after Daisy Fay's. Daisy's was full of money; this one was full of... *joining*... one of the most balanced, integrated, together voices I have ever heard. I think that, unless you've met someone with a voice like that, you don't know what I'm talking about. I don't notice that quality in media dolls - actors, rock stars, politicians - that sheer balance. But maybe I'm just deaf to it; I have that mistrust of fame, that I presume its aspirants have forsworn all realler altars, not true enough to themselves long enough to develop the ring of full spirit in that voice to which I ran. Its owner was a succeeder, a contributor, someone who put good energy back into life.

That evening I returned her call and found her voice as miraculous live. P. J. was a school psychologist in a tiny Monroe County town who believed one of her second-graders was displaying legitimate psychic powers. She wanted me to meet the girl and maybe help the staff understand.

The end-of-the-year rush was on at the Gow School, and it was actually another month before we could arrange a meeting at hers, on my first New England ramble of the summer. I was planning to OD on sports up in Stowe and maybe visit friends on the Vinyard; but the big plan was just to get a change of scene, clear my head, and, as always, do some sustained reading and writing. I work more on vacation, I swear.

I checked in at the school office and walked with P. J. Anderson to an empty classroom. Though she didn't fit it exactly, she was as good as my mental picture: a self-assured, outdoorsy woman of about twenty-six, curvaceous and athletic, with a mane of curly ash-brown hair, big turquoise eyes, and full lips. Her handshake was so forthright that it tingled, her eye contact so complete that it was disarming. It took you all in.

She set some folders on the table between us and took out a color three-by-five of a dark-haired girl with a resemblance to Anne Frank. Her classmates were telling teachers that this little girl could do "magic" tricks, which P. J. had gathered involved moving small, light objects without physically touching them, like making pencils spin like helicopter blades on smooth surfaces, so far never when adults were around. For the kids, this was a private, hysterical game, sharing the trick behind the backs of the teachers. The story was so prevalent that folks at the school began to think there was something to it, and made a videotape (which I presumed I was never to see) of a milk carton breakdancing on a lunchtable. At that point I was called.

Everyone was pulling for Isabel. All the breaks seemed to be against her, and yet the seven-year-old maintained a sunny demeanor that filled everybody in the school with hope. They could tell, though, when the night had been hard. Sometimes she showed up in the clothes of the day before, looking like she hadn't slept, sometimes even bruised. It was hard to figure the source of her happy influences.

The on-and-off boyfriend (a goon named Ion Begala) was most of the problem, it seemed, in constant trouble with the law but a virtual Svengali to Isabel's low-esteem mother Tina Sanford - good-natured enough, but hardly providing a stable environment for her children. Relations weren't good between her and her own own immigrant parents - I think they were Bulgarians - who nevertheless never declined to care for Isabel and her two sisters when the mother ran off looking for said boyfriend at some substance-abusing party. Since the grandparents' involvement displeased Begala, Tina Sanford had started leaving the girls alone, at two, five, and seven. Isabel sometimes called her grandparents when there was trouble, and for that, school authorities suspected, she was roughly treated. Her grandparents were in court to gain custody of the girls, since their mother was interested in little more than Ion. I'd classify that raging passion as a great love if it took account of some things you can't ignore - like three little daughters.

As we waited for the girl's arrival, I remembered a story about a "biter" from the Erie County kindergarten of one of my best friend's children. Kids were coming home with nasty marks on arms or shoulders, but none would turn the culprit in. Adults presumed that they were terrorized by a young psychopath and set about searching through likely methods. Nothing they did could expose him.

The matter was eventually settled by an adult male social worker - a big, bearded guy, incidentally who went through three weeks of full-time school with the kids. He ate when they ate, napped when they napped, and un-selfconsciously aped every other school activity. It had to be something to see, but within a few days the kids fell totally at ease. It was then that the social worker noticed one kid solemnly approach another, make eye contact, and, as if giving communion, extend his forearm to the other's jaw, receiving a rabbity nip that broke skin. Without reacting, the bitee tucked the wing away and rejoined his mates. Half an hour later at a pause in the activity, he whimpered and cradled the limb as if the wound was fresh. The social worker stuck around a few more days and witnessed the ritual again, with different victims but no other tooth-artist.

Adults speculated that the victims liked the attention of the biting, even taking cues from adult discoverers how to act, though they still kept the secret. How the biter was delegated is anyone's guess; but the schoolfolk and parents realized that their rigid villain-searching mind-set had been a complete block to finding the truth. I keep episodes like that in mind constantly when dealing with the paranormal - or children. I wondered if the matter at hand would be equally curious.

Knowing that they would have some relevance to a fellow teacher, P. J. showed me Isabel's academic charts. All the standard tests of coordination, maturity, and cognitive skills revealed that she was a bright little girl, but nothing prodigious - except maybe for her all-encompassing heart. She seemed kind and mature for her years, caring about the whole world, about animals, oceans, forests, and people. Maybe some of this was politically-correct educational conditioning, but what they were getting her to say certainly agreed with me.

I told P. J. what I knew about psychic children. They're seldom geniuses, less often bright and blissful than shy and troubled. Often they're disadvantaged in many respects, and if they keep their special abilities into their teens (which isn't the rule), they may attempt to turn them to social and economic gain, exposing themselves to pressure of unlooked-for types. Children have psychic talents more often than adults, and females more than males.

I'd seen films of Russian psychics like Nina Kulagina moving grains of salt and sand in controlled conditions with, apparently, nothing but mental-power. The effects were modest, though, and left them exhausted. If Isabel could do bigger things for a game, we had something the world needed to see.

At around two-thirty the little girl was brought in to us, and by two-thirty-one my heart had melted. I'm not used to seven-year-olds. She looked so scared and frail. She was dressed in a worn skirt and a Madonna T-shirt, with a pilled-up cardigan sweater around her waist. She had glossy brown eyes and black hair, with an olive complexion. It wasn't easy to get a smile out of her.

On the table before us P. J. had arranged a number of small light objects - pencils, erasers, wood blocks, and the like. "The kids say you do magic tricks," she said. "Can you do one for us?" The little girl tee-hee'd. I wanted to be a father. Psychic or not, she had to be something special to bring out my paternal instincts.

"Can you show Mr. Winfield a trick?" P. J. said. Isabel laughed shyly again, looking around the room, up the walls, out the window, at us.

"The other kids say you can spin pencils without touching them," said P. J. "Can you do that?" The girl squirmed affably, and P. J. prodded a few more times. Once Isabel stopped and fixed on a pencil in a way that reminded me of one of my old Classics professors reading, boring into a Latin line as if to set fire to it. One could imagine favored passages showing definite wear. Isabel's look looked so practiced that I could envision small objects responding; but in a second she broke up laughing. It was clear that she was not ready to show us anything, but, while we had her I had to try to find something out.

"Why don't we play cards?" I said, taking up a Zener - or ESP - deck, five sets of five distinct symbols on normal-size cards. The tester draws one at a time and the test-taker tries to guess which symbol comes up. Over the long haul - hundreds of tests - anyone should average about five right. I hardly ever mess around with these. The subject is controversial enough, and to have even arguable validity the testing has to be done in a lab. Furthermore, signs of ESP in a card-guessing test should have nothing to do with a person's psychokinetic - "mind over matter" - abilities like were rumored of this little girl. Many late-twentieth century parapsychologists suspect that information talents (ESP, or "micro-PK") and "supernatural" physical abilities (psychokinesis, or "macro-PK") are not even related.

"Let's see how Miss Anderson does," I said. When the stack was done, P. J. had called seven right, which might indicate some ESP talent, though you couldn't say from one test. Next P. J. took the deck and scoresheet, and I got four right, which was about what I expected. They say everyone has psychic talents, but if so, mine are low rollers. "Isabel's turn," I said. She did a lot of giggling, but we managed to get her started. Something interesting came up.

Isabel got the first, third, and fourth cards right. I felt my adrenaline kick in; seventy-five percent! Then she seemed to change her mood as if she could hear me thinking, and missed fifteen in a row. When I saw the way things were going I managed to slip a few of the discards underneath the table, shuffle them quickly, and fit them back into the stack yet to be called. I know this wasn't scientific, but nothing was on the record anyway, and I didn't want to break her mood. It was saying something to me. Of the last forty, she got one right.

Bells rang in the halls, meaning that the older kids were done for the day and that Isabel was late for her bus. This was a good time to stop, anyway. P. J.'s car was at another branch of the school, and she asked me to ferry the two of them to Isabel's house. The girl left the room with an aide to get her books. I must have looked as stunned as I was, because P. J. asked me what was wrong.

"She got three out of four right, then missed about thirty straight," I said, shaking my head. "Four out of forty-five."

"So she doesn't have ESP?"

"You can't miss thirty in a row on a fixed-response test like this," I said, starting to get excited. "The stats are what they are. Even if you're trying to miss, you should get one right about every five. You can't miss thirty in a row."

It clearly wasn't registering. P. J. is far from dumb, but this subject was new to her. I slowed down. I didn't want my excitement at what we'd just seen to come across as frustration with her lack of understanding. I told her about the "sheep and goat" effect, in which believers in ESP (the "sheep") generally score slightly above chance, and hard doubters ("goats") just a little below. "When the pattern holds across thousands of tests, it seems to indicate that everyone has modest ESP, and that the goats deliberately suppress their information talents."

It was her turn to look stunned. "So what does it mean?"

"That Isabel may be a real prodigy. That she knew the symbols on the cards to an amazingly high percentage, and deliberately picked wrong. It's the only thing that makes sense. It's as if she could read my astonishment at how well she started out. It also says to me that getting through to her will be a process. After the first few, she decided to do exactly the opposite of what we wanted."

My mind was working. The world could get its answer on the ESP question soon and for good if this girl was what I thought she might be, if she would ever directly cooperate, and if the researcher who found her - which, at the moment, was me - judged that the exposure would be positive in her life and set the process underway. Those were real ifs. The girl came back as I was considering them.

P. J. sat in the front of my Subaru, a light 4WD wagon whose back space, loaded for Vermont, held rackets and mountain-bike. In the rear-view mirror I could see Isabel, regarding the countryside none too happily. When she hit these spells it was impossible to lighten her up.

The road along the ridge narrowed, and the houses on it were generally the proverbial tar-paper shacks of my century. Maybe heat and refrigerators are the only real upgrades. The road took a sudden dip at the top of a hill, and the car just caught air. "Ooh, pickle-worms!" Isabel laughed. P. J. looked back, and I turned my eyes to the mirror. "That's what we call it," Isabel said. "In your tummy when you go over that."

We'd passed under the only cloud in the sky as I'd looked at Isabel's reflection, and in the sudden fall of shadow then light, light turning from gold to silver, her complexion paled, and hollows appeared under her eyes. I could see the crone in her, the seven-year-old, and was reminded of the mortality of us all. The only difference may be how much time you have and how much good you do in it.

Isabel's home looked like someone had backed a small trailer to the front of a tiny house, then hacked openings where they met. The trailer door had been shut tight, but someone must have been watching, because a pudgy squaw came out on the steps and ushered Isabel in. She didn't greet us, and was about to close the door when P. J. addressed her. "Miss Sanford," she said, stepping closer. "I'd like to talk to you about Isabel sometime. Could we arrange a meeting at school?"

A sweating widebody with Elvis hair barged past her, thrusting Isabel behind him with little consideration. Ample bare arms sprouted from a torn T-shirt. "Nother social worker?" he growled at P. J. "We told you people 'nough times keep away. Who you?" he said at me.

I'm opposed to macho-posturing for ego's sake, and the look of this guy would make pacifists out of most people; but I did nothing to defuse the situation. I hated him. I didn't look at him the way you look at a man who challenges you; I surveyed him like a pitted scavenger, like a hyena or vulture that had just looked up from nibbling at its own scabs.

"We're sorry to bother you," said P. J., taking my arm. "We won't be back." She pivoted me toward my car. Her touch was magnetic.

"Call the cops," I said opening the door. "That man's an abuser."

We heard a light scream from inside the trailer. We ran to it, and I set my hand on the door, expecting the moment it opened a lethal fight in a confined space with a man who outweighed me by a hundred pounds. I snatched it back and saw something I wouldn't otherwise have believed.

Isabel's mother was before the television on a couch at the other side of the messy house, terrified. Crumbs from snack chips and the like were on table and floor around her. Eight feet away in the kitchen - which was in the trailer - Isabel huddled against the oven as if she'd been struck. Above her, but motionless in an awkward position, was her stepfather. He was no menace to anybody.

Ion Begala shouldn't have been able to keep his balance. Eyes slitted and fluttering, he was leaning over Isabel in what would have been a natural position for an instant, transferring weight from one leg to the other. One hand, semi-clenched, was raised, either descending in the awful act of striking, or rising for a repeat stroke. He was essentially frozen, though a slight quivering revealed that he was alive and animate. His clothes ruffled as if in a breeze. Oddest of all, little flecks of pale material - which I presumed were bits of lint and crumbs - clung to his entire frame as if he were a magnet for them. I have no idea what effect this was.

In a few seconds the spell was broken, but instead of picking up where he left off in mid-swipe, Ion Begala collapsed to the floor wheezing. It was as if the force that had held him motionless had also kept him from breathing. I wondered if it could have killed him. "Get out of here!" screamed Isabel's mother, ministering to the wide fellow. His heart may have been bad.

"Can you believe that?" said P. J. as we drove.

"That girl is a miracle. I don't know what to do."

"We have to get her out of that house. Her or him."

We drove for awhile in silence. "You know, this is a dilemma," I said. "If she's ever to prove anything to the world about human psychic abilities, she needs to be looked at soon. But that would involve publicity, possibly a cycle that could be very damaging to her. And who knows what it might do to her life at home?"

"It seems to set her stepdad off when other people get attention," said P. J.

"I know what the right thing is on that front," I said, "which is to back out and wait. I don't have the right to make a decision like that for her. But I see a great learning experience for the world going to waste. The odds are that she won't be able to do anything in a few more years of society telling her she can't, or else some other facet of adulthood will wreck the mechanism. She may forget, or stop believing she ever had special abilities. I only hope they protect her long enough."

"Maybe she'll kill him first," said P. J.

A SITTING FOR ISABEL
(Pickle-worms, part II)

But his loving look
Like the holy book
All her tender limbs with terror shook.
William Blake, "Little Girl Lost," *Songs of Experience*

A SITTING FOR ISABEL

I

All the week in Vermont I thought about her, telling myself how silly it was. I'd only spent an hour or two with P. J., I reasoned. Our conversation had been totally professional. I didn't know that she was unattached, even single. But when I ran or biked in the woods, I saw her in my mind. It was hard to keep from thinking about her every five minutes when I read and wrote. When I had interesting experiences - funny, human, maturing - I thought about how I might tell them to her.

She sounded happy to hear from me when, every nerve firing, I called her from Stowe. I told her I'd be passing through her area midweek and asked her out to dinner. "Ah, yeah," she said boyishly, as if conceding that a carload of kids could have ice cream. I slept in my car in a pub parking lot in Saratoga Springs the night before, dozing off to a Silly Wizard tape, trying to visualize her face in the stars through the open sunroof. I ran in the park, scrubbed up in Saratoga Lake before the four-hour drive, and arrived at her home around seven. We walked to a pasta restaurant and laughed on its deck till midnight. I stayed with her that night and was in love with her for six months. Our affair lasted, regrettably, for nine.

I went the complete cycle from infatuation to apathy. It's so unfair to a woman, though it probably can't be helped. Just as she opens up and is ready for something real, some of us men cut and run. It probably relates to insecurity and a lack of self-belief. In the long run we get what we deserve if we don't learn, though in the short run we hurt others.

Many of my first impressions about P. J. had been wrong. The self-assured voice still spoke for the big picture, but she did have vulnerability, and, as well, the courage to show it - as a matter of fact, so much more courage than I had. She loved me, and I think I met her halfway. She needed me, and from that I withdrew. It made her cry. I found that terrifying, miserable to feel that I could hurt someone I cared about by something I couldn't help. It felt like I'd been trusted with something too big for me to handle and too valuable for me to deserve, like defusing a nuclear bomb in a city through phone instructions.

I always respected her, this P. J. Anderson. She was a fighter, a fine athlete - a runner, a skier, a cyclist, even a natural, if intermediate, tennis player. We actually won a mixed doubles tournament at her club, and I admired her fight then. She had a taste for winning of its own sake that was absolutely admirable. I think my competitive qualities come from an obstinate distaste for losing, even a sullen, almost military focus upon a task, a circling of the shield-wall when the going's grim. For her, winning was a thirst, a birthright, a glory, the unreachable star that falls so often into hand... like giving birth, expected, but a joyous miracle nonetheless.

They say it's important to be with someone who shares your interests, but I wonder about that. I went out with a lady poet for awhile and all we did was argue about art. I could enjoy running and cycling with P. J., and one image that still comes to me in heated moments is of her in a

jog-bra and spandex bike shorts, swaying out of her seat climbing a trail
just ahead of me. Ski-touring, though, makes naturalists out of many brisk
people, and I was like a leashed greyhound beside her on those long
February trails. Even the tennis came back to haunt me. One morning I
took probably my worst hard-court loss since high school. I know what
happened; my rotator cuff was acting up and I couldn't serve, and my forehand sucked all by itself; but on the drive home with her I had to listen to
a play-by-play about "seventh games" and "big points" all over again. Our
amorous mutual fund took a big dip over that one. No, I think when your
interests are as strong and diverse as mine you need someone who understands you pursuing them, not one who has to be there all the way.

Finally, after a fight I'd gone so long without calling her that I did-
n't know what to say, and that was how we ended. I knew I would miss
her when the door closed from her side, but I'd seen this pattern before,
and didn't recognize what it should have told me. An emotional coward,
that's what I was. I thought winning a couple ski races and backing down
a drunk or two in a bar meant I was a man. I had to be, right? I hurt someone who cared about me because of my own fear, and that doesn't suit my
definition. Now I most admire the sustaining courage of a spouse, a parent, a provider. The best I can say of me then is that I was still a boy.

II

"It's P. J.," said the winning voice when I answered the phone one
May evening, over a year after our parting. I stammered something cordial
and generic back, too surprised to fear entanglement in emotion. Her voice
had registered with some guilt, but also that little warm nether flicker I
hope I never lose. One aspect of our relationship had always been good, at
least for me, and recollection of it quickened every time I heard her voice;
but in seconds everything inside me sank, envisioning the scared, sunny girl
who never talked about home.

Quickly she laid it out: the bumps and bruises, the unexplained
absences from school, the legal attempts to separate her from her stepfather, the mother's indifference, Isabel's disappearance, the hundred-person
hunts, the open-ended suspicions, the quirky behavior of absolutely everybody in her family...

I would read half of this in the morning's paper, but P. J. figured
it might be better for me to hear it this way first. She sounded like she had
pulled herself together after hours of tears. She said she had to get out of
her home. I told her to come to mine. It was an hour and a half drive; she
was there in two. We walked the campus of my school in the early lilac
theme. We climbed the ski hill through the woods, daring the dark, and
rested on it, closer to the stars. We talked in my still room with the blue
spring air coming in and nothing but the moon to light us. We held; she
cried; we lived again. For a few weeks we could even believe. Maybe our
shared sadness suspended her disbelief; maybe it did mine.

In the coming weeks the media murder-opera dominated the
Western part of the state. It did nothing to stabilize impressions: a nightmare of slow law, contradictory details, and infuriating behavior from

A Sitting for Isabel

Isabel's parents. On the night of the first search, they were in his home, watching TV with a twelve-pack. When the authorities asked questions that might have helped track the little girl, they were already in boggling defense mode. How the searchers must have cursed! Everybody suspected that creep of a stepfather, even beginning to include the mother in some utterly baffling way. Accusations were even made against the grandparents, but without a body there was officially no murder, and for weeks that seemed endless that was where things stayed.

III

Our reborn affair had no official end. We shared a June weekend in which P. J. was in need of emotional confirmation and my mind kept wandering to a story I was writing. If ever a confessional phone call was needed, it was a day, maybe two, after, but I didn't know what to say, and within a week I realized the deadline had passed. So easy in retrospect. A month later I was playing a tennis tournament at a Rochester club and saw P. J. at the banquet on the arm of a member in a suit, an arrogant, bearded, balding man I instantly didn't like. There seemed no need of anything but a smile and a casual greeting. It was not awkward to talk with each other when P. J. called in early October to invite me to the reading of a police psychic who was attempting to locate Isabel. I thanked her. "You're in this to the end," she said. That's real class, the only kind that counts, the kind that has nothing to do with the money you were born with.

Maybe driven by the impulse to collect ourselves before the other's arrival, we surprised ourselves, each half an hour early, at the old inn in the horsey lake town. We used the time to catch up.

Months before Linda Malone, the psychic we were waiting to see, had introduced herself to me after one of my talks. Though half Tuscarora, she looked like a red-haired Irishwoman. A newcomer to our region, Linda had worked with the police in her home state of North Carolina with very good results, but I was still surprised at her quick reception here. Most law people have to discover for themselves the value of "alternative information talents." Those in our region were so troubled by Isabel's disappearance that they were in an exceptionally receptive mood.

Today's reading was off the record, at the private pressuring of Isabel's grandfather. Only he and Isabel's mother were expected. I wondered why her stepfather would not display at least the gesture of concern or curiosity about Isabel, but a simple reason offered itself. The legacy of trouble between the two men in her life was now on record. Orders of protection had been issued against the grandfather, an imposing man whom, it was rumored, the stepfather feared. It was not deemed peaceable for the pair to share a room.

Our short walk from the inn to Linda's bookshop-home seemed surreal in the bright day; the leaves were dry, dark and furled, and in the gusts frisked around our steps like puppies. Ignoring the "Closed" sign, we rang the bell on the door of the modest Victorian farmhouse. Linda's tall husband, a yoga instructor all in white, walked us to the parlor where Linda waited with a pot of tea. We sat quietly in the murky smell typical of these old homes, their old chairs and implements, their dim windows and lace curtains, their cracked china and frayed furniture, piecing our thoughts together before the members of Isabel's family arrived. The down-time was probably good. The papers had made the Isabel case and all its cast famous, and it felt like we were waiting for celebrities.

I studied them carefully, Isabel's slatternly mother and her saturnine, massive grandfather. The papers had presented a scandalous tangle that seemed to smudge every player, and it was fascinating to look at these two and wonder which was a child-killer. My mind was made fairly quickly. Tina Sanford was a dark-haired, pale skinned hippie whose English was perfect. She never made eye contact. I am no psychic, but in my read, she was a person unable to make even temporary sacrifices of her comforts, controlled by her impulses. I was convinced she was no killer, but she was hiding something.

Stepfather Ion Begala had been solid, but he was small beside Rosen Gogouchev, a vigorous man whose handshake engulfed mine. Rosen's English was only fair. He was gruff, and painfully straight-spoken; his grey eyes looked at me as if he was counting my eyelashes. In tones as deep and gnarled as an ancient oak, he announced to us all why he had come, as if such formality was important to him. The grey stubble on his cheeks seemed as if it would scrape the tender flesh of a child, but I could envision Isabel climbing the recumbent mountain of him into a dear embrace, nesting her porcelain cheek on his granite. He was no child-murderer. I was not sure anyone was. So far this was a mystery.

IV

There are many styles in which psychics gain the inspiration to work, but two basic practices: telepathy - drawing on information from some human mind - or clairvoyance - tapping into facts and details that absolutely no one knows. In reality, every psychic is probably a bit of both, though Linda's work falls into the latter class. She's a "psychometrist" (literally "soul-measurer"), for those interested in terms; she holds an object and tells you about its background, even to the people, past or present, connected to it. Her impressions are often so subjective that devout materialists might never concede her successes, but the Monroe County police had their own reasons for coming back to her, and in a few weeks we would find them out.

Tina Sanford rustled around in her bag, handing Isabel's humble possessions one at a time to Linda. I almost cried at the circulation of mass-produced, synthetic artifacts. Linda held each for a few moments and seemed to go within herself, closing her eyes and brooding as if inhaling the vapors from a spicy cup. She settled on one of Isabel's shoes, clutching it to her like an infant. I studied the glossy miniature sneaker in her pale fingers, a discount special if I'd ever seen one. Suddenly now in its setting against Linda's dark sweater, it seemed the most significant artifact in the universe. It broke my heart.

It took longer to get a reaction from this object, but it came in a river, and once it did, I think Linda needed to keep up the talk. She start-

A Sitting for Isabel

ed by reciting her impressions as she held the shoe, chanting scenes and
sights with her eyes open as if describing the sets of a movie, as if holding
the attention of a tour bus. None of her images seemed to promise revela-
tion of a scene or a murder, a body-spot or a wound; they were places, cli-
mates, fragrances, feelings.

At our first meeting Linda had described her practice to me as
fairly detached: totally conversant, eyes open, and never fully going into
trance, at least by design. With us, she went under, but just once. It was
after a spell in which her patter thinned and stopped. Her eyes opened
wide, then narrowed, and she looked at Tina Sanford and abruptly uttered
a question in another language. I've never seen it spelled, but I've heard the
tapes many times and remember the sound of it: "My-ko so-shtoe nay-me
pomogna?" Then she was back with us, surprised at herself.

The phrase has become a mantra in my mind, and I've learned
what it means. Its effect was electric: the mother looked angry and astonished, and rushed from the room like an offended Scarlett O'Hara. The
grandfather's expression dropped, and he stared at the chair his daughter
had left and the course she had taken to the door. Then he sat where he
was, shocked as if forced to consider for the first time something he never
would have suspected. As it settled, he stared ahead of him.

"Go on," the big man said, with the gesture of rousing privates out
of a trench for a bayonet charge. In his bent English he drove Linda further, back into her space to find Isabel. It took minutes for Linda to recov-
er herself, to find her balance, and settle into wherever she had been. She
surrounded herself with all Isabel's belongings, making a pile of them on
the table over which she could huddle.

Rosen drove her, he drew it out of her, he impelled her descent
into whatever realm she described. Watching him scourge her with his
questions, I remembered Vergil's scene of the Cumaean sibyl, the mortal
medium, in the grips of the unseen Apollo. Vergil compared the prophet-
god to a rider, breaking her to his psychic bridle until, bucking and inco-
herent as if in orgasmic throes, she could communicate his wishes to the
world. This time the pressure was from our side, but it was no less marvel
or ordeal to watch. Rosen asked question after question, drawing our seer-
ess through Isabel's movements, through her last recollections. He knew
Isabel, her home, and her environment; he knew the questions to ask. I
sensed that to his ancestral culture this process was no stranger.

Several times Linda's husband interceded, but halfheartedly; these
questions deserved to be asked. Neither party noticed him, anyway. This
was a drama private to its players, headed unavoidably to its end, and
everybody present sensed it. The powerful, good man would have his
answer, and he forged to it. "What do you see?" he said. *What do you see then?
What do you feel? Where are you now?* He was able to push Linda through a
series of different locations, allegedly, if one bought the theme, those to
which his granddaughter had moved.

"I see a barn... a tractor... a man on it," she said once. "I hear it."

The trauma to both of them was almost unbearable, the strain of
concentration and vicarious experience in Linda, the pain of discovery in

Isabel's grandfather. A point came, though, where something had to give - our credibility, their resolve, or the husband's ability to watch. "Where are you now?" the grandfather asked.

"I don't know."

"What do you feel?"

"I don't know."

"What do you see?"

"I don't know."

"*What do you see!*" he nearly snarled, as if giving a command to a firing squad.

"Nothing."

We could see the realization settling in as if it were something for which the big man had to listen. Linda looked at him with tragedy in her eyes. "I'm so sorry," she said. "I'm so sorry," again and again, weeping. His realization came in an instant. He cried, an avalanche of shuddering and sobs as sudden as an explosion. It ached to hear him.

I felt sure that what he'd been told was more or less true, and that he'd suspected it all along. It didn't make it any easier, and I stepped outside into the warm, windy day, not knowing anything I could do for him except to give his sorrow the respect of privacy. I waited, looking at the sky and the fiery hills clearly visible from the valley town. It was about three.

P. J. joined me on the steps of the inn. We had an ale before the old redwood bar. The leafy intricacy of its work brightened merrily in the sun through old windows and felt worlds away from the earlier part of the afternoon; but several puck-faced green men beamed at me through it, and turned my thoughts again to the mysterious. "What language was Linda speaking?" I said, breaking a long silence.

"Bulgarian. The only thing Ion Begala permitted in the house."

"Does Linda know Bulgarian?"

"Not a word," said P. J. Her turquoise eyes met mine.

I exhaled quickly. This was becoming unexpectedly heavy. "People under trance have spoken or written a language they don't know, but usually it's one they might have encountered. The debunkers come up with some theory to explain it: trickery, the unconscious mind, whatever. What did the phrase mean?"

"*Mommy, why didn't you help me?*" said P. J.

That was enough. I was beginning to need a release; I was beginning to get inspired by the day. I needed to run on the windy trails, in the hills and sun. I needed to run from this situation, from my own guilt about P. J., from Isabel's torment, from the stale smell of that house. I needed to pound every ounce of frustration out of my body, to breathe in only clean atmosphere, to wash off the day's old cycle and turn to a new one. It would take hard running. From the side I stared into the rusty half-inch at the bottom of my glass. That was all that was left of our affair, I realized. This was the last conversation we would ever have.

"What does P. J. stand for?" I said. Why hadn't I asked before?

"Penthesilea Jane," she said wearily. I think she was still in despair as were we both; but by then she may have trusted me so little as to doubt that even mockery was out of the question. The name had doubtless done the rounds in third grade.

"*Great* name," I said, meaning it, images of Greek mythology and Neoclassical art coming back. "Penthesilea Jane. Penthesilea Jane Anderson. Do you know who Penthesilea was?"

"Queen of the Amazons," she said exhaling, probably tired of everything to do with me. I turned, astonished to see her smoking. I think the new guy smoked. I was strangely let down.

"Ever read Robert Graves' poem about her?" I said. "Achilles, Greek champion, fell in love with Penthesilea during their duel at Troy. Over his shield he kept begging her to surrender; but all it got him was another spear-thrust at the throat. At the end, heartbroken, he stripped her body of its armor. The whole army leered. This was the custom of war, but Achilles found the sneer of the lout Thersites particularly offensive, and with a backhanded swat took his life. When Achilles, too, went to the Elysian fields, the afterlife of heroes, he was confronted by Penthesilea; but instead of cursing him for her death, she thanked him for appeasing it with sacrifice.

"This is bizarre logic to the non-Classical mind, but Graves hit it on the head. There was - or should have been - an understanding between these two that was bigger than their conflict. They were only following their natures. Achilles had played by the rules."

I got up and looked at her: the amber-curls, the liquid eyes holding only curiosity about what I'd say next. Love may really be something I can realize only in retrospect. I'd deserve how I would ache for her, I realized that then. "I'm sorry I hurt you. I assure you, I will sacrifice for it, and I think someday you'll acknowledge it."

V

This whole part of the state was depressed about Isabel. Everyone sensed she was dead, but until found, she was merely lost. Linda Malone had provided several images in her various readings that hadn't located the little girl, but we understood why the cops continued to trust her and kept to themselves about it. Isabel's killers - her mistreaters, I should say, since no one had meant to kill her - had transported her several times. When the police checked the sites to which Linda had sent them, they often found evidence that something had been removed; and clues from her past locations remained on Isabel when she was finally found. The story of it was in all the papers and is simple to relate.

A farmer ran a tractor up and down his fields on a day clammy, biting, grey, windy, forty. All afternoon a stray, strangely nurturing beam of sunlight pierced a path to some single patch in the fallow field beside the one he worked. Something about it looked suspicious to him, and, at the end of his day, on impulse, perhaps recalling tales of the gold at the foot of the rainbow, he went to the spot the beam of light had so devotedly shown. He started pushing earth aside, and in only a few seconds uncovered, shallowly buried, as if reaching up for help, toward the beam of light, like a flower blossoming to the sun... her hand.

THE HEART
OF A BLACK BIRD

The dogs they do bay, and the timbrels play,
  The spindle is now a-turning;
The moon it is red, and the stars are fled,
  But all the sky is a-burning:
The ditch is made, and our nails the spade,
With pictures full, of wax and wool;
Their livers I stick with needles quick:

There lacks but the blood...

Ben Jonson, "The Witches' Charm," *The Masque of Queens*

THE HEART OF A BLACK BIRD

[People ask me if I've ever blundered into something I couldn't handle; if I've ever been persecuted by a psychic entity; if I've ever been cursed. I usually smile those questions off. Paranormal research is far less sensational than almost anyone presumes; but since the question is so persistent and the matter so alive for some people, I have to answer it, and in the affirmative.]

I

Synchronicity (besides the title of a song by The Police) is a term from Jungian psychology which I hope it will be justice to describe as a sort of causal principle, a means of proposing that apparently random events tend to fall into patterns that seem orderly. Imagine that on your birthday - say, January 13 - your change at the day's first purchase comes to $1.13; you look at your watch at exactly 1:13; you fill your car to $11.30; and that night when you are in a restaurant with friends, someone else is loudly celebrating a birthday, maybe even declaring some of his own synchronicities to the date.

There's a reasonable argument to be made that this is all coincidence. Think of how many opportunities our culture offers for things like that to happen, and how seldom we notice. Yet if the coincidences you observe seem to have a point more than to declare themselves, you may turn to other theories. One that comes up is "magic." Something like that may have happened to me.

One day near the end of August 1983 I was cycling east down Comm Ave in Boston and turned right onto Harvard toward Brookline. A girl in a VW Rabbit nearly nipped my wheel as she pulled into an illegal parking space in front of me, and then flung her door instantly into my path, catching my right handlebar and spilling me into the street. Every move she made had been as if I didn't exist. The sound of brakes behind me announced that another driver was more attentive.

I picked myself up. The driver - a twentiesh White girl - didn't react as I would have had I nearly taken a life. (An impish "Oops.") My only injury was a dig into the middle joint of my right middle finger.

In a few days I was back at school, readying for the year to come and helping several colleagues in the kitchen with dinner. A teakettle that had been simmering cut loose with a tempest. I nearly dropped a laden wok. The unlikely blast caught my right hand and raised a blister on the back of the middle finger.

In mid-September during an indoor doubles tournament I hit a dipping return from the ad court. My partner at the net lunged into my side of the court to gobble the expected floater, which drifted right back where he'd been. The other team was getting used to his over-pursuit; but so was I, and dashing behind him, I caught the ball about six inches from the second bounce and ripped a forehand over the middle. Our opponents were so shocked that they blew the shot; I never saw it, though. I'd run full-speed into the nylon net between courts and grabbed it with both hands, hoping to stay up and get back into the point. I spun out, and the netting lifted a grisly flap of skin under my right middle finger. It was a week of healing before I could even stand to look at it.

In a relaxing moment not long after I surveyed the triple-scabbed digit. The middle finger is an evocative one in my culture, offensive if brandished in anger, yet symbolizing an act which, seriously proposed back to you by someone hotter than you've ever expected to land, would weaken your knees. This is a mixed extremity, and three injuries to it in three weeks had me wondering.

II

There were no more suspicious dings to my finger, but events that I regarded as truly paranormal (and thus an escalation) followed, the first of them at the end of September. At about ten-thirty one evening I had just come out of the study of my apartment. The window was open and the moon cast tree-shadows on my wall. A woman's sudden, shockingly abrupt inhalation, almost a gasp, came to me from the yard to the east. I looked out the window and saw no one, and heard no footsteps or bushes rustling. In seconds I was around the door, peering into the yard ringed with fence and foliage. Only the most determined conspirator with perfect timing could have made that noise and escaped - and to gain what? The odds seemed more in favor of a paranormal cause.

They would improve with a similar effect a week later, this one in my bedroom on the other side of the same apartment. I was drowsy, just setting my journal aside after turning out the lights. I heard a woman's laugh, surprised and delighted as if by the hand of her lover scooting up her dress. This sound was sharp, sudden, inside the room. There could also have been a tone of mockery to the voice, like its bearer was appreciating a witticism at my expense. I snapped to wakefulness, thinking hard. Things were getting closer.

III

The effects I have described may seem insignificant, unconnected, and unthreatening, and they surely could have been. Yet if they were part of a pattern, it was one of the fastest-developing and targeted I had ever heard of. Many people are terrified by the very thought of psychic phenomena, and at lectures they often ask me how I dare to tread near angels - or worse. Most of the reason is that I believe psychic effects are rare, modest, and remotely (if ever) threatening. Also, I've always thought that if I ever did get into a psychic jam I would know where to go for help, and in my leisurely way I set about getting it. I described the matter to my pious friend Father Holden. Our dinner had been cheerful up to that point, but the old friar fell quickly somber as he thought.

"You were wise to consult me. There are many stages ahead before I assume this is a case of direct psychic persecution. Only you can know that now, though, and I would tell you to trust your feelings. The pattern you have described may indeed be coincidental, but it's very rapid. It would be foolish to let it get out of hand." He reflected.

"If someone launches a curse, they'd better be sure it doesn't miss.

That's one of the oldest adages in magic. Whatever they sent at another may come back looking for them. In that line of reasoning, all you have to do is stay stable, healthy, and safe for awhile longer. We all have ups and downs in our lives; you have to make sure you are as up as you can be right now. Strengthen yourself. Live a disciplined life. Pray, and do no harm to anyone. Actively try to do good, if you feel it's sincere within you. Whatever has been aimed at you may start to affect your assailant, who may look within and reconsider."

"That plan has its drawbacks," I said.

"Agreed, if things are moving too fast for waiting. Another old theory has it that you can evaporate the curse by killing the sender. You have to identify them, which you would have done already if it were to be easy. You have to kill them yourself, though; you can't just pay to have it done."

"Neither option sounds like me."

"Hardly," he conceded with a twinkle. "You know that the Church of Rome doesn't exactly fight fire with fire in matters like this. We believe in a payback at the end of the game. That doesn't help you if your goal is to play it as long and peacefully as you can.

"I have been praying for you since we met and I recognized that you would continue with this work. I will continue to pray, and I can't help but believe that it would have some effect before a situation became too drastic. But you might want to take some steps of your own, since I see that you are curious anyway. That does sound like you. I suggest that you go to the source."

"I thought we agreed we weren't going to do that."

"I mean, identify the source of the 'magic.' Its rationale. There are a host of new ritual systems out there."

"Wicca, Neo-Paganism," I suggested.

"Precisely. It's rare for the groups I've heard of to attempt to hurt anyone. Whatever force has been sent your way may be driven unconsciously, almost as if it's beneath the better natures of those who sent it, and they may have no idea what they're causing. If they have not appealed directly to demonic forces, they may not admit to themselves that they're even wishing evil. A simple wake-up call could turn things around."

"How do I sort it out?" I said.

"There again, I think you should trust within yourself. I believe you know, or have some means of finding out, already." I did.

IV

Lily Dale is a Western New York treasure, the world center of Spiritualism but a summer community with diverse programs and speakers. The site on Cassadaga Lake was a formidable power point to Native American cultures for ages, and it's not just for Spiritualists and psychics now. I speak there several times a summer. It would be ludicrous to expect instant and literal answers from any source; but I've always felt support from the community, and took occasion the second weekend in October to ask for it.

I was there to speak at a fall conference and, after the first talk on Friday evening, walked with several of the presenters to a restaurant just off the Lily Dale grounds where a roistering party was underway. Spirits - pun intended - must have been high, because bottles of wine kept materializing on our table. When the evening was over, I took a wobbly solo walk through the ancient trails to the woody amphitheater called Inspiration Stump. They've become a Lily Dale ritual for me, these dark walks to the grove. They're either inspiring or unsettling, but they never fail to have some effect, and that night was bright, windy and haunting, just what the Romantics would have called *sublime* - that combination of beauty and terror the mind finds most provocative. I sat among the benches, opening to the influences. My feet were unsteady, but my mind was surprisingly clear. I considered the possibilities.

First of all, I realized how unpredictable psychic energy is. If a curse was starting to show itself, its manifestations might give no clue as to who or what was after me or when the energy had been launched. Even effects as humble as the ones I was experiencing could indicate a directed and escalating psychic assault. I knew of no enemies to suspect or rule out, and, as in all paranormal cases, kept a range of possibilities in mind.

My thought turned to one of the dozen occult groups I'd investigated and written about over the last decade, or, more ominously, maybe one I'd never heard of that sensed I was on its trail. Maybe my troubles were warning signs; if so, I just wished I knew from whom. Just as likely a scenario was an individual, probably a stranger, with a few issues on hold who, perhaps offended by something I said or wrote, had made me the symbol of every fury he or she ever had. The weirdos are out there.

Once I moved into an apartment whose former tenant - a graduate anthropology student - had left a closetful of belongings. To anyone else they were trinkets, but I recognized the objects as votive, even sacred in nature. He was a practitioner of some third-world ritual, well before the new paganism had become popular. How many such twirled personalities are in our cities or small towns, working their private rites? Slight them if you dare; how would you know?

But from all I knew about human psychic abilities, there was no guarantee my troubles were even intended. Poltergeist phenomena may be produced unconsciously, and many famous mediums could only work under trance. Was my persecutor even aware of what was happening? Were these effects coming from someone's unconscious mind? Was I being stalked by someone in his or her dreams?

"Trust within you," Father Holden had said; I could hear his words. I thought I should be able to summon some clue within myself, but gave up for the night. Only a focused period of meditation, I felt, and a flash of insight could do a thing like that - something for which, sitting in a deserted circle of benches in a dark, windy wood after celebrating all night, I was in no condition.

V

During the night on the return trip from the loo of my guest house I was shocked by a sudden, loud, aggressive growl as if a mastiff behind one of the doors in the hall objected to me walking by. It was not my imagination. In the morning I was informed that I was the only guest, and that no animals of any kind were in the building.

My fellow lecturers chuckled when I recounted it over brunch. That building was one of the oldest at Lily Dale, they told me, widely known to have "company." Visiting the grove under the influence was toying with the energy of a spiritually-charged place; it was advertising a party - with free beer - in my unconscious and abandoning my post as the ID-checker. I should have expected some consequences; no telling what Klingons had come in betimes. This made sense, and I was pacified for the moment. I think of Lily Dale as a very good place, but it's powerful, and its energy can go either way with you. I suspect all sacred places are like this.

My part of the conference was over by noon Saturday, and I decided to clear my mind of the matter with a visit to the lakeshore cottage of my friends Todd and Kay Jacobson. It was on my way home, and Kay's big Irish family was visiting, circumstances that promised an instant party. I slept in a tiny guest building that the Jacobson kids used for a rec room. A dartboard hung not too far from my bed. The missiles seemed well in place when I fell asleep, but when I woke up Sunday morning, a dart stuck in my pillow, a foot from an eye.

There was no guarantee that this accident was paranormal, but I was reminded again of how little force it takes to wreck a human life. Who needs to summon up Godzilla? I wondered how long it would be before a tiny vein in a human body could simply shut off, before a critical connection in an automobile would short at the worst possible time. I wondered if other booby traps were waiting, and began to think my suspected curse nothing to be trivialized. I went back to Lily Dale.

Surprised to see me again, my fellow speakers were serious when I related the second disturbance, and admitted the look of a pattern becoming hostile. That afternoon after the closing ceremony, several resident psychics and visiting lecturers put together a sitting in a private home to address my worry. One began by announcing my situation to the group, seeing that all were focused. They relaxed during a short, modest ceremony, and in a fairly orderly fashion set about discussing the impressions that came to them.

Nothing I heard rang a bell. They couldn't give me even the conviction that I had an enemy, certainly no name or description of a mortal witch. Most of the concrete images I heard were architectural and environmental. It sounded like they were describing any of fifty little Yankee towns I might have passed through in the last year. They seemed to be drawing from information related to my life, coming back to images of buildings, summer sunsets, pine woods, hilly trails, heavy breathing, and generic impressions: questioning, heat, and haste.

"Questioning, heat, and haste" were the feelings left in me by the unspecific reading. However, several of the psychics felt strongly that there was a chink in my aura. They could see an interruption - a cloud, a depression, a greyness - where natural energy should have shown. At the end as they made their goodbyes, a famous teacher from Florida took me aside for a note of comfort. "This is not near enough a crisis," she said. "It's too new for us to get hold of. But it's not too big for you. We'd have felt that. You'll get your guidance before long; I feel that strongly. Look within. The answers are there."

VI

That again: Find answers within myself? The looking part, at least, I was good at, and I set to it in earnest. Once I'd had some time to put together what I'd heard from Father Holden and the Lily Dale folks, I was fairly sure that neither cult nor conspiracy was involved. Almost from the beginning I'd had the feeling that my stalker was a woman, possibly one who'd been offended during a relationship or its lack. The sound effects were largely feminine, and all my injuries were to the finger of an obscene taunt. Serves me right if I ever flipped the bird confrontationally at a woman, I said to myself, and the whole picture was consistent with an affront to the wrong one; but repentance wasn't helping anything. I searched my past for an amorous enemy.

Stay single long enough and you see it all. I swear there are times when my life sounds like a Led Zeppelin song. I've been called another guy's name at a tender moment; I've been called from Colorado by a vengeful waif crowing that she had given me an STD (untrue, incidentally), of which I should immediately inform my current flame; a rich and beautiful substance abuser called two men to her backyard hot tub while I slept in her room at 3 AM; and I called my answering machine from out of town one Sunday morning to be answered by another Betty Ford Clinic parolee who'd broken in and fallen asleep waiting for me to come home the night before... who threw my radio out of its plug when the alarm sounded, pounded a mosquito into the bedroom wall with a shoe, and spewed cherry seeds down my sink. You get the picture.

But I couldn't think of any woman anywhere who was truly mad at me. Even the above suspects had so fully vented their disaffection in person that we'd been able to share retrospective chuckles. The fact of the matter is that I've remained on fairly good terms with my exes of whatever degree, among whom (after the fury hell hath none like had settled) conjecture runs that my sins were of simple withdrawal, and my own demons simply stronger in me than Cupid. Nevertheless, introspection wasn't identifying a sorceress, either.

It was surely possible that quirky individual psychokinetic effects were behind my troubles, and no attempt at understanding would take. I just had the sense, though, that some ideology was behind it all. Serious occultists are extremely rare, and I'd know if I'd ever dated one. It had to be a user-friendly discipline that's potentially powerful. Wicca fits.

I've found Wicca - modern "witchcraft" - to be a generally benevolent, consciousness-elevating movement (unrelated to Satanism) that draws ethos, energy, and imagery from many non-Christian systems. There is still great public misperception about Wicca which not all of its factions go out of their way to dispel. Many women I know have been exposed to Wicca, at least attending a ceremony or two. That could be enough to focus psychic energy on a goal if the paranormal is as unpredictable in this respect as in every other I've observed.

I had friends among several prominent Wiccan covens in my part of the state, and I asked them all for help with the current matter. They held services and ceremonies for me, two of which I attended, and though I felt blessed and confirmed by their concern, even my own contacts acknowledged that Wicca is a movement fragmented down to the coven. If someone of the persuasion had gotten it in for me, he or she might have channeled the energy of a whole group. A load of karma could be coming and little re-routing the delivery until we had a return address. This put me back where I started. Things came to a head with a strange dream.

VII

It came in the middle of the week after I returned from Lily Dale, and it was so unsettling that I hated to entrust myself back to sleep. My apartment seemed eerie and unfamiliar, night hostile, and the dreaming unconscious an abyss of lurid predators, manifesting with ghoulish luminous eyes out of darkness like the deep ocean. This dream was so severe that the dream itself woke me.

As in so many dreams, I had the sense that I'd roused into a continuing story, chaotic as it was, to which I was asleep all other times. Much preceded my recollections, and more would have followed. This one began with the understanding that I was targeted by a slow, inexorable, deadly force, set in motion by a foreign enemy and powers we might call magic. It was greater than magic, though: it was a force of destiny and nature, simply triggered - alerted - by a human agent behind the Stone Woman.

A stone-grey idol came into my view, with the impression that it was greater than human size. Its inky environment seemed both religious and cave-like, and neither its features nor its shape were unlovely; but they were rough, blocky, just on the edge of attractiveness. She was either naked or lightly garbed, perhaps with a sash or loin-cloth. Her slaty breasts were bare, and her full arms close to her sides and parted as if to embrace some infant or offering that could be placed in them. She didn't move while I saw her, but I realized that she was in motion, relentless as a glacier, targeted like age, never-erring. I could run, drive, fly, move, all my life, but sooner or later our courses converged. Every step I took took me closer to my appointed time at her web-shrine. What waited was death undoubtedly, but also, an encounter with something totally other, so flinty and inhuman that I could not fight it. Fighting was simply out of the discourse.

It was possible that this was an image I should recognize, a statue I had seen before, but the features were so dim, without human coloring and perspective, that it didn't register. The hair - up in some third-world fashion - was unique. I couldn't even identify the part of the globe where it might be custom. I had the feeling someone was behind it, driving it, in the cavelike scene of my dream. The atmosphere and environment seemed to me Indian or Native American. I woke with the sense that the fateful thing was starting in motion from that moment.

I know other people have dreams that are more violent and overtly threatening, and as I read this, my own looks melodramatic and even comical by comparison; but tell all that to my unconscious mind, upon which that dream did a number. I'm not immune to the Jungian and Freudian possibilities in it as well, and think I might turn more to Erich Neumann for an explication of the female archetype. My dream had suggested Native American elements, and it occurred to me that my Iroquois friends could help.

VIII

"There's a couple ways you can go with something like that," said Peter Arvidson one mid-October night before the fire in his house. The glow illumined his forehead. Always cold these days, he was wrapped in a blanket like a shawl.

Eric Reynard and I looked at each other after a wait. "You care to enlighten us, Uncle?" said Rick.

"I was getting to that," said Uncle Peter, and we smiled. "I have to figure the one for you. How mad at 'em are you?"

"Not mad at all," I said. "I probably deserve what I'm getting for something or other. I think I've learned from it by now, though, and I don't want it to go too far. And I'd like some answers."

"He's half-way cured already," chuckled Uncle Peter, stirring the fire, which was his habit when he was thinking. "Why don't we do the one Arthur Parker wrote about? That would probably be a good one for you. That way we can get some answers, and we don't have to hurt anybody. Let's do it like that.

"Give me a call next week. Oh, and the night we pick, you have to bring something." Rick groaned, and Uncle Peter said, "The heart of a black bird," as if he sensed that I was the kid who hated dissecting in biology class and it gave him some satisfaction to make me confront it.

I was that kid. "What?" I said. "A real bird? Do I have to kill it? Can it just be roadkill? Do I have to take the heart out myself? Can I get it from a butcher?"

"Just what I said," said Uncle Peter with a gleam of triumph. "You have to bring it, and it has to be from a black bird. Even a black chicken."

"The heart of a black chicken," I said, mock-momentously.

"Uncle, can't we get it for him?" said Rick. "We've got the farms out here. Somebody has to have a black chicken that they're willing to cook that night."

"Do you want this to work or not?" said Uncle Peter. "*He* has to carry it to the fire, writer-guy or not." Rick made a little OK sign like he had it covered. Uncle Peter looked at me like he was wondering what kind of wizard I would have made.

IX

A shiny weeknight in late October found us around a small fire on one of the heavily wooded Allegany hills between Salamanca and Ellicott-ville. I had the sense of a few other folks in the trees, but the only one I met was the middle-aged woman who sat with us, the storyteller and historian Hilda White. I'd heard that she'd been a dancer earlier in her life. Her long hair was still dark and enveloping, her features clear and straight, and from the way the fire played on her I'd bet she had been a looker. "I don't expect anything to get out of hand," said Uncle Peter as he introduced us, "but we want to have help around in case it does."

That wasn't so reassuring. I couldn't tell which of them - Hilda or Peter - was supposed to be the ranking wizard. Peter was older, but the Iroquois were matrilineal, and the decision-makers at the end of the line in their culture were traditionally women.

The heavy woods were soaked from a recent rain, and we sat on chairs around our fire. I'd carried my bloody baggie up the trail alongside Rick and Uncle Peter and, to their direction, fishhooked the rosy bauble to a wire that dangled above the blaze. I was so careful not to touch any fluids that all three of them smirked. "Swing it down in there," laughed Uncle Peter. "Don't want to be here all night, Writer-guy." That was his favorite name for me ever since Rick's introduction of me years before, and right then it seemed to mean, "useless-for-anything-else."

"Not that close," said Hilda White. "We don't want this over with before you get some answers. There. Just let it steam."

"Now what?" I said.

"We wait," said Uncle Peter. "For someone to talk to you." He threw something into the fire that I presume may have been tobacco, an all-purpose North American offering, but it may have been a grainier substance. I didn't remember this from Arthur Parker's writeup of the ritual.

"In the old days they believed that whoever's witching you will show up in spirit form in the leaves above us," said Rick. "Can't say you'll see them, but they'll at least tell you who they are and why they're witching you. We'll see."

"You tell us when you think you know something," said Uncle Peter. *OK*, I answered to myself. We sat listening to the nip of the fire and the night-noises, looking into the glow. This was a natural space that my friends had chosen, a spot in the old forest never used as home or campsite. I doubted anyone more than fifty feet away could see our fire, but for us our whole little clearing gleamed. It felt like we were in a cave, an almost visible spiritual haven formed by the golden light.

I looked up through the branches, marveling again at the shades of the night, the cool near-full moon and lavender clouds, the slick slant of hill against indigo sky. There was a charm in the natural night-images that defied description. It was gothic, poignant, inspiring. I was hoping for literal visions.

I intended to clear my mind of all minutia, to receive in an almost Zen state the natural influences around me and the spiritual ones that might be coming. One was a path to the other, I believed, and couldn't imagine better circumstances, with three mystical Iroquois friends in their ancestral woods; but I couldn't keep the flow. I couldn't let go of the thought that this wasn't as much my home. I am not a Native American. I am a Euro-American, of English, Scottish, German, and Irish ancestry - as far as we can tell. I have no discontent with this, but I couldn't forget that my direct forbears had only been on this soil a few centuries. Here I was with people who went back millennia. Forgetting why we were here, I drifted into my thoughts, reflecting back, strangely, on seemingly random events in recent years of my life.

I thought of all sorts of episodes, some trivial, some comical, some affirming, some educating. One led into another, until one of them became very involving. I started thinking about a small resort town I pass through often on my way to Vermont. I'd lived there in the 70s and have always found its mood and architecture curiously charming. I still like to stop there, walk through the town or its park, and steep in its atmosphere. I remembered something from ten years earlier.

One hot August twilight on my way home from my last New England swing of the summer I was resting between legs of my drive in the ample mid-town park that's always been instant inspiration for me. I was staring into a swan-pond, writing notes in my journal from my umpteenth reading of the *Tain* (Thomas Kinsella's translation), and getting my thoughts together, summing the summer nearly past and formulating my hopes for the upcoming school year. A woman spoke to me, a solidly-built, handsome blonde of about thirty. She noted the book I was working at. A poet, she talked about her own spirituality, taught her by a Southwestern "Stone Dreamer," touched by the earth. ("Some of my best conversations are with stones.") Not really my type, but she was offbeat enough to be interesting. We had a nice talk and seemed to be friends.

Those were the days when I traveled a lot but had very little money. Sleeping quarters were someone's couch or my car. Hoping against the latter, I gave Bo a call when I passed through her town again one December night. She insisted we meet at her house. She was in a bathrobe. Another woman, looking as if she had just showered, hugged her warmly as she left. I asked if I could sleep on the couch. She hoped I would sleep with her. I'd presumed she was involved with the other woman. She asked angrily why I would think that. She showed me a book with one of her poems, a raging lyric whose delicacy notwithstanding made me think it was written to a woman. Thinking it a clever pun, I flattered the line, "those little poisoned errors," envisioning an insult I could hear hiss like the bolt of a crossbow... one that sank into a sonorously deflating blimp when she said that it was a blunder for "arrows" that had gone into print. My dyslexic students accustom me to comical misspellings, but not accompanied by literary hauteur, and I laughed immoderately. I had to run out for an errand. Her door was locked when I came back. The Subaru-sleeping was damn cold, let me tell you. I think my back carried the indent from a ski binding all the next day.

She was the "Stone Woman" in my dream. The image had been so grey, dim, and mineral that I had never linked them, but as I thought of

THE HEART OF A BLACK BIRD

Bo, it was her impression in sarsen, even by her hair, done up in some deliberately antique style when I had first met her. How could I forget the hair?

I recalled the last time I'd seen her, the following summer, in line at a coffee house. I greeted her, hoping bygones were by. Her response, so short and furious that heads turned, suited shooting her dog more than short-sheeting the pillow-talk. Even her woman friend looked at me with contrition. It had never occurred to me that Bo would feel like the wounded party; I still remembered that night in the wagon. This was the most strident display of offense I'd ever seen in a mature woman not playing Medea. Surely it had to be more than vanity, and I remember at the time wondering what.

Bo's spirituality was a veritable passion that surfaced in the first minute of our meeting, and she was very opinionated about history. My left-brain stickling over facts, particularly when making pejorative judgments about someone's ancestors or religion, didn't rest easy with her, but she seemed to be suspending it while prospects of a relationship between us looked stable. When they teetered, out it came in a rockfall. It was entirely possible that I symbolized some sort of type to her whom it was letting down a standard to have ever approached. This "culture conflict" could have been what called out the "secret, black, and midnight hags" over little. It all seemed logical now, but she'd been so small a part in my life that I'd never considered her among the suspects. Maybe that was part of the offense. Why the energy took so many years to show itself - and as it did - I'll never know.

It came to me that the images the Lily Dale folk had been finding in our reading weeks before described this town in which I had met Bo; they were the ones I get in my mind when I think of it, but of course, the town was so far from my mind during that reading that I didn't make the connection. Their recollections of pine woods, hills, and activity had described the morning of the day I had met Bo: trail-running and tennis in Vermont. Even "questioning, heat, and haste" made sense, exactly my impressions on the night I met her in the park: questioning my life (as always), hot on the August night, and in a hurry to get back on the highway. I recalled my parting with Bo in the cafe, a dupe of an old *Black Adder* routine I had the chance to walk into live.

["Hi, Bo. How you been?"

"Did you hear something?" (Frostily, to female friend.)

"You don't sound real happy to see me."

"He's brilliant."

"I try not to go against public opinion."

"And you think you're pretty funny, too, don't you?"

"At least I'm only funny when I want to be."

"Why, you little....(expletives)."

"Ah, yes. Glad to see things going so well."

(Expletives.)

"And now, Madam, as you're obviously mad as a mongoose, I'll just be on my way."]

Most often I lament the dullness of my wit, but at the worst times it can be too quick. I'd grown a lot in the intervening years, but I resolved again to do better, to respond with patience to pain, never to add hurt to others' mere expressions of hurt. If I ever saw her again I had some conciliating to do, and could start by thanking her for a lesson I would not have learned without her. My impatient, fiery, younger self... Ah, he saw challenges in too many situations, and could be such an ass sometimes that it was literally comical; reliving scenes with him, I laughed inwardly again. I must have done so aloud, and come to with the sound. My fireside companions were studying me with amusement. I wondered how long I had been under.

"Well!" said Uncle Peter. "Get your answers?"

"That was something. That was really something."

"Find out who witched you?" said Hilda.

"I did," I laughed. "I never would have guessed."

Uncle Peter chuckled along. "It's always where you never look."

"You want to get back at her?" said Hilda.

"No way!"

"Then take that heart out of there now," she said. "We'll get rid of it right." I untied the wire from the tree beside me and pulled it down from the bough above us.

"I hoped you'd feel that way," said Uncle Peter, accepting the line with its simmering trinket. "She shouldn't have done that, but she doesn't deserve hurting. That's a pretty old trick. Anybody you could get with that one anymore isn't serious."

"That's right," said Hilda. "A Six Nations witch would have been real trouble. You don't look like the type to get one of them that mad."

"I bet that was a White witch," said Uncle Peter. "She oughta stick to White magic. Or finish the course. Hah. She'd a been here talking to us if you'd done the heart all the way like I told you."

"She knew enough to make some trouble," said Rick.

"Some people do a few sweatlodges and think they know Indian magic," said Hilda. Rick and Uncle Peter were grinning broadly. "It's only trouble when they try to hurt somebody, and that mixed-up garbage gets going. I bet she was at a ceremony, maybe even a couple, where everybody else was praying and she sent something special your way. Took everybody else's energy and got the whole thing going. I bet even her own folks wouldn't like that. You must have stung her," she finished smiling.

I smiled back. "One of my many talents. Don't ask how I do it."

"You come and tell us if this thing doesn't straighten out," said Uncle Peter. "She's had an uncomfortable night, too. I expect she'll learn a little something from it. You and Rick can get on back now. We got some straightening up to do."

"MY VENGEANCE LURKS"

By refusing to admit their existence, the world gives a very long start to those who practice the occult arts.

Dion Fortune, *The Secrets of Dr. Taverner*

"MY VENGEANCE LURKS"

I

By the end of my teaching career - at least the full-time high school stretch of it - I was getting pulls from different directions. I'd started young at the Gow School with the idea that it might be a year or two stint, but found before I knew it that a sense of calling had developed within me. I believed in the school and in my colleagues; and in the often indirect struggling of our dyslexic students I found both drama and marvel. In short, it seemed a campaign always due another hitch, a good fight worth fighting. I also loved the teaching, which I regard as one of the greatest things anyone can do. However, other areas of boarding school life that weren't as inspiring took up a lot of time, and my research was becoming utterly captivating. I'd always wanted to reach a bigger audience than thirty kids at a pop, and I found myself growing so dispirited by the trends of education at large that I wondered if I was still in the right business. In the fall of 1993 I started to write and research full-time, aimed at a freelance career eventually becoming what it seems to be now. I have to be thrilled that it only took four years to get it launched. Few things are what they would seem from the outside, and I knew there would be some trial and error; but still there were surprises.

For most freelance writers, the writing is the easy part. The time and effort of chasing work is the problem; but authors of a successful book will often find work of all related types starting to chase them back. The October 1997 publication of *Shadows* caused a bit of a stir which was a boost not only to the research effort for its eventual sequel, but also to other areas of my income: lectures, tours, and other writing projects. As an unlooked-for consequence, several amateur research groups formed, sending teams of eager beavers into the field after spooklore.

I was flattered to have served inspiration, but had my worries about the unsolicited help. Winning the trust of strangers and getting them to communicate was one of my gifts when I started this business, but it's not everyone's. People who have information about some paranormal event can be touchy, and, if not approached just right by their first questioner, they may so completely shut off that later ones can't even gauge that there's a subject worth investigating. That's the real tragedy.

Generally, though, these well-intended newcomers merely retraced my steps, using *Shadows* as a tour guide and, almost in the nature of a "spook of the month club," digging further into the mansions, graveyards, incidents, or characters surveyed in its pages. This was also a mixed blessing. They weren't burning bridges ahead of me, but they turned up new details about old cases, and on occasion embarrassed me with them in public, usually on radio or TV. Ah well.

One such moment came in October 1998. I was upstairs at a Halloween party doing a radio program - that of the venerable and literate John Otto - by phone when Peter Jerome of Williamsville called the station with some pointed questions about William Mulley, a mysterious occultist from Buffalo who tried to tell the world about something in his city and its region, for him a haunted, demonic place. Anyone who thought I had the goods on everything spooky around here had overestimated me, and I found myself just listening to Mr. Jerome. Weeks later he and a few others in his group introduced themselves after one of my talks.

Peter Jerome is a burly former Marine and general devotee of paranormal inquiry. He's also a bail bondsman, an expert and relentless tracker of both people and information. His wife Marie is a Wiccan and a psychic. Gabriel Hatcher - a twenty-three-year-old wunderkind who has already authored two books - is a blond, bespectacled scholar at work on a graduate degree in anthropology. Dark-haired girlfriend Emma Falzone is a lit Ph. D. These were not only good research contacts and bright, capable people, but they put me onto a winding tale that would go in strange directions and involve a famous American horror writer.

II

Nowadays I read almost no horror fiction. (To answer the curious, I read original sources: dry historical documents and studies, paranormal research and philosophy, mythology, mysticism, and comparative religion. I'm interested in what at least ostensibly happened, and what I can piece together from it.) Of course literary greats like Borges, Kipling, and Henry James occasionally step near the genre, and I have also admired specialists like Brits Arthur Machen and M. R. James, and the Canadian Algernon Blackwood. I favor tales that are mythic and literate rather than merely sensational. Though I'd read H. P. Lovecraft (1890 - 1937) with relish in high school, he never really set his mark on me. His lasting, cultish appeal to others seems to state that I've sold him short.

Rooting Lovecraft's fiction were the "Old Ones," a murky oligarchy of demonic gods undetected by mainstream religion: giant, evil, twisted beings with melodramatic epithets ("The Goat with a Thousand Young!") and names like expectorating coughs - Cthulhu, Tsathoggua, Shub-Niggurath, Yog-Sothoth, Azathoth, Nyarlathotep. (I stubbed my toe in the dark last night and snarled something I'd swear came out "Tsathoggua!")

In the age of the dinosaurs thrust back by powerful, benevolent forces sometimes called "the Elder Gods," these "Old Ones" vengefully strive through the aid of human and semihuman agents to manifest fully in the world. Humanity's "dark" gods like Loki and Satan are mistakes in apprehending the real "Old Ones," and our other folkloric baddies - satyrs and Sasquatch, for instance - are merely ground troops, buck privates in this hellish hierarchy. Perhaps hoping to give his tales a heavier pedigree but oblivious to comic possibilities, Lovecraft routinely cited a number of horrific and totally mythical books (the *Necronomicon*) and scholars (Abdul Alhazred, "the mad Arab").

The setup wasn't really unprecedented, but Lovecraft's development of it was innovative, and I liked his "down to the roots" plot development, delving back through time across disciplines and in layers - layers of history, archaeology, religion, folklore, literature, and his own creepy mythology. That's my take on the real business, except that I work from the roots up. To me, though, there was something formulaic about Lovecraft's stories, most of which are narratives of a man's steady path of discovery, driven by occult forces into madness, worse-than-death, and full apprehension of the "Old Ones" (a fate next which Hell is summer camp); in me, Lovecraft touched no archetypes.

III

Known as the "Cthulhu (*Ka-thoo-loo*) Mythos," Lovecraft's theme was gleefully adopted by other writers of the 30s - like *Psycho* author Robert Bloch, Robert E. Howard, August Derleth, Clark Ashton Smith, Henry Kuttner, and others who soon contributed their own innovations which Lovecraft picked up on the rebound. In sharp contrast to their literary horror, the kinship between these writers was full folly, replete with whimsical nicknames. "Conan the Barbarian" creator Howard was rootin' tootin' "Two-Gun Bob," and Derleth the effete "Comte de Erlette"; Smith and Kuttner were the Egyptianate "Klarkash-Ton" and "Khut-nah." Lovecraft himself was "Grandpa Esh-pi-el" (for "HPL"). Even a wordy war-game was afoot, killing each other off in successively devilish ways. Lovecraft tags a Bloch-clone in "The Haunter of the Dark," but Bloch does Lovecraft back in "The Shambler from the Stars" and settles Kuttner's hash in "The Shadow from the Steeple." Their letters chortle over telling portraits and rollicking do-ins. Not so Buffalo's Mulley, perhaps the only serious contributor and undoubtedly the strangest of a strange bunch. Gabriel Hatcher filled me in on the literary aspects of the search.

Like many sincere mystics, William Mulley (probably living from 1880 to 1960) was an independent scholar, generally a failure at his outer life who took his inner one seriously... and that's about all we know. I've said before how academically dangerous it is to go to print claiming some paranormal subject or event is impenetrable, particularly one as rooted in material facts and figures as the life of a man of this century, *particularly* on the sayso of others; but it seems safe to say that William Mulley represents more than your average mystery. Because of his correspondence with H. P. Lovecraft, several prominent scholars developed curiosity about Mulley over the years, and they dug up even less than we did. From his one published and widely anthologized story "The Diary of Alonzo Typer" (*Weird Tales* magazine, February 1938) Mulley's heirs would be due some royalties, and the apparent failure of any ever to turn up is more fuel for the fire. I can only talk for sure, though, about our journey. Every question we asked about Mulley led to another.

Mulley is harder to track down than anybody should be. Along the way we considered that the name might be an alias, except for other details that no impostor would bother to fake. We aren't even sure when Mulley died, though it seems he may have spent his last years in an indigents' home in Erie County and may now rest, such as he would, in an Alden grave. Almost all we know about him in any other sense is revealed through the occasionally chatty letters of Lovecraft (which refer to Mulley as already old in the 1930s). None of Mulley's are preserved, but from

Lovecraft's we gather that he and Mulley evidently traded occult as well as personal confidences, comparing bouts of flatulence and other medical delights. Indeed, it appears that Lovecraft's last letter (February 1937) was sent to Mulley, mentioning the belly trouble that finished him two weeks later. ("Cripes, but I'm about all in.")

Lovecraft's letters to his fellow Cthulhu-kins reveal his impressions of Mulley: "tremendously likable - with a spontaneous gratitude and generosity that are almost pathetic"; but also a real occultist whose reading was "unusually wide." A speculator about ancient American and Asian prehistory, even fringe archaeology, Mulley was familiar with such classic mystics and alchemists as Paracelsus, Hermes Trismegistus, Albertus Magnus, and Apollonius of Tyana. In that he was one up on Lovecraft's bunch (except for maybe "Klarkash-Ton").

Yet Mulley also claimed familiarity with nonexistent texts like the *Necronomicon* and made-up horrific scholars like Eibon, von Junzt, and "mad Arab" Alhazred (likely "All has read"). One of Mulley's human contacts he calls "the Oriental Ancient" was allegedly in Buffalo in 1932 for a long pow-wow. Mulley claimed to have gained "strange and marvelous results" from cryptical incantations and rites with clay images; to frequent a "haunted" valley in Western New York in which he met elemental spirits and a misty "white presence"; to have slept in prehuman ruins and witnessed monstrous rites in deserted cities; and to have beheld Cthulhu and Nyarlathotep with his own eyes. For Mulley, Lovecraft and his band of hacks were channeling for the "Old Ones," speaking true whether they knew it or not. For Lovecraft - and this is saying something - Mulley was one bent boyo.

I see from "The Diary of Alonzo Typer" (and one gothic God-awful poem) why Mulley made no literary splash. The "Diary" holds few plot elements but a "hellbound train" sense of horror with which the reader loses faith rapidly. The tale of a man exploring an old mansion replete with untranslated books and unopened cellar doors is completely derivative of Lovecraft, to whom it was even handed for editing. The greater author adds a foreword and some literary frosting that makes for a smoother read, yet his conclusion did no service; fearing Mulley's ending too indirect and atmospheric, Lovecraft has his diarist manage a final scribble, as the dark manifesting arms draw him into a cavernous netherworld more forbidding than Hades: "Too late - cannot help self - am dragged away toward cellar..." (Lovecraft's one concession to credibility is the editorial comment, "Writing here grows indistinct." One would think.)

It's curious that only after Lovecraft's tinkering do local references deck the 'Typer' tale, whose key features - its lost settlement, ruined mansion, and ancient monument (a hill with standing stones) - Lovecraft sets near Attica. (I think of the now-vanished Abel House in the extinct community of Williamsburg, not far from Avon and Mt. Morris. I've also heard of a pre-Iroquoian megalithic site in the general region, but have yet to view it.) Maybe Mulley's original tale is truly generic, and Lovecraft got his references off a map. Lovecraft's own father was Rochester-bred and might also have steeped him in Western New York wonders; but no one exposed to the debate presumes the need to look to any other source than Mulley, who obsessed so much on his own about the mysteries of the old "Holland Purchase" and felt the need to cry out that he was writing from experience.

IV

So much for the books; the legwork remained, to track down anything else that could be known about Mulley, and this was the domain of Peter Jerome. City records listed Mulley's occupation as "watchman." Watching for what? Night watchman? A likely job for a solitary occultist, and likely a penniless one. Old postal files revealed that Mulley's longtime residence was on Buffalo's East Side, on, I have to observe, one of the original streets from the Masonic city plan of founder Joseph Ellicott, one of the three that geomancers have identified as the "leys," or energy lifelines, of the city. Most urban hauntings seem to be on such lines.

Mulley's neighborhood had once been elegant, but it had slipped even during his life, and was all the way gone by our November 1998 visit to his building. Pete, Gabriel and I were disappointed to find the 1885 row house vacant, boarded, and for sale. We poked around a bit outside, trying to figure which were the windows of Mulley's apartment 3-C.

I knew from my own research that there are tunnels in this part of the city, some tapping into cellars. They've eluded archaeological curiosity and are officially unexplored. People presume that they date from the early 1800s and were used for human transport for the Erie Canal or the Underground Railroad, or contraband imports during Prohibition. On the East Side, the last would seem the most likely. If these tunnels are that recent, though, how could people have forgotten all mention of their construction? That was a lot of dirt to move around. They put me in mind of Lovecraft's themes, levels beneath levels of macabre significance, all pointing back to a single source: the "Old Ones." Are their avatars in Buffalo's basement?

We turned up some neighborhood rumor about that building, but most of it was unspecific, third-hand, and possibly even made up on the spot. People will do that, you know, and the researcher has to develop a feel for it. Returning to the archives, Pete did manage to identify some former tenants of the building, even a few who may have lived in Mulley's old apartment. He readied to interview them.

V

Two weeks after our visit to the site, Pete Jerome called with an update. Although no former tenants or neighbors remembered Mulley, there were rumors of witchcraft ceremonies or other dim rites in the building. Considering that Wicca wasn't developed in Britain until World War Two and didn't become popular in the States until the 70s, we took this as a sign of a potentially serious occult interest on the part of someone in the building. Maybe Mulley had made converts. Pete finished our talk by mentioning that he had left a tape at a Williamsville cafe (one of our frequent meeting-sites) to which he just wanted me to "give a listen."

It's not Pete's nature to waste time by being deliberately mysterious, but when, a day or two later, I settled in to hear the tape, I would understand: he had not wanted to prejudice my listening. It was a five-year-old demo of a couple of rock songs into which somebody's idea of fun was to put a few fruity, cavernous laughs. All were in the same seasoned male voice, reminiscent of Jackie Gleason's *Honeymooners* har-dee-har, but faster: quirky, natural yuks. Its acoustics were so different from the music that it sounded dubbed. No wonder the band flopped.

It turns out, though, that the laugh was unscheduled. When I first heard it, I didn't get the stereotypical "cold shot," that is, knowing paranormal effects as they are instantly. I got that feeling when Pete told me the tape had been made by a rock guitarist who had lived in Mulley's building, likely in his former digs, and that nobody, least of all the musicians, knew whence the laugh came.

The guitarist had mentioned to Pete that he suspected a hidden space in his erstwhile quarters. Every other corner apartment in that building had a stairway (leading to a small windowless attic) where, in his rooms, was only a wall. Was this Mulley's old place? Had we recorded his own discarnate voice?

We took the tape to the studio of Dave Clements, the young engineer who recorded the CD-audiobook of *Shadows*. Dave subjected it to a variety of tests and isolated the voice fairly well. It was not pleasant to hear this way. Dave was even able to get the laugh to manifest on a graph on his computer screen and compare it to a natural recorded voice which, no matter how abrupt, has a rising and falling pattern that shows up clearly. The mysterious voice was nothing like that. It just seemed to appear and then snap out of existence.

VI

You very seldom get to the "bottom" of a paranormal case, though all the time you reach points from which no further progress seems likely. I've learned to be at rest with it, and the matter of William Mulley was pretty far from my mind when, at nine o'clock on a surprisingly warm December morning, a call from Pete Jerome caught me in the shower. At first I didn't recognize him in the static of his cell phone.

I arrived outside Mulley's old pad - which had been scheduled for demolition that morning - to find Pete discussing the fine points of building-bashing with the young crew of longhairs whom he introduced by name. They greeted me like I was famous. Pete had evidently briefed them in his usual complimentary fashion, which was also his form of ribbing; I can be easily abashed by too much attention, and was prepared to feel guilty if nothing mystical turned up that morning. Pete had also prepped the crew about basement doorways and blocked-off staircases and arranged for them to go easy with what we suspected was Mulley's corner of the building. I never asked him how he had kept such close tabs on the site. Pete's always arranging stuff like that.

In fifteen minutes Gabriel Hatcher was on the scene, and the two of us withdrew to wait for things to get started. Forty-five minutes later there was still nothing to watch. I'd skipped my coffee for this? That left me sluggish on top of bored. I left and came back half an hour later with a couple of to-go's, startled to find the building virtually down. The others had their own reasons for astonishment, all gathered on the outside of the crane like sightseers behind a guard rail, in such a stunned sympatico that none acknowledged me when I clambered up.

The rubble prevented us from deciding anything about tunnels, basement doors, hidden rooms, or the lack thereof. Everybody was looking up at the only corner of the building left standing, a jagged, top-heavy, brickwork tor thirty feet or so high. Only Gabe kept enough objectivity to answer me, accepting his coffee with an absent hand. "What's left of a bricked-up staircase," he said pointing, "and a hidden room." This had to be the apartment in which the musician had made the troubled tape, and, probably, the former home of Mulley himself.

The focus of everyone's attention was a patch of floor from the room behind the staircase, still wedged inside the wobbly crag. We leaned and stretched to get better looks at what might be on it, but no one would walk close. This last forbidding corner of the building was ready to pitch at any time, and there was no telling how far it might reach.

The tattered tray of floor space sagged a few degrees, spilling some of its sparse contents. From the dust and flapping, moldy books we could tell that what had just been exposed to daylight had been hidden from it, probably for decades. The rough steeple with its shard of floor keeled slowly and unevenly toward us again, catching on a timber and dropping a staggered cascade of small objects like apples from an apron into the rubble beneath. To me, forty feet away, they looked like votive implements: incense-burners, idols, a little altar. What was left of the floor was still too level and too high up to see.

We couldn't stare forever, and the workmen had a job to do. At the last love tap of the wrecking-ball, the jagged corner pitched down and inward toward us, burying the trinkets beneath it and powdering the bit of floor in our focus. It came into view just an instant, though, and I did catch a glimpse. The base of the tiny alcove had contained some kind of pattern, possibly a mosaic, whose remaining parts suggested that it had been a pentagram, replete with symbols. Odds are that whoever had arranged for that had been a Satanist, if nothing more. We all stood in the bright sunlight, in the steady hum of the urban noon's activity, staring. I felt like a man in a whirlpool trying to pull himself out by clutching at question marks.

"My vengeance lurks..." chant the last hieroglyphics translated by Alonzo Typer in his Attica mansion, speaking for the saurian sub-basement slitherer of William Mulley's only published story. Is it Mulley's discovery that lurks? Is it his recognition as a true and formidable occultist, something the citizens of this city would be astonished to think was ever in their midst? What happened to him? What is there about this region? Which was his haunted valley?

THE HO-HO KILLERS

I fled him, down the nights and down the days;
I fled him, down the arches of the years...
                Francis Thompson, "The Hound of Heaven"

THE HO-HO KILLERS

[The narrator of one of Poe's oddest tales relaxes in a busy city and studies the throngs around him. He decides to kill a little time by following a stranger, but the one he chooses is stranger than he could ever have suspected. As he gives up after more than a night and day of walking, it seems evident that "The Man of the Crowd," though outwardly a natural human, has no purpose but to walk, contributing to the city's moving human backdrop. If his story is to be believed, a Rochester detective may have had an urban encounter at least that unsettling.]

In three Autumn months of 1888, an unknown fiend killed and mutilated five women beneath the gaslights of Victoria's London. The public was outraged; herculean efforts were made to find the killer. British wit gave "Jack the Ripper" his memorable name, but it's always been stymied by his real one.

The utter absence of any firm leads fed the wildest speculation. Occult conspiracies - even black magic - were presumed at work, and "Ripperology" soon became a hobby. At least a hundred and thirty suspects (almost all of them disqualified out of hand) have had their advocates. The murders were so explosive and demonic that it was hard to believe their perpetrator had never struck before; it had to be a visitor to England. The blade-work seemed to bespeak a knowledge of surgery; the "foreign doctor" theory settled in and stayed.

Early in 1996 I heard the rumor that the Ripper, a Yank after all, had a Western New York connection, perhaps even resting in a Rochester cemetery. Unless there was something paranormal about them, serial killers didn't fit into *Shadows*, the book I was writing; secret occult societies, however, did, and old conjecture that the original Ripper, whoever he was, had had a deep-seated Masonic affiliation, perhaps even operating to Craft directives, made the rumor worth investigating. The process I picked - the only one I could think of - turned out to be long, indirect, and fruitless.

I'd have been happy to settle that issue - and any of about eighty other topics I was chasing - at long range and with little effort. My first step was to call historians all over the area and put the question to them. I turned next to scanning Ripper-books by the batch and looking for Rochester connections among the candidates. Then I made lists of suspects and compared them with cemetery records. Finally, I visited the city for days in the autumn of 1996, interviewing historians and sifting archives. None of it got me anywhere. Still sensing a story that I couldn't write, I turned my energy to other parts of my book.

Months passed, and I half-seriously considered working up an article anyway, treating the local Ripper link as a charismatic, so-far baseless rumor; but I'm glad not to be caught in print overstating the matter's impermeability. Someone would soon have informed me, probably through the media, of an entire book on the subject. I found out about it almost accidentally, on a lark as casual as that of Poe's character mentioned in the foreword to this.

One spring afternoon as *Shadows* was weeks from its deadline, I was waiting for something from Special Collections and punched in "Jack the

Ripper" on Buffalo's Central Library computer files of recent newspaper articles. Up came several months-old reviews of *Jack the Ripper: First American Serial Killer*. They couldn't have been on the data base for long, and the book had just hit American shelves. Information about it might have been available during my earlier searches, but its British title (*The Lodger*) held neither Jacks nor Rippers nor any other word that would have clicked.

Many of these reviews noted that the newest leading Ripper-candidate - American quack doctor and herbal healer Francis Tumblety - had been a Rochester resident. Some, even stressing the local connection and a family plot in Holy Sepulcher Cemetery, had appeared in Rochester papers. I understood why I hadn't come across the book or its suspect - both new - but why could no one give me any leads on the story?

I develop all this less to point out my own inadequacies as a scholar than to make some key points about research into the "fuzzy fringe" of the paranormal. Obviously, there's no road map. You may be the only person who has ever seriously looked into the question at hand. Information that could settle it for you, perhaps even causing you to conclude that there's nothing questionable about it, may be inaccessible, in the possession of, not a small band of published scholars, but individuals among the general population who may be hard to identify. One of them will surely turn up after you have gone to print. Never forget that most of your inquiries begin upon things that are in plain sight - somewhere. They may simply not be in *your* sight.

Also, you can never tell where a lead might turn up. (You don't go to the newspapers *after* the libraries, historical societies, and interviews, but my idle gesture at the computers was what filled in the blanks by my deadline.) Finally (and perhaps most critically), you can't be blind to what you might uncover when you're looking for something else. The rest of this piece is an illustration of that. It was on that Ripperless Rochester visit that I called a research contact I'd interviewed before, and he put me onto a story as terrifying as any I've ever heard.

Historians I'd consulted the year before while tracking down a UFO report from the Southern Tier (the famous Cherry Creek incident) had put me in touch with Carl Meyer, a man who'd taken part in that 1965 investigation. A Rochester resident, he had answered my questions over the phone and suggested we meet the next time I was in town.

I arrived at halftime on a Monday night at his favorite bowling alley. The big screens were on, the Bills were kicking Dolphin tail, everybody felt good, and everybody knew Carl, a man I instantly liked: plainspoken and sincere, about sixty, big-boned, with thin brown hair, little eyes, and a big nose. He seemed so at home there that I suspected he was an owner. He liked beer a lot better than I do, and the environment doubtless loosened his information files. We went to a back booth from which we could see the screens. The first part of our conversation was over in ten minutes.

I have no way of knowing if there's a real "X-Files" department somewhere in our system, but there surely is somebody high up who takes an interest in strange cases and deputizes certain parties to follow through;

and if there is a UFO coverup, it hasn't become evident to me. Carl looked me in the eye and told me what I'd heard from other sources: that the whole Cherry Creek deal - panicked animals, malfunctioning milking machines, freaked farm lads, and puzzling purple substances - was a mystery to him as well. He said the same thing to those who had investigated him. I had no reason to doubt him.

Law people rank alongside church folk at the top of my interview list. Paranormal situations seek both professions out. Many an old lawman is still reflecting about the one that got away, either the crime unsolved or the case never understood. Whenever I corner one I set to finding out what he might have to tell me. Few people know everything I might be interested in, though; I gave Carl a little crash course on the modern paranormal, taking him through my projected table of contents for *Shadows* and asking him what he could add to it.

He blinked a bit at the novelty of my query, but when it had settled he knew something I might be looking for, and his mind went immediately to it: a situation from start to finish involving perhaps forty minutes of his life, a revelatory moment and a conversation with a stranger on a bright September morning. I could see him searching his conscience to see if even he believed it, a normal feeling after most encounters with the paranormal. He decided to talk, and I reconstructed things from there.

Carl had worked on the team that pursued Rochester's own late 1980s serial killer. All sensed that he was a local, but there was always the chance that he was a traveler who had struck elsewhere, and that information from other regions might be helpful. The Rochester team communicated with others all over the States. In every office was a maddening data base by which the profiles of cases both solved and unsolved could be called up along many perspectives. Carl (like other investigators) had scanned them again and again, hoping for some clue that could be decisive.

A special handful of cases haunted him, revolving their fetid details in his head like the chorus of a popular song long past the point of irritation. Photographs of victims, sonorous names and locations, murder-details... What was there about them? He could still recall them.

In Oregon, a former boy scout leader - portly, single, fiftiesh, and evidently a violent pederast - was found in his basement with many blade-wounds. The search for his killer took an unfunny turn when a number of male bodies - boys and teenagers, probably runaways or hitchhikers - turned up under his back lawn.

From the midwest came a freezer with body parts from children of both sexes between the ages of eight and sixteen who'd been abused, beaten, then throttled. The hunt for the home's tenants - a divorced White male and a twenty-year-old school dropout - ended at a rural second home. They had suffered countless blows and, lastly, strangulation.

Hikers peered into an Ozark Mountains cabin window and saw the owner's decomposed corpse. His car had been parked all winter at the foot of the hill, half a mile below. The thinking was that a hitchhiker - or a mad hiker - had been behind it; but the ground nearby was an ossuary, decades-old, for other victims.

The Ho-ho Killers

In northern California, police found a basement room decked with photographs of miserable women on a sort of torture-couch, and the final male victim on the real device. The women were later identified as missing prostitutes, some found along roads and highways over the last few years. The true murderer, of course, could have planted the pictures and other evidence; but everyone guessed that the dead man was involved. It was his home.

There were others like these. On the Baja, even a whole cult was found sacrificed in the old Aztec way, their peeling heads decking an altar in a grove of their farm, a rack of skulls amassed over twenty years. At first nothing connected them all in anyone's mind. Conjecture ran that these were freak incidents in an already freaky pattern; that each last victim was done in by psychotic brethren, still at large, perhaps retired; and that, clearly, the eighties were a dangerous decade to be late with dues to the psycho killers' club. Maybe it was graffiti, maybe a candy wrapper, maybe the sheer pointlessness of the acts, but some clue at a scene sent the phrase "the Ho-ho Killers" into the lingo of the research teams and stuck it to the pattern of the spider dead in his own web. "Another 'Ho-ho' case?" someone might ask. And then it came to him.

One morning in one of those idle, screen-staring moments that often produce insight, Carl summoned for the hundredth time the cases with the "Ho-ho" profile. A pattern unfolded behind his eyes, one so obvious that he wondered why it had come to no one before. He had never had a feeling like it.

A single purpose, some single entity or outfit - someone was directing all these scattered operations. He was as sure of it as of a well-documented fact of history, as if he had read it on the front page of the *Democrat and Chronicle*. Something was out there doing away with the human monsters in exactly their own terms. It was the only thing that made sense. It had been the uniqueness of each "Ho-ho" murder that had thrown off the investigators, hung up on their modus operandi. The killings were different; the killers' killer was the same. The last victims were the murderers of all earlier ones, done in in their own style.

His face shining in the grisly glare of the screen, he sat and stared, figuring possibilities. He trembled as they settled in: a rogue outfit of his own bureau or some other that had ways of tracking these beasts, and the will to deal them their own medicine - that alone was impressive; a vigilante group of great ability and resources, and resolve as horrible as those they stalked; a cult or individual with supernatural powers. It was hard to say which was more terrifying, but the last was unthinkable. He got the same feeling he had when he thought about the birth of God. Then his thoughts turned back to himself. He went cold.

A lawman on to it would be its worst enemy, to be stomped upon recognition. Its reach must be enormous. He cursed himself for his obsession with these cases! He should have been careful even about what he called up from the computers. Were they factions of his own profession, he'd declared himself to them already. Maybe he was the only one around him not involved. He looked at his coworkers and wondered which of them he could trust. Two secretaries shared a laugh by the coffee and he weighed their last line for secret meanings. He sat motionless and developed the thoughts.

That worry faded with the first rush of his alarm. He'd seen from the inside the best resources of law enforcement put to the search for the serial fiends, and knew that whatever caught them so well could be no conventional agent - to say nothing of their hideous Hell-sending. Another impression lingered: the occult one. It grew on him that the killers' killer was a force - an individual or group - completely outside legal channels, possibly outside society. At first it was a relief to feel that it was not his own fellows around him, who would know of him before too long; but then a feeling came that was worse. How did they do it?

He had wild ideas: secret high-tech surveillance tools, even enhanced telepathic research, even the exchange of UFO technology with the inner circles of government, the recruitment of devils, angels, aliens; he didn't know what to think. Maybe just for thinking about it he was threatened. Suddenly the headlines of the yap-mags seemed not so crazed. He was beginning to doubt the stability of the world.

Whatever had the power to find the human monsters, seeking to hide from everything, could surely find him. Whatever did that to them would do it to anyone. Suddenly even breathing was hard. He wondered if this force now knew of him, thinking of him as he thought of it. Maybe putting it out of his mind was the only way to hide. Was it targeting him? Where would he be safe? His family? His grandchildren?

He thought of the Rochester murders that had put him on to this, and wondered if the being or force whose existence he had just inferred was turning its energies to the city in which he worked. Maybe it was already here, looking for the same quarry. He began to realize that, rather than protecting him, his capacity as a peace officer made it even more urgent that it deal with him before he could identify it surely enough to persuade others. And now it was here.

He felt caught in a Catch-22. He could tell no one until he had proof; if he waited, he might never get it. He resolved to keep his words to himself, to hide from the being or group or force until it could no longer hide from the world. He even tried to quell his obsession, to keep his thoughts as controlled as possible, as if they alone could give the alarm. The feeling mounted like a weight on his chest. Even sitting in front of the screen that held these cases made it hard to think. He had to walk.

The world seemed filled with a new uncertainty. He savored the city environment that brilliant, ambiguous autumn day with the astonishment of an infant, but the suspicion of a man who had traveled time. Faces seemed new and variegated to him, and he felt as if he were in a different country, studying the inhabitants. He walked lightly and automatically, wondering whether even to trust each footstep as he put it down, as if the pavement beneath it might change its material into something liquid or powdery, a sand-tunnel or glacier-cave, to give way and spill him into a nether world beneath it, into a dimension of formless chaos.

The weeks ahead played themselves out in his mind as if he had already lived them. Little peace they held. He looked for this force, what-ever it was, to make itself known. How many times would he fear a blow from behind when he walked from a restaurant under the dark sky, when he returned to his office at night, when he called his wife or children from a phone booth, when he unlocked his car in the shadows? Would it be a rifle shot he would never hear, a poisoned cup in a restaurant? What would it look like when it came? Was it a single righteous avenger, a comical caped hero that might try to enlist him? Was it an angel, a predator? Was it even human?

Blocks from his office, he leaned on a bridge over a canal and tried everything he knew to calm himself. Cars roared beside him, and the day's windy gusts whipped their scorching exhaust into his eyes and nostrils; but above, angelic clouds sailed the thrilling sky, and the sun seemed to promise hope. Before him, out from him, the city's profile radiated, still-ing as it withdrew, and he could fancy that it aged as it receded, becoming a mural whose soundless distant peaks were fabled, glorious, ancient cities. It seemed incongruous to him to be so alone amid such commotion, and so plagued beneath heavenly skies; but he felt an influence within him, a fear about life and his place in it, that had never touched him before. He stared fixedly before him at city and sky. He sensed a strange energy around him, rising like a faint electric current. It tingled as if he was near-ing power lines.

"Why are you trying to find me?" said a voice beside him with a trace of an accent. He didn't remember what he mumbled in reply.

A red-haired kid, twenty-five at the most, leaned beside him on the rail of the bridge, looking over the river. He had green eyes, pale freck-led skin, and a jewel in the side of his nose. He was dressed in the street fashions of the day - denim, boots, some waxy substance in his bright hair, multiple earrings. Though he outweighed this kid by a hundred pounds and had a .38 beneath his arm, the FBI man had never been so afraid.

From the lawman's description I had the absurd image of one of the kids I'd taught, an identically-colored Canadian of sixteen who was six-one and probably a hundred twenty-five, the proverbial skinny weakling - but no kid at the school would fight him. He was put together pretty well, just reed-thin, and he had a savage self-belief. It was rumored that he'd fought in the street-bouts of Montreal, earning plenty for his handlers. His appearance was utterly deceiving, except for that expression. Keen.

"You must want to ask me something," the youth said, mimick-ing the officer's position. "I'll just visit with you till you think of it."

"You're...?" He could hardly talk.

"And he knows it," said the kid with a squinty grin.

The lawman's eyes wandered, as if he were searching for his secu-rity in random fixtures of perception, taking comfort in at least their refusal to morph. Time was distorting. He had wondered about this being, now right beside him, so hard and deeply that it had seemed to last for weeks; inside himself he'd known about him forever. He looked over the railing at the bits of city. Just below them to his right was a little park - trees, swingsets, tables.

Down the long bridge on the same side at the rail were a couple of street kids, possibly younger than the lad beside him. A longhaired, bluejeaned bird of about nineteen looked quizzically at his companion, who smiled back and nodded her off. The little flock moved down the bridge, ending up in the river-park. One did tricks with a skateboard, hopping on and off a table, and the others watched. There was a calm about them; they had an inhuman patience, a surreal ability to be amused in the simplest material things; they seemed human leaves, drifting in the wind, needing little entertainment, finding it in everything.

"Maybe I'll meet him down there," said the red-haired fellow, nodding to the park below them, a nighttime pickup spot the lawman knew. "He comes there, you know. He can't help himself. Maybe he'll make a mistake before then, and you'll get him. His time's running out, and he knows it."

The officer, hiding terror, thought of his obligation. As if reading it, the young man beside him snarled. "Hah! Don't put yourself in the way!" He skipped something into the water below them and turned to look at Carl. His stare was otherworldly. The lawman felt transparent; the green eyes aimed toward him seemed focused on the cityscape and sky right behind him.

The lawman tried to quiet himself. It was horrible. He found himself fixing, in his terror, on the pale fingers before him, drumming on the rail at the ends of their denim sleeves, innocuous, vulnerable things, the index and middle digits of the left stained, doubtless, from hand-rolled cigarettes. What had they done? He could envision the panic, the pain, the cries, the desperation, the dead-ended sites... They came back to him, looking at those hands, as if he had seen them. He had to break the silence. "How do you find them?"

The urchin coughed and laughed scornfully again. "Find them? They find themselves!" He spat over the water, scanning the city.

"Like I could avoid them. It's like a sense that comes to me, a mental stench, like... decay. It's like there's an open grave or wound, but it's the whole world that stinks, and if I don't see to it I have to live in it. I sense it somewhere, it creeps more strongly into a corner of my mind, a little at a time. Pretty soon I know the direction I have to go.

"I know when to leave by the feeling of a day. I know which way to go from maybe the look of a part of the sky. I get a feeling for the part of the country. It may take weeks, even when I'm in the same town. I may stop a couple places along the way. Sometimes I don't even want to keep going. But I never know for sure till I get there and settle in.

"As I get closer, I know streets, neighborhoods, buildings, just by the look. I may even start to go the same places. Usually I never learn their names. When they see me, sometimes they know. Then it's the most fun. Then they're really bottled in. Where can they go for help? What could they say? 'Officer, can you save me? I killed all these people, and now something's after me?' They deserve their panic. That really helps clean it up, some sense that they feel what they did. And the only way to put it out is to do it all the way. That way you cauterize it. That's the only way there's peace, the only way there's revenge. If I couldn't tend to it, I don't know what would happen.

"I get one of them fixed up and I think it will be the end. Then the air seems fresh, and I feel like I can get on with things. Like it might not always have to be this way. Then I get wind of the next one, and I have to go to it, to put it out. The only way to do it is to do it all the way. And it starts again."

"You can't..." thought the lawman, with terror of the young face he was looking into. He wasn't sure he said it. "Sooner or later..."

"Can't?" the young fellow laughed.

The lawman stared straight ahead. Was this a real human being? "You could help us," he stammered.

"Why would I?" said the youth, looking at the lawman with his delirious eyes. "You want him so you can nurture him! You people don't do anything to them." He looked into the water, which seemed to calm him. "You keep them in cages and protect them, you pamper them like pets. Oh, that wouldn't be right at all. Because the stench goes on. And I have to live with it. That makes it more important that I put it out everywhere else."

The lawman looked straight ahead at the expanse of the city, swept by a gusty wind and the feeling that he had never understood the world at all. For the first time in his adult life he didn't know what to do. He had a responsibility and not the faintest idea of how to discharge it.

"You won't see me again," said the voice to his left. "Don't put yourself in the way." The lawman heard pert footfalls behind him which, in a few seconds, turned on a heel and came back. A hand light and hard as a raptor's claw clapped on his right shoulder. Looking down, he could see the boots. "You can have this one," said the same voice. "I'll give him one mistake. Better hurry, though." The light, hard steps retreated and seemed to fade, and a voice muttered, "Who would want him?"

The lawman looked off to his right, down into the park at the base of the bridge. The young people he'd seen earlier were milling about, following the movements of the wind, moving with no more volition or purpose than the leaves and litter in their swirls. They seemed to be entertained by the movements of a pile of dry papers and leaves, pointing and laughing as the breeze took them up and out. Then they drew themselves and started to walk after a scruffy spiral in their midst, scurrying to keep up with it. The lawman fancied he saw them speak and even listen to it, as if it were a person visible to no one else.

In January 1990 Arthur Shawcross was apprehended in Rochester, charged with the murders of several women and suspected of many more. Ironically, Shawcross' execrations began an exact century after the Ripper's London ones, in the American city that shelters his likely bones. This should be just coincidence; but if some spirit of the Ripper returned for his centennial to that graceful city at the mouth of the Genesee, into which of these beings did he incarnate?

The Whistlers
(The Gift of Forgetting)

It is difficult to understand how this reference to a secret order has passed unnoticed for so long, for it is scarcely less than a proclamation of the Society of Unknown Philosophers.

Manly P. Hall, *The Secret Destiny of America*

THE WHISTLERS

[Bear in mind that I have nothing but verbal testimony for this tale - except for my recollection of two gritty whistles, and a newspaper article about an unidentified blind man shot dead from long-range.]

Still in my coat and tie, I hustled up South Grove Street outside East Aurora's Roycroft Inn. It was a rich May dusk in 1989. An hour earlier I was running evening study hall at school, and mistake number one was checking my answering machine from the phone at the podium. Someone whose name I didn't catch said he'd be at the Inn at 8:30 that night and wait five minutes. It sounded like a desperate situation, related, I presumed, to my study of the paranormal - in which things like that happen about as often as a cabbie gets told to 'follow that car.' Though my curiosity was wickedly roused by the guy's sense of mystery, the rest of my faculties were frustrated. If I could have called him back I'd have changed both place and time.

This was exam week at school; I had to pull strings to get off, and as it was I was running late. I had papers to grade and an exam to print up. Even worse, the Inn was closed, two years into what would be its eight-year fallow period. I'd arranged for the caretakers to meet whoever it was on the porch and take him in, but I had no guarantee this would go without a hitch, hence my haste. I had my hand on the latch of the big oak door of the Inn and brooded again into its suggestive, oddly-punctuated motto (*Produce great people; the rest follows:*). Day and night, though, were at such a delicious point of transition that I had to stop for a look. Above, into the cool sky, a magpie struck with a heavy flap to its obscure rest; in the green billowing around me, treetoads and fireflies quickened their impish tag of flicker and peep. Someone spoke from the garden shadows.

The voice seemed warm, civil, and possibly Australian. I was so startled that I didn't immediately connect it with the message on my machine. I never got a good look at the speaker in the tree-shadow, but had the impression of a tall, well-built man. He seemed disappointed that the Inn was closed, and asked me several short questions. One thing he could not forget, he said, had been this place - its aura of peace, purity, and stability - in its May glory on his last visit years ago. "Forgetting can be its own gift, though," he said, and trailed off.

As if they were signals, I heard a pair of raspy, penetrating whistles. One seemed to come from behind me, from the hazy trees near the Gift Shop to the west; one followed it from the other side of the Inn, behind the wood fence at the northeast of the building, near the old Print Shop. I stepped out from the Inn and looked both directions, but in the twilight saw nothing that was surely a human form. When I turned back, the man in the garden was gone. He could have ducked under a bush, hopped the porch, and been out of sight in the time that I looked away and back, but it was masterful.

A small party was underway in the back dining room of the darkened Inn, ground level of the squat tower supporting the storied and mystical Ruskin Room. Five people about my own age sipped Bass in the glow of the fireplace around a long, low coffee table. Beside the married caretakers, Ted Hollis and Kim Emerson, I recognized Peter Kraus, the young architect who shared their house next to the Inn. Mark Jantzi, a neighbor and Roycroft craftsman, had come over because of the lights. There was one stranger, but I gathered that we were waiting for one more.

Geoff Desmond was a good-looking fellow of average size, mustached and with thinning blond hair. His discreet speaking voice was a bit like that of the man outside: a British accent with something added. As we shook in the dim light, I noticed a tattoo on his right hand, in the fleshy web between thumb and index. It was a dime-sized, faded, yellowish sun, with eight or so navy ripples going out from it indicating beams. One of the rays had faded to invisibility, giving the design an odd, unbalanced look.

Geoff introduced himself as an antiques dealer from Clarence who did business in Roycroft art and furniture. He, too, had been summoned by a conspiratorial message; he knew the caller, though, once quite well: his old friend Martin, whom he had not seen since the mid-seventies. Over the last few years Geoff had received five or six calls from his former schoolmate, from various parts of the world. He sounded hag-ridden.

Since his desperate friend had seemed bent on coming to Western New York to impart some message with occult undertones, Geoff - who knew of my work and needed help from somewhere - had hoped to put the three of us together. That afternoon Martin finally called, waiting to the last hour to declare a meeting-site and leave messages on Geoff's machine and mine. His secretiveness had led to our conference in an officially empty building. The Roycroft was doubtless one of the only sites in Western New York famous enough for him to know. Only locals knew it was closed.

I related my experience outside. The small group presumed the stranger was Geoff's missing friend, and that he would eventually come in, but when I got to the whistling, Geoff's expression hardened. "This is all beginning to come together. There's no need to wait."

He turned to me. "Mason, have you ever heard of a case where someone has put false memories into another person's mind, mental images so convincing that the person believes they are his own experiences? Or, conversely, can a person have had real experiences - even dramatic ones - that someone else has obliterated from his conscious memory, repressing them so deeply that they only come out when another person directly prods them?"

"Everyone's heard of the repressed-memory syndrome," I said, "and recovered impressions of childhood trauma. People at least testify that they have these memories, buried by circumstances and brought up by others. Few psychologists believe these recovered memories are reliable, though. As for the process working the other way - manipulating someone else's mind, particularly an adult's, to repress selective true memories... Well, I've never heard of that kind of mind-control, adding or subtracting memories, and I can't imagine it. The mind's a terrible thing to paste."

They snickered at my awful pun on the anti-drug slogan, but Geoff stayed serious. "What I'm getting at is, if I have memories coming back to me that only my friend Martin can activate, is he giving false memories to me, or has someone else repressed real ones? I need to know if one alternative is more likely than another, or if either is impossible."

"I can't tell you what isn't possible," I said. "I've encountered some bizarre things - altered mental states, extrasensory communications - but this is new territory."

He seemed let down by the lack of resolution, and took a different tack. "You've written about secret occult societies. I wanted to ask you something else. Ever heard of a Middle Eastern society of blind men that specialized in assassination?"

"The blind part is a problem," I said, "but several come to mind if I can get by it. I'm thinking first of one some of you may have heard of, the Assassins - the *Hashishim* - so called because their rites involved the essence of the leisurely weed. The accounts in the books are doubtless simplified, but maybe not beyond usefulness. I'd thought the Hashishim were wiped out in the Middle Ages, but you never know anything for sure. Groups under enough pressure may seem to disappear, but they may simply go underground or merge with other groups. Depends on who you read. But I don't think the group you're talking about has ever made it into the books."

"Have you ever heard of 'The Defenders of the Nine?'" said Geoff. "That's what they call themselves, anyway. Everyone else just calls them 'The Whistlers.'"

"Great names," I said. "Both of them. I've heard of 'The Nine.' Nine geniuses in various disciplines that an Indian ruler sometime around the fourteenth century put together to work for good. Supposedly they're still on the job somewhere in the world. The Himalayas, maybe?"

"Working for good, eh?" said Geoff. "Not if my friend Martin has anything to say about it. They're murdering, pitiless bastards, and I believe him now."

"Well!" I said. Others shifted in their seats.

"I believe I had some encounters with this group," he continued. "Years ago I and others may have found out something that could have made us a problem to them. The memories have been buried. For years I've been getting calls at strange hours from my friend Martin, from all over the planet. He wants to warn the world." We looked at each other.

"Does anyone remember something odd - what was called a hunting accident - from last fall?" From his pocket Geoff took a clip of a *Buffalo News* article and unfolded it, watching as each of us turned it toward the fire and scanned it. "Martin told me to look for this in the news. A blind man no one could identify was found on Greiner Road in Clarence Center - where I live - shot dead on a bright afternoon. It was deer season, and everybody thought it was a stray round from the ridge. He was a dark, bearded White man about fifty, so lean he looked almost undernourished, in old worn-out clothes, and with no identification. He had a few tattoos which were not described. His eyes had been violently put out at least twenty years before.

"I also hear there's a blind man around East Aurora," said Geoff keenly, looking at each one of us again.

A few nodded. "I've seen him," said Mark. "Just noticed him a few weeks ago. He doesn't have a cane or a dog. If he's really blind, I don't know how he gets around."

"Just sort of appeared didn't he?" said Geoff. "And no one knows him, right? Does he have a bandanna or dark glasses?" Someone answered the latter. "Have you looked behind them? Have you ever seen his eyes? Where they would have been, I mean?"

"I saw them," said Kim. "They were scarred... scabby... gross."

"Stitched shut, right?" said Geoff shortly. "Don't feel sorry for him. He did it to himself. Or he let it happen." As he reached to his beer and sipped it, the odd tattoo on his hand came into view.

"You saw that, did you?" he said to me. "Got that when I was in India. Woke up from a pub-crawl and there it was. It was back in the late 60s, about the time the Beatles were into their Eastern phase. I was traveling with my roommates from boarding school in Jamaica, Ian and Martin, looking for enlightenment instead of college. We studied with the same guy the Beatles went to. Maharishi. We met 'em all. Oh yeah. John and George... Paul... They were just fellow peons in that environment.

"A lot of us were like that, back then, you know. We turned to Asian disciplines without even the preparation of having lived in the culture. We took to intense periods of devotion, caught our buzz, and then got out and went on to other things. Most of us went home and got jobs and families. Well, that's dangerous. Just like experimentation with seances, Ouija boards, and Satanism, you can get into trouble you can't protect yourself from. You have to go a long way, or none of the way." He sat and gathered his thoughts quietly. He had a way of being at peace with himself - and silence - in social situations that was beyond most Americans.

"You know, it's amazing how you can forget big chunks of your life and not really question it," he resumed. "How you can simply never even wonder about the big conspicuous blank spaces. You'd think, at least, there'd be some sense of incongruity to the missing time when you look back on your life and reflect on images from your past, people, places, and things, and there's a grey, shimmering spot in between certain episodes. And as if something told you not to worry about it, you just go on, not even conscious there was something you missed... Now that's forgetting. That's a real talent, whoever can make you do it.

"So much of the year I spent in India is missing. I never even questioned how little I remember about the six weeks it took me to get from Bombay to Paris. I suppose I always attributed it to the drugs. We all did 'em. But now I think that was too handy an explanation.

"As a result of my talks with Martin, memories have started coming back. They were just flashes, unconnected, random scenes that I couldn't draw up into anything coherent until this afternoon. Even the ones I have now have little connection to a big picture; they're just the entry-level memories, but they're the most dramatic, shocking things I could ever witness, things you'd never forget. Why did I? As it is now, they're just the first things I can remember. That's the only thing that makes sense. They'd be the first to surface with a little prodding. If something could make me forget those, what else, what more subtle things could still be buried? I sense they were the tip of the iceberg. Not only do I remember the scenes, but sometimes I remember where I was when I last remembered them. It all comes back in a big wave of impressions.

"This afternoon Martin plugged them in. Talk about a head-rush. He was calling me from some little town, Palmyra, I think it was, and he just gave me a word or two, kind of inserted naturally into a sentence. I almost dropped the phone when I remembered the first violent episode.

"It was in India, the night we woke to gunfire. The Sikhs and some of the Hindu fundamentalists weren't getting along, and the government thought trouble could be coming that would involve any Westerners. The ashram was guarded by private agents, the Indian Army, and even a few Gurkhas - stealthy devils, little fellows, but masters at anything to do with paramilitary operations. Masters. They're the men for knife-work - at least I thought so until that night.

"Some of us had been outside the ashram walking in the hot fragrant air, a night out of a poem - jonquils, magnolias, eucalyptus. And as we walked, we heard whistling, just a phrase of notes, like imitating a bird call. A few seconds later from somewhere near came a different musical sentence. Then faintly, from a long way away, on the other side of the mansion, a different whistle. I remember thinking it was no bird.

"That night I woke to shouting, and we came running out of our rooms to a bloody sight by the stairs, two men dead in a last grapple. A thin, middle-aged, European man in Indian clothes had a cord about the neck of one of the soldiers. One of the other guards had blasted away in a panic and killed them both. Apparently, when he was jumped the dead soldier's rifle went off. Had the safety been on, the whole thing might have happened quietly. He'd saved the life of the man that shot him, and who knows who else? Nobody would have heard a thing. The assassin had a kerchief over his eyes. A crowd gathered, and we went from place to place.

"Several guards had been garroted to death with thin cords. Someone had snuck up on one of the dogs and slit its throat. Imagine! It was dead before it could bark. Others were choked with those evil wires.

"There was commotion in another part of the mansion. Three of the Gurkhas had surrounded another intruder. He had a thin rag across his eyes, and in his hand a short, ordinary-looking blade that might have been a sharpened butter knife. He held it like a pencil. He had his head high up and back like he was perceiving everything very intently with his other senses.

"The Gurkhas circled him with their curving kukhri-blades, trying to wound or disarm him. They were having trouble landing hand or edge. He anticipated their every stroke; he didn't even need to be fast, but he was - really fast. Suddenly he made an impossible move and slashed the throat of the one blocking the window behind him. Didn't even turn around.

Went right behind him, facing the others. I can still remember the gurkha's eyes, wide and astonished. The blind man was at the window in a thought. Guns fired right behind me, and he was dead before he came down, skinny legs on the sill. I lost the hearing in my left ear for two days. That I remember really well.

"The next scene I have was from Washington, where I lived for a while. I remember something that at the time seemed unconnected. On a spring evening a friend and I had just come out of a restaurant near her apartment. A blind man in sunglasses was walking haltingly. We'd been hit up by street people a couple of times, not always of the friendly type. I was wondering how this guy was going to fare if he had anything of value on him. Sure enough, three of them flanked him as he walked. I still have a very vivid image of them escorting him across a street. One of them was a Black man with a big upper body and a green silky shirt.

"The next morning as I was leaving her apartment, I saw crowds and police at the alley. Three bodies were laid out like logs at the mouth of it, one of them in the neon shirt. I was sure these were the same guys who'd been with the blind man. How could I have needed reminding to remember that? But it was Martin's memory that really shook us both up, that he said came to him in the same way as it came to me. Somebody helped him. Who? Martin's been living with it for fifteen years.

"This one happened when we were still in Europe. The three of us - Martin, Ian, and I - were walking in Paris on the way home when Ian must have seen something that reminded him of an episode in India - one of the hidden episodes. I don't know what it was. It must be different for each of us. He snapped into a sudden daze. Maybe we were being watched even then.

"Martin and I got him back up to our room in the hostel. I didn't know what we were going to do if he didn't snap out of it. He looked like he was dwelling someplace in his mind, like he was in the grip of several desperate emotions - outrage, astonishment, disillusionment, despair - at war to see which one would come out on top, each one of them enough to destroy whatever balance he'd had to begin with. I take it from that that his spell of remembering was like some of Martin's - or mine.

"When he lapsed back on the cot I went out to get him some sleeping pills and came back to the hostel to find our room spattered with blood. It looked like a blender in a tempest had hit the room. Ian was dead, with apparently a hundred knife-cuts. How could it have happened without waking Martin on the cot next to him? Why had no one in the rickety building heard anything? How could it happen in thirty minutes?

"We ran. There didn't seem to be anything else to do. I'm sure the Paris police would have wanted to talk to us about what happened if the scene was unchanged when they got there, though their questions would have been the same as mine." He looked around the room at us. "I tell you I'm questioning everything."

"You remember all that?" I said.

"And I have the sense of more," he said. "So much more... But I'm losing it... That's part of the reason I had to look you up. I can't explain to you what work it is to remember these images and scenes, even since this afternoon. It's like treading water. I have to tell these impressions to someone that might know what to make of them, because they're fading, even as I try to hold on, like a dream when you just wake up and try to get it back. Even now I can't remember the thread, but Martin believes he has it, oh yes. These, though, you won't want to hang on to. They're like nightmares."

"Evidently Martin was farther along the route of recollection," I said. "Or else he never forgot. What did he tell you about 'The Defenders of the Nine'?"

"'The Whistlers'? That was the point of our meeting tonight. We were going to find out. But I sense some things about them. I think there are a number of them still extant. There's something they want, and they stalk it slantways through history. They're patient, and utterly ruthless.

"I don't know at what point in their initiation the blinding comes," he said, shaking his head. "Maybe it's more or less a graduation ceremony, maybe even an initiation. Talk about giving yourself to a group. It could be voluntary and possibly pain-free, but maybe the pain and terror are part of the process. They may do much of the first part of their training with sight, grooving the discipline that way. Maybe the prerequisite of the blinding just makes it easy to tell the serious recruits," he continued, shaking his head, "or get rid of the ones who don't pan out. What a gruesome sacrifice.

"But don't feel sorry for them. They're arrogant, pitiless bastards. Any group that would do that to themselves would have no pity on anyone. They thirst for nothing but their goal, which I assume is power. They don't exactly like to hurt; they have this virtually inhuman detachment from suffering that to me seems even more terrifying.

"Imagine an opponent, a stalker, to whom total darkness is no disadvantage; who knows your every move before you make it, who knows what to do in any form of conflict, who, no matter what he does, can lapse back into the defense, the public guise, of being a simple blind man in need of protection! You go after him in broad daylight, and you can't touch him. How many would come running to his aid from all quarters! How they'd judge you, giving him just a little bit of what he deserves! You go after him at night, and he's got you.

"I think, if they don't want to kill you, they can make you forget. Maybe if you remember too strong, or if something in your lifestyle or occupation takes you too near them, then they take you out. Maybe they would just kill you, if you knew something that could hurt them; maybe it's someone else that gives you the forgetting, and then they don't bother about you. Maybe nothing that could be predicted ever really surprises them. Maybe Martin and I are doing just what they want us to. I'm questioning everything." He stopped and gazed into the air ahead of him.

"They're horrifying," said Geoff. "They must be telepathic in some sense. They seem so fixedly working toward some goal, like communal insects controlled by pheromones. I've never seen one of them speak." He finished with a sardonic chuckle. "At least I can't remember it."

"None of that needs to be supernatural," I said after a suitable pause. "Martial artists can acquire amazing powers through their disciplines. A yogi can stop his heart and go into virtual hibernation. At least in the folklore the Zen masters can do anything blindfolded that they could sighted. Maybe these guys - the Whistlers - just took it to the next level. The blinding may have a honing effect on the powers they already possess.

"A connection between your 'Whistlers' and the Assassins of history would at least be logical," I said. "More logical than to other killers like the Thugs, nationalistic and fanatically religious. Your Whistlers sound like they have broader goals. The Hashishim were suppressed several times before their supposed extermination by the Mongols. They had an uneasy peace with the Islamic rulers, and when the Crusaders took over the Holy Land the Hashishim were their situational allies, too, though I'm not sure they and the Templars ever made nice. These Hashishim were players, a small order, but cross them at your peril. Only overwhelming force could have put them down. Maybe they were easier to handle in an era that accepted supernaturalism, in which every culture had wizards of its own.

"I think the Mongols were unique among overlords in that they didn't bother with allies. *Vassals* would be more the role, and the surviving Hashishim may have declined to audition. Inadvisable, usually fatal, with the Mongols. Something about the case might have been special, and the survivors made examples. Blinding always made a clear statement in the ancient world. The surviving Hashishim might have learned to get around the drawback. I could see such a thing becoming ceremonial, sort of a dire initiation. I'm sure the reformed group - as part of its new beginning - would change its name.

"Have you ever heard of 'seeing' through other parts of the body?" I continued. "There have been a number of psychics who could 'see' color and numbers, and even read a newspaper through their fingertips. Some well-known psychics of the last century could play chess while blindfolded. Maybe your Whistlers don't need their eyes for what they do."

"Like the power to make people forget," said Geoff, whose mood seemed to be changing. "You know, that's what really puts them on to you - the remembering. Even now I don't have a firm hold on what I just told you. I can't hang on to these reflections. Now I see why I'm no danger to them if they truly exist, and why only someone who might be able and determined to make others remember - like my friend Martin - needs to run.

"But now I wonder if the forgetting is the tool of the Whistlers, or if it might not be some gift of the Maharishi to keep us out of a struggle," said Geoff. "If so, it was a true one. I only wish he could have given it to us all the way." He looked at us as if he had said his piece; but I was at work.

Maybe the choice of this building alone by Geoff's furtive friend should have said something to me earlier in the evening. The Roycroft Inn with its sacred lines was a building at a site of power; the home of its

Rosicrucian founder Elbert Hubbard would have made an ideal fortress from which to wage arcane war or a logical last stand from it. What would we have learned if only Martin could have made it inside? But I saw no reason to remind them of all this, and said into the talk of forgetting, "Have you heard of the Masonic secret? It supposedly can come to the proper candidate after years, maybe most of a lifetime, of dedication, pondering, and study. No one can tell anyone else what it is, and there's no guarantee that it's the same for all beholders; it's probably just a flash of understanding, a moment when the big picture falls into place. Maybe it's so simple that no one would consider it a secret. Maybe that's why your 'Whistlers' are so protective of theirs."

"It's like that old joke," said the caretaker Ted Hollis, "where the guy sacrifices career, family, everything to go to the Himalayas and ask the wise man for the secret of life. He sits there ten years waiting for the answer, and finally the old man says something like, 'Life is a bowl of cherries.' The guy says, 'What!?' And the wise man says, 'You mean it isn't?'"

"I remember when everybody in my high school was trying to figure out the Who's album *Tommy*," said the artist Mark Jantzi, "like it was something really heavy. Of course, that was before the film came out. A friend of mine who liked to let on that he was a brain had just listened to *Tommy* all the way through several times, and we were all hoping either to get it explained or to see him stymied once and for all. He let on like it was very heavy, but the meaning could only be explained as... just... '*Tommy*.'"

They laughed, and the story's spell seemed done. I could see even the Englishman sharing the chuckle, already forgetting the grim tale he'd just told as if only his missing friend could make him remember, as if once it was given it was spent, letting the others fancy it no more than a tale for a crisp night by a fire in the Inn. To me, though, savoring its ending tones, sitting back in the massy Roycroft armchair and remembering the hissy whistling, it still had impact. My thoughts were already off, weighing possibilities and chasing connections, trying to imagine the desperation of the man from the garden, squinting down the rifle-sights that windy October day.

SOUL OUT OF MY SOUL

Mon âme, grande fille, vous aviez vos façons qui ne sont pas les nôtres.
St.-John Perse, *Anabase*

"My Soul, great girl, you had your ways which are not ours."

SOUL OUT OF MY SOUL

I

Sweet Spirit! Sister of that orphan one,
Whose empire is the name thou weepest on,
In my heart's temple I suspend to thee
These votive wreaths of withered memory.
P. B. Shelley, "Epipsychidion"

I felt like a traveler descending a frigid mountain into a spring festival, or emerging from a tunnel to a serenade. Riding in the Colden hills one glorious October Sunday and hoping to fill a water bottle, I'd dropped into the valley to find an art show underway, and the tiny village as lively with human activity as the trees in their raucous change. Something struck me in the untoward abundance, of July warmth and sun so late in the year, and of human color and motion at the sleepy crossroads. It sent me into an odd mood. I walked my bike staring curiously, as much to hills and horizon as at the people and displays around me. I must have displayed the tender wonder of von Sydow's knight in *The Seventh Seal* who, between chessboard bouts with mime-faced Death, rejoices at simple facets of life, finding affirmation in a bright day, a young family, and a meal of strawberries and whole milk. The knight and I were joined in our appreciation; we both knew how precious it all was. What about it set me questioning?

Remembering that I'd come for water, I went into a bar, joining a table of friends on the packed outdoor porch above the creek. This was its own form of abundance: a lively group, and with scenery - either social or rural - in all directions. I could enjoy human company and stay with the natural environment at once. By four-thirty these friends were off to their next stop, dinner at a tavern in West Falls and more merriment to a big-screen Bills game; but I let them drift away. It was too strong for me, this honey-day in October; I couldn't leave it in its prime, I couldn't hide from it indoors, through its transition, until darkness; but even more than that, there was a feeling rising, that a message I hadn't heard was still here for me, and that if I stayed with human voices I would never hear it.

I rested on my bike at the bridge over the flat shale creek, watching the thinning crowds and projecting to the ride ahead and that offroad stretch in the middle, up one of the gaslines on Route 240 and along the trails. I was already savoring the leaves under my wheels, the look of the ridges in full harlequin flair from one spot on the top. Then I would hear it, if I still didn't figure it in the town in stillness; there it would be, whatever was coming to me, at some point along the way, if I looked and listened well and knew where to stop and reflect. Maybe by waiting a little more at least the question would come. But I was already staying just too long. The last miles would be dim, and every minute was precious. What was it, this savoring of something effectively past - life, activity, season - but still tantalizingly here? I sensed it waiting, even if amounting to no more than a journal entry and an observation about nature or my life; but that choice, this step back into the natural brightness, was one into a super-natural twilight.

Still waiting for whatever it was, I took a last jaunt through the displays, some of them being dismantled, and paused at some surreal paintings I had admired earlier in the afternoon, neon affairs in buccaneer colors: alien skies, candy landscapes, and Classical columns. I talked with the artist, a pretty woman in her twenties. We traded interests. She had heard of me and mine. She had a story.

Her stepfather was a cop in whose career only one thing made him shake his head. He'd talked to his family several times about her, the young woman who was abused and killed and the paranormal effects thereafter. When the artist recognized the seriousness of my interest she seemed to feel that she had said too much. Only her stepfather, if he would, could tell me more. She agreed to give him my number.

Two days later my caller-ID machine showed a hang-up from Alden, the artist's community, and I wondered if it could be the puzzled lawman. I noted the number, but never called it. Whoever it was could speak to me on his own terms.

II

I measure
The world of fancies, seeking one like thee,
And find - alas! mine own infirmity.

The winter following was a busy one. I think I worried more about my life, my work at the school, and other cases in progress than the paranormal story I sensed was out there, so prodigious or terrifying or who knows what that no one would talk about it. I was surprised when the call came, on the first day of spring break. It caught me in an unlikely pose, glumly plotting the next move of my day, Coors in hand, in my living room on a midweek afternoon in March.

All through exam week I'd been looking forward to some more skiing. Those last long tours of the year are the icing on the cake, when you really figure out what it all means; and now that I finally had time for them, the snow had left us under overnight rains. Even New England was bare, and my intended trip seemed a Quixotic pilgrimage. For consolation I'd gone on a vigorous hill-running session in Emery Park. Wind and rain had come up halfway through, and I was drenched to the skin and chilled deeper; still, I had to wait to shower. A maintenance worker from the school hacked overtime in the bathroom of my cottage like a Wagnerian dwarf fashioning the outhouse of Siegfried. There was a silence after I answered the phone, as if someone was deciding whether or not to talk.

It was Jack Cochrane. His artist stepdaughter had told him about me in the fall. He had been retired for a month, he said, and was still trou-bling himself over a certain case. He'd heard of some new developments in it, and had finally called me to have his curiosity eased. We met that night in a pub in the Old First Ward, Buffalo's traditional Irish section. The sturdy, bespectacled man had a manila envelope.

Soul out of My Soul

She was dead before I met her, the girl I'll call Amelia. Out of school at sixteen, by nineteen she was a mother by three different men. It was then that she started to turn things around. She'd found an apartment, gotten her diploma, developed a passion for writing (at which she was said to excel), and started college courses when her time ran out.

Her high school yearbook photographers had evidently shared my estimate, because Amelia appeared in several cameos. One overexposed shot particularly captivated me: in a dark sweater, facing the camera but unaware of it, with a transcendent, world-weary detachment, eyes half-open, probably reading, looking down and to the side as if she was above and beyond it all. Dark shoulder-length hair framed her oval face. In another shot, her hair was up in an Afro wrap, and her profile reminded me of Nefertiti's famous bust. I wondered what was in her, what heights she might have attained in life with any breaks at all. Had she been born in Nefertiti's place - and the reverse - would each have ended as the other? Did she have a queen in her, too? I found myself oddly fascinated by this girl from so close, but, as the cliche goes, so far away.

According to Jack Cochrane, there had been paranormal reports from the girl's former apartment, as well as from the foster home of her children. Some of them had come to the attention of the police, though they were all speculative at this point. Cochrane wouldn't give me any details, but the cycle had started before the aborted exhumation of her body, which his stepdaughter had suggested to me.

Cochrane had stayed in touch with his former colleagues. What he heard about this case made him need to talk to someone who could explain it, and that was where I came in. He allowed that there was to be another exhumation in the coming week, and if I happened to be there, no one would stop me from getting some idea what was going on.

|||

The spirit of the worm beneath the sod
In love and worship, blends itself with God.

Graveyards are very meditative places. Something about almost every one of them - trees, creeks, even the bird-songs - seems to me just a bit off from the nearest patch of land on which people are not buried. I know that observation is subjective and probably illusory, but when I really study one, I always believe it. My journal and I were way early.

It was a chill, moody day. The light sky held a hopeful tone, though from time to time some sterner bully barged among the silver clouds. I found myself looking more at the raw green of the earth, the brown soil where it showed through like open wounds, the grey of the stones, man-crafted and natural. The team trickled in, a carload at a time. For some reason they were videotaping the thing, and this was probably good: without it, I don't think anyone would believe what happened.

Amelia's stone was in a little depression by a creek. From a rise above it I leaned on a Celtic cross, peering around it. A couple of times Jack Cochrane came over to see how I was doing, but I preferred not to join him up close. I would have felt like an intruder, a voyeur. I couldn't stand to peer into Amelia's privacy like that. It seemed so pathetic to think of her exposed to the staring. Besides, I have no interest in seeing a body that's been in the ground. No, right where I stood was fine.

Shovel had just thunked on coffin when a wind came up, as sudden, vicious and localized as if we were in the eye of a budding cyclone. It was determined and alarming. If it came to it, I figured, I could let out my belt and lash myself to the stone I stood behind. As terrifying as it was from my vantage, I could see that things were worse a hundred feet away in the little depression. A Grand Cherokee rocked on its shocks. Most of the crew took shelter by trees and vans. I could see them jawing. They must have agreed to break things off, because the guys with the shovels ran out, crouching beneath the gusts, and started putting all the earth back.

They weren't even finished, though, before the wind lifted, tearing itself up and out into the wide reaches above us like a wanderlusting genie that had been given work here for just a brief spell. I could almost see that little pocket of fury rocketing to its content, bruising clouds in an expanse that could give it play, like Ariel freed. The diggers stood looking at each other, waiting for direction. The supervisors came back out from their shelter and appeared to give the go-ahead to start digging again. They hadn't gotten to where they were the first time before the wind returned, this time accompanied by one of the most ominous low black skies I had ever seen. Where had it come from? It fairly rushed into position over us, blotting out the sky. Lightning teethed.

The exhumation team took its cue. The dirt was repositioned in no more time than it took for the cameramen to pack up their equipment. The day cleared even before the last of the vehicles left the graveyard, and I could see the front two vehicles, a patrol car and the Cherokee, idling next to each other as the occupants talked. Apparently they had learned their lesson for one day, because they left. Something wasn't ready.

IV

The spirit that creates
One object, and one form, and builds thereby
A sepulcher for its eternity.

Jack Cochrane called again early on an April morning, inviting me down to a station in Buffalo. The troops were due back at school in two days, and I was savoring every opportunity to sleep in. Still, I was up, into the shower, and out within twenty minutes. Jack led me to a conference room and left me with three men whose names I have forgotten. One was in a suit, one in a lab coat, one in uniform. They regarded me with the noncommittal look I'd long come to associate with law people. If you turn on them, they won't be without a plan. A yellow file folder marked a space for me at the head of a long, shiny black table.

These three men looked at me so curiously that I almost felt like a suspect. They didn't know much about paranormal research, and were of the impression that I claimed to be a psychic. They were hoping for some leads into the case Jack Cochrane had told me about, and were willing to give anything a try. One of them tapped the folder half a foot in my direction. There was a photograph I didn't want to look at: Amelia in her coffin, in her open grave. It was alarming.

There was the face that had begun to haunt me, eyes fully closed this time, with the expression of a queen grieving for her subjects. She looked like she was sleeping, like a famous Mayan sculpture of a thin-slitted, ambiguous face with feminine, and suspiciously European, features - thin nose, long face, sharp chin. Her full dark hair spread beside her like a headpiece. White, filmy, clothlike things emanated from behind her, suggesting overarching folded wings. Traces of similar white material, seeming half-liquid, were on her cheeks and beside her head. Whatever substance this was might have come out her nose and spread behind her. I was stunned. "Have you shown this to anyone?" I said.

"Only people who need to see it," said the man in the suit.

"Have you analyzed that substance?"

The man in the white coat looked at me evenly. "It completely decomposed before we got it back to the lab. All that was left was water. Salty, human water."

"Tears," I said with a little loveless chuckle. "How long was it visible?"

"As long as we had the lid open," said the uniformed officer. "Fifteen minutes. Seemed to break down some during that time."

"Jesus H. Christ," I said, rubbing my eyes with a 'too weird' smile. The man in the suit lightened up. "What do you make of it?"

"I don't make anything of it, but it reminds me of something. Have you ever heard of 'ectoplasm': a mysterious, not-quite physical substance, usually invisible, that some people in the paranormal business, particularly in the last century, believe can be manufactured by the body of a psychic and maybe cause physical psychic phenomena? It usually shows up white in the alleged photographs, and can emanate from every bodily orifice including the navel, though mostly from those above the neckline. This is very controversial, though. It's completely disregarded in some quarters, but there are still people who say they can demonstrate it."

They sat and thought about that. I addressed the man in the lab coat. "Have you ever seen a body that well preserved?"

"Not like that," he answered. "Damn near impossible."

"I've heard of saints being miraculously preserved, and members of philosophical cults. Most of that's in folklore, though, from centuries back. I don't know of any cases that well documented. Obviously, she was below the frost line." They just looked at me. "I think we have a problem."

V

In solitudes
Her voice came to me through the whispering woods.

I can't develop for you the way the poor girl began to run my thoughts. My first emotion was simple sadness as I thought about the circumstances of her life, the poverty, the neglect, the total lack of guidance, the sudden brutal end. There was none of the attachment from siblings, grandparents, or even a single caring parent that you would wish for any-one. The more I thought, though, the more inspired I became. That guid-ance eventually came so strongly from within Amelia grew to be for me one more testament to the human spirit. She made so many other mortal miracles believable; and I could really see the invention of zero, the heal-ings of Christ, and the middle-class country kid from Stratford writing the world's greatest plays. Her charisma had something like those effects on others, including the Buffalo cops. The fact that the case was going on so spiritedly after her death was probably its own testament.

One afternoon in April I met one of Amelia's writing professors in a Williamsville coffee house. Jan Dufek - a slender woman with prema-turely grey hair - filled in some blanks. Amelia had kept a journal as part of Jan's community college course, and had developed a real passion for this pursuit - "ownership," I believe, is the lingo, and it's a good thing. Amelia had found her own voice in these smooth, simple paragraphs, a few of which Jan had brought along. Efforts were underway to get her work some attention at Hallwalls, and a full ride to UB seemed a done deal. Amelia had been truly making her own life; until, of course, someone - someone who'd drank and smoked with her in her apartment all that night, almost certainly the father of her middle child who always enticed her into throwback behavior - smothered her. In her weakened condition the effort would not need to have been wholehearted, but someone was responsible, and many people wanted to prove who.

Teachers and classmates attended her funeral, and the journal went into her coffin. Veteran cops were there as well, and word of it went to the top, thence the exhumations. The people in blue had come to know Amelia pretty well during her turbulent life, and they wanted to see if the journal held any evidence. Of course, after the first complications, includ-ing the controversial photographs, there had to be another exhumation.

I finished my interview with Professor Dufek and went on with my day, which included hours behind the laptop in the historical society. Still, I doubt I went ten minutes without thinking of Amelia. At midnight I entered my East Aurora apartment (in what had once been a Roycroft barn) without turning on any lights. The bright moon shot through the eastern window of my bedroom and silvered that whole half of the apart-ment. My answering machine flashed cycles of two. Brushing my teeth, I hit the playback button and listened from the other room.

One call was from a tennis bud looking for a game; another from the treasurer of a country club, calling to request a talk. That should have been the end of it, but after the last beep, there was a pause, then another beep. Odd. Could there have been another message? I went into the room and played them all over again. There was the hint of talking after the other two. There should have been no way for it to be on the machine.

I checked the caller ID, which accounted for the two clear ones, but no other. The answering machine hadn't signaled a third call, either, but one was on the tape. What was this? I cranked the volume as high as it went and bent close to the machine in my moonlit room. There was a voice, unnaturally faint, of a young woman, speaking three slow, almost indignant syllables. It was not like whispering, but like natural speaking from an environment that came through dimly into ours. Long distance?

The voice was unlike any of the women I knew, and the message was delirious. Its tone was personal and almost scolding. After innumerable replays, I decided that "Close your tent!" was as close as I would ever get to what the stern girl was saying. The consonants - C and T - were voiced almost into G's and D's, as if she had throat congestion.

If you knew anything about my life in those years, a single, portentous female late-night message - even an outraged reverie over an abortive camping trip - wasn't so surprising. Its deliverance was the problem. The suspicion that there might be something paranormal about this third message was with me, but so many material explanations were possible that I made little of it. I did think about it, though. It was strangely chilling, that voice; such conviction in it. I felt abashed, like a boy observed doing something scurrilous by a girl he had always wanted to impress.

VI

I questioned every tongueless wind that flew
Over my tower of mourning, if it knew
Whither 'twas fled, this soul out of my soul.

My April meeting with the Buffalo cops seemed to break some ice, because in June one of them called me back in. "This is what we took from the coffin," said Officer Tom Leonard, shoving a three-ring binder across the table to me. It held photocopies of the pages of Amelia's journal. Someone had spent time at this. There were red markings on certain pages, and they were all numbered. It was clear that he expected me to read it.

"I don't feel good about this," I said. "This was her diary."

"I see that," he said. "Do you feel good about her killer getting off?" It seemed like a stupid question to ask if they would let me take it home, so I set to it. All the hours in libraries and historical societies have made me a fast, alert reader. If there's something I'm looking for in a document, I'll find it, though I may not have great retention of anything else.

Amelia's journal was a special chore: two hundred handwritten pages, smudged by the copier, and in poor and variable script - capitals to cursive, all sizes and shapes and positions and (I was told) ink colors. Years with the scrawls of dyslexic boys - so many of whom are dysgraphic - had made me a trooper with bad writing. You get used to any hand after awhile, but Amelia's tightened up considerably by the end, and her six-by-nine journal was hardly epic-length. In an hour or so I was through, and found nothing I could interpret as a clue - other than beatings by the suspected boyfriend. To hear her refer to an aching arm or jaw was more than I thought I could bear. I was just so sorry. And mad.

I came to know her well. I was relieved that she said nothing of an intimate nature. I didn't want to pry into something she might try to conceal from the world; but her emotions spilled out, her frustrations with her kids, her difficulties with money, her lack of self-esteem, her bad choices in men, her pain at their physical and emotional abuse, her doubt of herself... And then there'd be this rhapsody of fancy, this bird soaring among the paragraphs, some clever urban analogy or metaphor that would just glitter in its concise grace. And she could be so easily hurt.

By the last sixty pages things had changed. Her handwriting had tightened up, becoming smaller and generally cursive. Her spelling was better, probably due to the reading she'd started to enjoy. Her writing had become less a vent for frustrations in her own life than a venue for observing the world around it. She seemed as spellbound as a Wordsworth would have been at her growing children. Bearing in mind that these productions were virtually unedited, I saw literary potential in them. Some began to read like subtle prose-poems, disarmingly chatty. I went back and reread earlier ones as that realization started to dawn on me.

One thing about the middle of the binder caught my attention, though. It was an odd stack of words in shaky capitals, written right onto another paragraph. It reminded me of the writing I sometimes do in my journal when I wake with a dream-phrase and don't turn on a light. My letters come out as spooked as these. Someone in the department had put a red circle around the odd verbiage in the middle of the photocopy page, but I would have spotted it anyway. It was pretty much the phrase from my answering machine:

GLOZE
YER
TEND

When I was done, I told Tom Leonard I'd seen nothing I could regard as evidence, though there were clues to the bad relationship with the suspected killer all over. I did call his attention to the scary capitals and asked him why someone had set them off with a red pen.

"Those appeared in the journal after we returned it the first time," he said, looking at me keenly. "I can show you the copy we made of that page back in April."

It settled in immediately. "You've ruled out the obvious?" I said. "That someone in the department..."

"We have videotape of the way everything was when we first took it out of the ground and when we found it the second time. The writing was done with green ink from the pen that was buried with her, while it was in the ground. The journal was open to that page when we dug her up the second time. That's how we spotted it."

VII

In many mortal forms I rashly sought
The shadow of that idol of my thought.

By now I was fully haunted by the lost Amelia. I found myself catching my breath at the sight of a magazine in the library whose cover model had something of Amelia's look - oval face, olive skin, curly dark hair. In a crowd at a concert I might spot a woman like her and even move to get a glimpse of her, satisfying myself that this could not be her. Why I had the impression that she was not irrevocably out of reach is a mystery to me. My fascination with her was departing from the professional to the peculiar.

The night I had read Amelia's book I told the officer about the slate-writing of the nineteenth century. Small tablets were sealed, sometimes buried, with a few pieces of chalk and then opened after periods of time to reveal messages, even elaborate drawings. The assertion was that "the spirits" did the writing. Of course something like that could be faked by a simple switcheroo at any stage of the process. The question is, had it been in every case? Some of the successes had looked pretty controlled.

My mind kept returning to the phrase, both the message on my answering machine - of which I told no one - and the mystery writing in Amelia's journal. Almost any combo of phonemes can be a word, however arcane, in some Western lingo, and I know each of these is; but in their sequence they were meaningless to me. My exposure to Medieval mysticism had left me alert to code-language, and the moment I saw these words spelled I sensed that they might be a cipher. There were no signs of technical occultism in Amelia's work, but there was plenty of other word-play, usually take-offs on people's names. Even when she doodled it was faces. I sensed that I was looking for a play on a name.

A week later I went back to the station. "If this is what it might be," I said, "it isn't the only case of a complex message coming back to us. A couple of the founders of the British Society for Psychical Research, determined to give the world evidence of after-life survival, had worked out a tricky code with that in mind. Several of them died near the same time (around 1900), and soon after, messages using literary references were received by psychics on both sides of the Atlantic. The messages had to be intricate to stand against accusations of coincidence, and to prove that the people channeling them weren't making them up. They were a little too intricate, though. It took even the supporters of parapsychology a long time to recognize what they were getting, and the debunkers still claimed it was all gobbledegook."

Tom Leonard was less interested in the history of parapsychology than in evidence, and I set my rundown of the grave-message before him. Though the Devil to decode, the old ciphers could be quite basic in some respects, sometimes even to order of their reading. We won't go through my unsuccessful perambulations; the only one that made sense to me was the simplest. The letters in rows downward give us GYT LEE ORN ZDE (or ZED): "Guy T Lee Ornzed." Since in many schools students are taught to say "zed" for the letter "Z," "Guy Lattornzi," I thought, might be the best candidate for an actual name.

The officer looked at my renditions. "Jesus," he said several times, shaking his head. "Nobody's going to believe this. What the Hell do we have going on here?"

"I'd think it's the other place that's interested in justice," I said.

VIII

And bid them love each other and be blessed:
And leave the troop which errs, and which reproves
And come and be my guest, - for I am Love's.

As I write this in the spring of 1999, the very long and public trial is over. There has been simmering outrage over the death of the young woman, and little doubt over the party responsible; but getting pounded in a rumble in an Elmwood Strip bar is as close to earthly justice as Lee Quattornzi has come so far. Lee's come to fancy himself a painter and thought, after hanging low for a few weeks, he might come out for some nightlife on the Buffalo artscene. Still, it was unwise. Some of the dead girl's wellwishers took exception to him enjoying himself so publicly at the post-opening party. An artist-friend described the whole thing, and I wondered aloud to him who - beside the bar-staff - might have come in on Lee's side. "That's about it," was the answer.

I wondered if the manic jingo had been the last words playing pinball in Amelia's brain as she shook with his knee across her throat, and coming back to haunt my answering machine as if she murkily sensed a sympatico. Ah, maybe better this way. I don't picture her as a vengeful spirit, merely, perhaps, as a communicator still earthbound in some dreamy way. Maybe through me she was seeking the articulation she would have gained for herself with time she was never given. Maybe now she can fly.

Though I'll finish this piece with a lift from Shelley's elegy to Keats ("Adonais"), all through it I have been thinking of his long lyric, "Epipsychidion." This title is a meld of Greek words often pronounced, *A-PIP-sa-KEY-dee-un*, and translated, "This Soul out of My Soul." Possibly the best pure "singer" of lyrics in English, Percy Bysshe Shelley (1792-1822) is my image of someone so into the spiritual realm that he's not really on this planet as most of us are. Shelley was always forming crushes, likely Platonic, on oppressed, unattainable women, and, envisioning their two spirits as astral mates, he wrote "Epipsychidion" to Emilia Vivianni, a young Italian woman virtually imprisoned in a convent.

The young of both sexes have unrealistic crushes and fits of puppy love, but taking the propensity into adulthood and developing it into art may be one thing that distinguishes at least male Western poets. So did it Petrarch, Dante, Sidney, Shakespeare, and all the Romantics, among too many others to name. The old concept of "The Muse" may be built around some syndrome of the sort, though little its advocates would concede it. I'm not sure I would, either. I can accommodate both theories, since I may display each feeling myself in my fascination with Amelia. We were cultures apart in so many ways, but her soul, for me, "like a star/Beacons from the abode where the Eternal are." *Shanti*, Amelia. Peace.

BIGFOOT
AT BLACK CREEK

"I'm havin' a reg'lar hell-fire kind of a trip, I am."
Algernon Blackwood, "The Wendigo"

BIGFOOT AT BLACK CREEK

I

By now the word "paranormal" is used simply to mean "outside the accepted theory," and, as might be imagined, the modern business of it is a big one, concerning itself partly with subjects that people would type as "supernatural," like apparitions of dead humans and extra-sensory talents in living ones. Paranormal inquiry also addresses things that might be totally natural, even commonplace, but simply out of setting. "Ancient mysteries" - like the possible Phoenician exploration of the Americas - are generally of this variety. Some paranormal subjects may just be undiscovered - like UFOs, earth energies, and mystery monsters - and, if the general presumptions of their advocates come true, might someday be the study of mainstream disciplines like physics, geology, and zoology.

The apish giant often called "Bigfoot" would be in the last category, and *Shadows of the Western Door* addressed the subject of its possible presence in Western New York. I compiled as many good "crazy critter" reports as I could about my home region, hoping for credible and electrifying "close encounters." What surfaced easily was a folkloric mass from a long section of the Alleganies running well into Pennsylvania. Until recently this was the best modern cycle, but it was murky: often third-hand reports lacking reliable witnesses or physical evidence. At that point it didn't surprise me; I expected the critters to be... scarce.

From 1973 to 1976 there was a better cycle of reports from a largely forested and rural region around the northern part of Allegany County. I had interviewed most of the key human players from this episode in the early 90s and they seemed very credible, but I'd left the matter out of *Shadows* because I didn't have even enough idea what was up to know which chapter to put it in. (Ghosts? Beasties? UFOs?) From what I could gather, the focus - if not also the stimulus - of the quirky activity seemed to be a small cabin built by some high school kids near a marshy region that had attracted generations of paranormal rumors reminiscent of UFO stories, like strange lights and mechanical noises. The lads used to sleep in this jerryrigged shack on weekends and holidays, but one of them stepped outside one night and found himself and a large critter checking each other out. He described it as anthropoidal, but light-colored. In other respects the cycle followed paranormal patterns: ripped farm animals, rattled cabins, spooked livestock, alarmed countryfolk, and reports of strange, smelly critters. Yes - Bigfoot is supposedly so redolent that they call him "the Skunk Ape" in some parts.

Shortly after *Shadows* was published I started hearing stories that made me believe I'd given too short shrift to a couple of its topics, including Ol' Stinky. In the fall of 1998 after a luncheon talk in Niagara County I was approached by one of the attendees. That very week her brother's family had cast a set of seventeen-inch footprints outside their Allegany County home. They were wary of publicity, but I managed to arrange an interview for a few weeks later. I used the interval for a little more digging, and reflected on Bigfoot in my area back through time.

There were historic accounts of Bigfoot, or the reasonable facsimile. One of the most elaborate came from Livingston County, where a strange beast was sighted several times in 1870 and 1871. Big, bipedal, and hairy, it maimed a number of harassing dogs. The accounts make no mention of details we'd consider critical: its skull size and shape, its body configuration. It's hard to know what was going on.

As part of the work on "Buried Secrets" - *Shadows'* chapter on the ancient mysteries of the region - I had discovered a tradition of something like Bigfoot in the histories and old records. When the Whites arrived for good near the end of the eighteenth century this area was fairly dotted with earthworks much like the Old World type, and a number of curiosities came out of them, including two bestial, humanoid skulls from a pre-Iroquoian burial mound on Tonawanda island near Buffalo. Giant human-like skeletons turned up throughout the region, chiefly in the Southern Tier near the Alleganies, and along river valleys like the Conewango. More reports of big hominid bones came from homebuilders and other diggers near East Aurora and Rochester. Nineteenth-century finds, seemingly quite well-documented, of numerous giant skeletons just outside Western New York - in northwestern Pennsylvania and the Susquehanna Valley - could point to a tribe, even a race of them in the region, except for the sheer oddity of the idea.

While some Native American nations of the west seem to have the tradition of the Bigfoot, among those of the Northeast Woodlands the matter is anything but clear. Iroquois legend held figures that might be interpreted as Bigfoot-like, both generic - the Stone Giants - and individual, like High Hat, a bogie local to the northern Alleganies. I'd even heard of something called "the Wendigo Complex," only found among Native American men, in which the sufferer believes he is becoming something bestial, cannibalistic, and dangerous to his community, even his own loved ones. Yet I had no confidence whatever that a Bigfoot was what we were talking about. I don't believe you should start out looking for something and ransack tradition for things that remind you of it. You don't understand the significance of the images that way. You start by getting into the context of a culture, and I really didn't think I was with the native people of the northeast.

II

It was an exceptionally mild October afternoon when I arrived at the home of Bill Pascarella and Sandy Stefan. Bill was a strong, red-bearded fellow perpetually dressed in jeans and flannels, a wood sculptor whose studio was in Wellsville. He traveled frequently about our region on various jobs, and, though he was obviously a firm presence about the household, he seemed to be a bystander to its social life and much of the decision-making. Sandy was a thirtysomething hippie, a free-thinking, long-haired artist who watched their brood of kids (ranging from five to twenty) and ran a gallery out of their house.

With input from the kids, Sandy gave me the particulars. They'd heard "funny noises" - no one had anything more specific - outside their rural house one moist night the week before. I got the feeling that there was something atmospheric, possibly even subliminal, about their perceptions. The next morning they saw the footprints in the wet soil and made impressions of the best two. Presuming hopefully that the big fellow's a vegan, they put bowls with a variety of fruit and bread on the porch that night. In the morning they found the edibles uneaten, though moved, as if picked up and examined. Strangest of all, a mirror, a heavy old job that took strength to move, had been taken from their porch a dozen yards into a small grove and left resting behind a tree in a position that could have reflected the light from the house, as if the unknown woodsman was fascinated by it or his own image. One of the kids reported that something in the orchard had dropped a behemoth biohazard of which I'm pleased to say no plaster impressions were made.

For the evening of our interview an informal signing and reception had been arranged at Sandy's living-room shop. I enjoyed her granola-cruncher friends and got a batch of new leads on the local paranormal for *Shadows'* eventual follow-up. Sandy's boys and girls were well underfoot. A sixteen-year-old pack of anxieties named Parker was the image of my younger self, distrustful of authority figures like I must have at that point seemed. Evidently I passed the test, for within seconds of our first exchange of words the compact, sandy-haired, buzz-cut fellow was spilling those details of his life - his girlfriends, his fistfights, his wisecracks to teachers - that he thought put him in the best light. He focused on me as if only he and I were in the room, talking for a minute or two, then circulating off with his sidekick Jake and returning later, expecting my full attention for his every observation - no matter what stage a talk was at with someone else. Jake - an affable widebody introduced as a poet - offered to send me his own work for review, which would have been fine. I always try to encourage writing in kids. Parker tried to talk him into reciting one of the bombshells that had impressed their circle, but he declined. He'd send me something, though.

III

The late drive home on those spare country roads gave me the chance to step back from the Black Creek situation. My first gesture was to take a breath.

The Allegany Bigfoot was something new for me all the way. Most of the cases I work with involve psychic ("supernatural") phenomena, which are never so concrete or dramatic that there's a chance of official acceptance; thus, there had never been much for me to gain or lose by them. The prospect of getting the goods on this one made me nervous. I tried to slow down and evaluate the case for its legitimacy.

This was the most persuasive twentieth-century encounter I'd ever heard of in Western New York, and one of the only Bigfoot appearances anywhere reported in an area this accessible. Northern Allegany County is hilly, wooded, and rural, but you'd be hard-pressed to find a spot in it more than a mile from a paved road. The region is crossed by hunters, hikers, and ATV's virtually all year. It was maddening to think of a big unknown animal living hidden here for very long.

The plaster footprints had looked imposing enough: blocky, brute affairs much like the ones from California and the northwest. It was impressive to see and heft them, as if their mineral quality indicated their maker. Of course a woodcarver like Bill Pascarella could have done the models for them; but he was one of the skeptics. And what would have been the motive? The family were trying to keep things quiet; and they were far from united in their belief.

Sandy and some of the older kids were serious about the natural mystery, though to the younger ones, passing around chalky footprints like family treasures, the Sasquatch-watch was clearly a game at this point. Husband Bill and college student Suzie had never caught the obsession, both seeming to feel that the family were the victims of a joker in the matter of the footprints and overactive imaginations thereafter. I drew no conclusion from this disparity. Even in some famous and apparently legitimate paranormal cases, members of a family don't always agree about the situation under their own roof. Had Sandy's entire clan been trying to persuade me of something I would have been more suspicious.

One thing even had me questioning Sandy's belief. I know she's a tree-hugger; but why, after taking its footprints, would anyone who believes in its existence invite this creature back near her children? This is a massive animal - or whatever - and, because of its presumed intelligence, potentially the most dangerous in the world. Then I thought of the UFO freaks in *Independence Day* imploring their own incineration from atop a high building. I know people who would do that. Brutally dismissive of other folks whose politics merely differ on points from their own, they can suspend all critical faculties with a UFO or an unknown animal, regarding any manifestation of either as a sacred event like the surfacing of an endangered whale. I reflected that anything is possible where people are concerned, and that my own attitudes were not above reexamination as well. I pondered my next concrete move. I wasn't sure there would be one.

Whatever I am (or think I am) accomplishing, I never saw my role as that of a paranormal P. T. Barnum, calling ever more mystifying events to the world's notice. My point has always been to remind us of the great language embodied in the world's myth, religion, and spirituality; to protest this legacy's neglect in the late twentieth-century's materialism; and to point out for us all again that our scientistic mind-set has not proven its case well enough to rule out all but its own gods. The discovery and documentation of a Bigfoot in a Western New York backyard had no direct impact on any of these goals. Most decisive, however, was the concerned family's desire for privacy. Any further publicizing on my part would be betraying them.

I decided simply to wait, either for Sandy's clan to change its position or for another pertinent development I could write up without compromising any source. Because of my book and my new contacts in the region, I thought I'd have a fair chance of hearing about it. I resolved to prepare for it by solidifying a personal big picture about the whole topic.

This was not a major scholarly undertaking, I might add. The literature is truly dense in almost no paranormal subject.

I found that most devotees see the Bigfoot question as a zoological one, regarding the beastie as a presumed-extinct hominid like *Gigantopithecus*. To them the only problem is that the hunt so far has been unsuccessful. The rest of us, though, run into some dead ends looking at it that way. It's hard to see how the North American environment could support a still-secret breeding population of large animals (unless they eat trees and sleep underground). A Bigfoot still hasn't been shot, captured, or even found dead.

There are counter-arguments, and good evidence of Bigfoot's physical existence: footprints, recorded sound effects, even a few unidentified reddish hairs. The sheer mass of testimony has to be worth something, pointing at least to a perceptual mystery. Almost every forested state of the Union has had Bigfoot reports throughout White history and, at least in the west, Native American tradition. There is also that famous short, amazing film. It could be a power forward in an ape suit except for its walk, which physiologists have pronounced as humanly impossible to fake.

There are reasons to believe that the absence of a Bigfoot - living or dead - is not such crushing evidence. Its alleged environment is huge and trackless. A dead grizzly has never been found in the woods, either, and many natural animals are marvelously elusive. Most people in my region, for instance, are unaware that coyotes live among us in abundance, even in the suburbs. Bears hide pretty well, too, and they're lumbering, and not as smart as hominids. The defiance of skeptics isn't so worrisome, either. There have been these in every generation about every issue; they admit no doubt of the standard picture, which changes, if ever, around them. The most credible position may be in the middle, especially for those who haven't done any digging. If you take only what's known about Bigfoot - that it has been reported - and work backward, a number of insights make sense.

Worldwide, mystery critters - lake snakes (like the Loch Ness monster) and freaky furries (like Bigfoot, the Yeti, and others) - have for some reason become associated both with the UFO cycle and the "Earth Mysteries" school of modern supernaturalism. There seem to be UFO-beastie zones, and even seasons, about the world. For instance, the third week of May 1977 found the British Isles a supernatural circus of "big cat" and Nessie sightings with a veritable "Star Wars" bigtop of UFOs above. Researcher John Michell noted that most of the sightings were near "places of ancient sanctity" - old religious sites - and related geological features, like geomagnetic electricity and underground water (also associated with hauntings).

Philosophers of the paranormal have found a Jungian (as in psychoanalyst Carl Jung) significance to most of the apparitions, too. Big snakes, big monkeys, and big discs in the sky are elements of such primal significance in the language of the unconscious that they would be likely things to imagine. It doesn't matter at all that the people who see them are unexposed to Jungian psychology; it's actually more persuasive that way.

The upshot of all this philosophizing, though, is that I formed no theory at all about Bigfoot. Evenly weighted in my mind were the possibilities that Bigfoot was connected to forces within the earth that somehow caused its apparitions; that it was some semi-physical mystery being totally new to science, possibly a super-natural "wild card," the classic "psychoid archetype" stepping from the collective unconscious in and out of the world; and that it and the whole business were make-believe. The prospect that Bigfoot could be a truly physical being was remote to me until my last 1998 visit to Allegany County.

IV

I'd agreed to a mid-November signing at a small book-and-gift-shop in the valley thirty minutes from Sandy Stefan's home. I was planning on dropping by Sandy's big old farm house in mid-afternoon, but was running late as usual, and by the time I arrived in her vicinity I still had to get in my workout. I decided to take a run in the woods.

I didn't know the trails around Sandy's home and couldn't afford to get lost, even off-schedule, so I found a hilly stretch of logging path that took about two minutes to get up, and did it a bunch of times - what I call a body-workout, not a head-one. One can become the other sometimes, but those long "big-sky" tours on just the right days are the ones you live for. I took my cross-country ski poles with me. I would be glad of it.

The carbide tips - plain affairs without baskets, made for roller-skiing on the roads - clacked behind me on the rocks and dirt with each push-off timed to a stride. I reflected on the recent Bigfoot reports from this immediate region, and couldn't help recalling that the national image of the big fellow varies from reclusive veggie to moody savage. Hunters stormed in their cabins, prospectors trapped in valleys, and even lonely campers dismembered figure in the accumulated lore. Great images to keep you company in the dimming woods.

It looks dorky, but running with poles like that gets the arms involved and raises the heart rate nicely. It also takes weight off my chronically bad feet, which, by the mid-1990s, were so beat up from years of sports that I couldn't run hard enough normally to get a workout. If time was limited and a run it had to be, that was the choice. I'd been plugging away at it for about ten minutes when some crows stormed up fifty feet away. My heart rear-ended my ribs; those wings sound like breaking bones. I was glad to know instantly what they were, but what made them take off? I was developing that nasty feeling of being watched.

Whenever I passed a certain spot about the midpoint of my course the bushes rustled, and I sensed a big dark body crouching behind them. I recalled the many calm, credible people over the years who had reported impressions of "things" in the Western New York woods - big lumpish forms, exactly as a Bigfoot should look at the distances reported. I'd had impressions like that many times myself, and made absolutely nothing of them. I'm used to the woods. Around twilight stumps and bushes at different depths around you can look animate when you jerk your head. I couldn't fight my own sensation, nevertheless, that something was stalking me, ranging out from that bush alongside me just out of sight for the first fifty feet of my curving course in either direction. It was always back waiting for me as I passed that spot on the return swing, following me again within reach until it saw me stop and come back.

It was pretty oppressive, leaving car and road behind each time and winding back up into the dimness toward that clump of bushes behind a maple. I was beginning to dread it. By my tenth up, I fancied that whatever was there had sensed that this would be its last chance to make a move. Sure enough, as I passed the fated spot for the last trip down, something broke one of the branches as if it were pulling it aside for a spring. I snarled and dropped into a karate crouch, raising the poles like twin prongs, announcing that this potential dinner felt militantly indigestible.

Ski poles are hardly weapons, though running with them, I fear no dog. I can pop the tips up to business-level in a thought, and the straps give excellent leverage for thrusts in any direction. Still, the metal point of each basketless tip is about half an inch long, unlikely to stick further in a heavy onrushing body or even to catch and splinter the pole into something really lethal. I glared down the long fiberglass shafts at the crouching form I imagined in the bush, filled with the adrenaline of righteous anger. I even staggered them. If a monster grabbed the pole in nearest reach, the other was going into its throat. Would serve it right for interrupting a law-abiding run.

Something was waving above the apparently crouching form, and I snatched a glance upward. Intestines swayed from a branch ten feet up. They had to be from an animal, though they looked big enough to be human. I cursed sourly. I was almost glad I didn't see them earlier; might not have finished my workout. I side-stepped down the trail, as angry as I was afraid. Hearing no pursuit in the thick leaves and trees, I relaxed and ambled normally the last hundred yards. The feelings came back as I unlocked the car, at that point most vulnerable.

V

I arrived at Sandy's house, still chuckling at myself over that comical little standdown. I had probably outfaced a dyspeptic groundhog. Young Parker let me in and showed me the downstairs shower, looking like he had something on his mind. When I came out, Sandy and other members of the brood were back, rushing around like they were battening hatches against a storm. "Don't go anyplace," she said, ushering her youngest up the stairs.

"Parkie shot a 'woody'!" chirped the little one.

"You shoulda been there!" crowed Parker, but he looked like he was covering his feelings. An hour before the young fellow (babysitting his little sister) had fired a shotgun at some suspicious bushes. The resultant bellow and heavy bipedal running had them believing that he had winged the Bigfoot. I wondered if that was the stalker I had envisioned on my run. Its scrub-haunting style was certainly the same, and we had our explanation if it had turned nasty - unusual, but not unreported, Bigfoot behavior. Parker even believed he had some blood samples and hair from the scene, which he seemed about to retrieve.

I raised my hand before he could spring up the stairs. "Can it wait? I have a signing to get to." Sandy, however, was distressed at the idea of Bigfeet on the warpath and the house with only one adult. I almost said, "What am I gonna do? Stick 'em with my ski poles?" But, reflecting on how recently I'd been offering to do just that, I held my peace and considered options. There was no telling how long I'd have to wait until Bill Pascarella returned, but I was determined not to stand up that little bookstore. They're the ones you want to show respect. A signing can be the high point of their year.

The cops wouldn't stay here all night on suspicion of Bigfeet, but another idea came to me. I called Jim Lynn, a retired civil deputy who lived nearby. He had attended a couple of my talks and even helped me track down a ghost story in these parts a few years back. He arrived in forty-five minutes with his brother-in-law Bob Gorski, a State Trooper, and Ed Gunther, a friend, hunter, and curiosity-seeker. They were brawny, middle-aged men armed for game, and I had no more fears for the family. Parker seemed to have some new heroes, and when I left he was on the porch with them chattering about law enforcement.

Signings - like lectures - are usually great opportunities to make research contacts, and this small one in the shop of a Black Creek woman was no different. I inquired about the local paranormal as well as the "mystery critter" population. I didn't mention the word *Bigfoot* for fear of getting whoppers delivered to order; but a few stories from the last century did offer themselves, and word that recent digging in the cellar of an old home on Sandy's road had turned up giant bones. Sandy had kept that from me, or else she hadn't known. It was also pointed out that this was "the Valley of the Lost Nation," the region from which a small Native American group just vanished from history with barely a trace, as if something had snatched them into the sky. What the Hell was going on around here?

I got back to Sandy's by nine-thirty to find Jim Lynn and his pals jawing with husband Bill at the kitchen table, praising Sandy's coffee and whole-wheat cookies. The three guardians had been all over the ridge with the family dogs and noticed nothing out of the ordinary. Everyone's spirits had lightened. I felt as if I had gotten swept up in Sandy's mood earlier that evening, and that my haste to get to the signing had tag-teamed my normal reasoning processes. I was even questioning my experience in the woods. I'd seen nothing, really. It was generally believed that Parker had sunk buckshot into his own bogeymen, and that our suspicions were the stuff dreams are made of.

I delivered something like a vernacular Puck's address (at the end of 'Midsummer Night') to the lawmen, filled with genial remorse for wasting time in their busy lives. Veterans of many a fruitless material stake-out, they were good sports about this failed paranormal one. It had even become the fashion of the evening to scoff at Bigfoot rumors. Some comedian among the bunch - I can't embarrass Bill Pascarella by revealing who - screamed upon opening a closet as if a werewolf were inside. It was so far from his normal manner that everybody laughed.

The evening now seemed so innocent that no one noticed when Suzie walked with a couple of the dogs out to the barn for an errand. She was taking her sweet old time about getting back, though. The others were hot into some topic, and I decided to see what she was up to. The minute I stepped from the house I knew something was wrong. The dogs were in full throat behind the barn. How could we not have heard them? I had two choices: turn back into the house and sound a warning or rush over immediately. For some reason I chose the latter.

Generations of owners had more or less connected the old farmhouse to the barn by an assortment of structures - a stable, pens, a toolshed - that seemed afterthoughts: walls without roofs, workspaces without walls, interlocking to produce jagged passageways and open-air spaces. I cut around the buildings from the outside and the front of the house, following the hubbub to the left of it. Expecting to see Suzie as I rounded the corner, I was readying a phrase, "What's all the racket?" I never used it.

It felt like I ran into a tree branch. I flew and fell in an awkward position, on my back across a stack of old doors beneath a low overhang. My hips were higher than my head, which may have been what kept me conscious. In the odd, crowded confines of the barn entrance there were wooden fixtures and heavy items at all angles, and only moonlight pouring in. The shadow that loomed over me looked as wide as a refrigerator. It reached for me with an astonishing peace.

Everything was slowed, as if the air had thickened into molten glass, and time into an invisible, permeating medium that even bogged thought. I had the impression of fingers thick and blunt as twinkies groping for me in my awkward perch. Several of them brushed past my eyes, inches away, as if expecting to fingerpaint into a palette of human features, as if reaching for an image a foot closer. Whatever it was was easily within reach of my legs or my waist and could have hauled me from my space like a wheelbarrow; but it seemed to prefer my throat, and to have trouble finding it in the half-lit jumble of flat planes, of table-edges and reclining doors. Its spatial awareness was not that of a human being.

From where I lay, I put my feet high against the figure above me. Its torso felt hard as wood. It leaned into me as if amused, sensing something it readied to grab. I'm not a big man at all, but I'm fit, and my legs are strong. Even as my knees flexed, bringing the figure closer, I had the absurd memory of a similar move in college, when I got my back against a guard rail outside Denison University's Bandersnatch and pushed a '67 Chevy out of a snowbank. The things that flash through you in the most desperate, speeded-up, slowed-down moments... The few life-and-death situations I remember have all been like that.

With the same motion, but viciously and faster, I gave a perfectly-timed shove with all I had when the figure was most unbalanced and my leverage was the best. The huge form shot back and up, hitting its head on the edge of an overhanging open attic-floor beneath which it had been leaning to reach at me. The impact had to be awful.

I was on my feet so fast it surprised me. As if it had been left there for me to grab, the haft of a tool on the edge of a bench came into my hand. It was an axe. I swung it sideways like a bat at a pitch and felt the hammer-end land with a sick thwack on a neck and jaw and carry right through. It made me remember a discovery from an ancient battle, some guy's jaw found a hundred feet from his body, doubtless slung off him by a single handy blow. As I say, the things that flash through you... I was sure something like this had happened in the barn in which I stood, and that the form that had to be at my feet would spell the mystery for good.

The tool fell from my hands, and I stood back stunned against the wall, the impact of the brushing blow I had taken either starting to tell for the first time, or really settling in. I came to at the incredible sound of a shotgun from five feet away, and the insane din of several dogs too afraid to do more than stand and yap.

Jim Lynn had fired at something toward the treeline and stood next to me staring in its direction. Whatever instincts the old lawman had had been good ones; he had left the house within seconds of me, out a different door, and come around from the other side. He may have saved my life. Suzie Pascarella stood frozen beside us, having witnessed everything from behind a waist-high partition. I looked down and saw nothing but scuffed dirt. Amazing. That blow was the most vicious thing I have ever done. I think it would have dropped a bear.

Others arrived, Bob Gorski with his pistol and Bill Pascarella with a baseball bat. Sandy and the older children followed. We stood, staring out into the night suddenly weirder than we had ever accepted, staring as if the field and trees beyond it was a screen upon which we had seen a film so moving that we could not rise from our seats until we had read all the credits. It had to be minutes before any of us spoke.

A QUESTION OF LEVELS

When you are actually in America, America hurts, because it has a powerful, dis-integrative influence upon the white psyche. It is full of grinning, unappeased aboriginal demons, too, ghosts... One day the demons of America must be pla-cated, the ghosts must be appeased, the Spirit of Place atoned for...
There are terrible spirits, ghosts, in the air of America.
D.H. Lawrence, *Studies in American Classical Literature*

A QUESTION OF LEVELS

I

One horizon pealed a glorious silver-gold, dusting gunpowder clouds that sniped sleet; but I stared harder at what was before me, a house of mismatched parts and, twenty feet from its north side, a contraption odd even in comparison: what I would call a Surrealist fence, a freelance barrier of all different types of material, festooned with rags and trinkets. "Better than rusting cars," I thought, knocking on the door. I would have stared longer, but I was eager to get out of the whipping wind, the season's first signs of the winter coming.

At rallies and parties I'd spoken many a time with the activist and medicine man Mad Bear, but that raw November twilight in 1983 was my first stop at the architectural concatenation he called home. His small house on the Tonawanda Reservation had been customized into a home-rigged fortress that could not only defy intruders but also conceal any sign of occupancy. Only by his car in the driveway could anyone tell that the burly Tuscarora was in and receiving visitors. Of course this was by design. Like many spiritual people, Mad Bear had periods when he was "indisposed"; there were a number of stories about why. He traveled often, and many magical trinkets were here unguarded; but some said he went on long astral journeys, as well - perhaps in the form of a bear - during which his physical body rested here needing protection.

Hanging out with Mad Bear and Eric Reynard was like being an extra in the stage adaptation (mostly comic) of the Cliff's Notes on modern Iroquois spirituality, and there was no need to cut things short. The school was on Thanksgiving break, and Mad Bear's coffee pot would guarantee that I'd be wide-eyed for the hour-drive home.

At about ten we noticed some queer sounds, which at first I thought might be from a radio inside the house. We were still; the wind was really at it, but we heard a harsh male voice, apparently shouting outside. Mad Bear didn't look surprised. He rolled out the window in the back of the little space he used as a living room, and we heard it clearly: "Mad Bear, turn it off!" Rick and I looked at each other. What was somebody doing out there?

"Turn what off?" Mad Bear called out.

"Bear, don't go out there!" said Rick. At points in recent memory reservation politics were pretty heated, and there was a very real chance that we were about to get shot; but our host had the door open, and we followed him to the porch. I could just make out a human form twenty feet beyond the Dali fence, a man, probably a Native American, whose clothes swirled. He had the hollow look of the first mate of *The Flying Dutchman*, or possibly the Seneca guide aboard the *Griffon*, one of the ghost ships of our own Great Lakes. He looked oddly unreal.

"Turn it off, Mad Bear!" the man shouted from across the barrier as if he was afraid to get any nearer. His voice was terrifying.

"You turn it off," yelled Mad Bear, his voice turning high. "You started it!"

"We're dying, Mad Bear!"

"It's what you tried to do to others!"

The man looked like he'd walked a hundred miles. "Not the children, Mad Bear," he pleaded, his voice growling like an animal. "Not the old. Hardly any of us are left!"

"Well, I'll see what I can do," said Mad Bear. "But I warned you about getting it started."

"Do it, Mad Bear." The wretched figure stared at us with cavernous eyes I could imagine, and then receded backward, facing us all the while.

"Sorry about that, you guys," said Mad Bear when we were settled inside. "There won't be any more trouble tonight."

"What was that about?" I said. Rick looked at Mad Bear.

"The less you get involved, the better," said Mad Bear, heading for the kitchen. "Hey, we've had our little excitement for the evening. Anybody hungry?"

That was it for me, though. "Meet me for a pint," I said to Rick on the way to my car. He lived in nearby Elma, and my neighborhood pub in East Aurora was almost on his way home.

II

Though it was after midnight, 'the Bill' was packed. I'd forgotten that the Tuesday before Thanksgiving was one of the biggest bar nights in the year, and on top of that they had a band. I waited in back on the only stool available and watched a replay of a Sabres game. It was too loud to hear much, but I could see a sour co-educational pantomime at the pinball machine between a young fellow in a flannel shirt and an older, tough-looking wide-body in jeans. She went to the ladies' room scowling, and he said to the air, gesturing at his crotch, "Ah better git sumpn' down here to-naht, 'r ah'm gon' be *pissed!*" His bristly mustache furled and trumpeted the last word like a bluesy donkey.

I had to laugh. Occult curses and voices in the night be damned, some things never change. I considered a few remarks in the direction of "respect"; but you can't change the world overnight, especially in a jet-engine bar, and it seemed like the fellow might learn the lesson better in due course. The lady in question looked as if she had no intention of dispensing her favors that night, and that she could also secure them against all single comers. By the time Rick arrived things had quieted down, and a table was open near the front. The neon sign on Main Street rainbow-striped each ebony pint.

"There are some pretty bad squabbles among the Longhouse Folk right now," Rick said when we had settled. "Bear's right about one thing: you want to stay out of the politics. As for the magic stuff, well, some guys up on one of the reservations in Ontario sent some bad business at Mad Bear and his friends. Mad Bear set up some protection in his own way."

"That fence-thing?" I said.

"I laughed, too, the first time I saw it," said Rick, "but he just said, 'You wait and see.' I guess we waited long enough."

"Who was that guy outside? What did he believe was happening?"

"These are black and white questions," said Rick. "The subject is grey. In my estimate, Mad Bear figured out a way to turn that hostile energy back to its source. It's still very dangerous, and it can take innocent people with it if they're too close. But that's the risk you run: whatever you send out at others, if it misses them, it may come back on you."

III

I was intrigued, but didn't think much more about occult wars and Longhouse curses until that December, when a number of New Age luminaries and like-thinkers held a winter solstice ceremony in West Falls. At the vegetarian pot luck that followed I walked into a big porch overlooking Route 240 and a discussion of Reservation politics that included Rick. Things weren't good for several of the Iroquois in their loop, and I was stunned to hear that old Peter Arvidson, Rick's beloved uncle, was in poor health. Most of the Whites there attributed it to age and related factors, but some breathed the notion of occultism behind it, and from the way Rick held his peace I figured there was more to it. We agreed to meet at his uncle's house near Salamanca late one January afternoon.

The Thursday appointed was my afternoon off, and I was on the trails of Allegany State Park by two-thirty. It was a perfect day: bright, still, and twenty. The tracks were fast, my skis waxed just right, and the day so exhilarating that I couldn't stop before I did every trail, probably twenty-five K's. I had a race on Saturday and should have taken it easy, but days like that are what the sport's all about for me.

At one point in my course the trail headed along the inside of a drop-off and hooked right. The natural scene before me fell most unnaturally composed: level trail heading into the white, wooded wall; flat ridge-top, thirty feet or so above; faint sun, an equal measure above that, strained through trees, exactly dotting the trail. Striding up the sun-track and entering the pall of blue shadow, I had the strange feeling that a bell had tolled, that something just beneath my conscious grasp and possibly profound was being put in motion at that moment, buried to me as I lived it.

This feeling only grew and stayed with me to the finish forty minutes later. It was odd poling and striding to it, and surveying snow, sky and trees around me. Maybe it was the day, maybe it was the afterglow of "the runner's high," maybe some of it was even the righteous delirium of starting to "hit the wall," but the visuals were hyper-real. The lemon sky had turned orange; the aging sun stroked citrus on the sculpted tracks, speckled diamonds onto the smooth surfaces, and swept titanium shadows into their declivities. The experience stood out in my mind, even to now, as if this afternoon was a turning point, and I was being given a last chance to take or not to take a step toward something I would either treasure or dread. I remember looking ahead to my meeting on the Reservation, wondering what I was getting into, sensing that quite a ride might be ahead. I would be right, though it would take years to fall out.

As I stepped from my car into the small hillside neighborhood, sky and day still had a golden tinge. The old snow lay dense on lawns and roadsides, and faint smoke drifted from the chimneys of humble wood houses. The venerable gentleman himself was in a big armchair before the TV, which was never off the whole time I was there. In the two years since I'd met him his companion Ed Jamison had lost leverage in his arm-wrestle with Jack Daniels. His hair was greyer, and he had all sorts of incomprehensible hand-gestures - "thumbs up's" and the like - with which he cajoled handshakes and high-fives out of all in reach. He seldom spoke directly to anyone but Uncle Peter, and his voice was ashy and absent. Uncle Peter, too, looked frail, and once he scared me with his coughing, which, when he sensed my alarm, merged into a laugh that warmed me to my core. "I don't smell strawberries just yet," he said, referring to the blossoms lining the path to the Iroquois heaven.

The back door opened and closed and a girly voice called from the kitchen. "Uncle, I saw one of those animals again. With the funny eyes."

"Aah," said Uncle Peter. "Tell me something new."

An Iroquois teenager came in halfway through his answer. "It was nearer the house than I've ever seen one." He saw us and stopped quickly.

"Thanks," said Uncle Peter ruefully. "Tell me something new and good, I mean."

The boy's eyes rolled up and around as if tracking a bat inside his bowl-cut cranium, so visibly taking the request literally that we all smiled. This was the inimitable Curly, Peter Arvidson's thirteen-year-old grandson. Every day after school he came to see to things: chores, cleaning up, even cooking. In two years he would be all knees, elbows, lacrosse sticks and rap clothes, but at this point he was a diligent cherub with a high voice and a thick black mop.

"What... animal is this?" I said, eying the shotgun over the door. If it was anything less than a T. Rex, its dispensation seemed at hand.

"The owl, under the clothesline," said Curly. "It had eyes just like that goat that nearly drowned Emmy..." A wave from Uncle Peter cut him off.

"I told you about that whole thing," said Uncle Peter. "When you know how things work, you don't complain about them. That's just the way they are."

"Yes, Uncle Peter," said Curly.

"These things make me tired, OK? I think I need some rest. Why don't we put on the news and you guys stay for dinner?" I had such a roaring hunger that I was getting hypoglycemic, but I wasn't appetized by what I presumed would be on the menu. There were few vegetarians on the Reservation, and I had reservations of my own about Curly's cooking.

IV

Ten minutes after leaving Uncle Peter's, I filled up at a Salamanca gas station owned by Alvin Green's father. I knew Alvin often worked here, and saw his familiar tall, lean figure in the office. He greeted me warmly, and I decided to sound him out. He was less into the mysticism than either Eric Reynard or Uncle Peter, but I'd found him to be less guarded about things, as well, and he usually knew what was going on. We walked around the corner to a bowling alley and were about to order up, but things got a little tense when Alvin and another fellow - a beefy, thirtiesh Iroquois with short hair and a mustache - took notice of each other. The big man had been at the bar with compadres on either side, and he turned with his thumbs in his belt to block Alvin's access. Alvin looked ready to make something out of it, but I steered him out.

"You've had your introduction to 'Big' Green," said Alvin as we walked to the Pizza Hut. "He and some of my people don't get along too good."

"I figured," I said. "What's the deal?"

"Some Indians are into gas and gambling, and others are into the lives of the people and the care of the earth. I'll let you make up your own mind who's who."

"You guys related?"

"He's my uncle," Alvin snorted. "Tried to kill me once."

We ordered a pizza and I got round to business. "Some bad stuff going on up there," Alvin said, referring to Uncle Peter's house and the hilly farms near it. "Most of it involves animals. I've never seen any of it, but there's a couple stories.

"Ol' Ed Jamison - not the most reliable witness, I'll give you - said he was riding in somebody's car one night last November and saw deer walking on their hind legs. They went back to natural when the headlights fell on them.

"Uncle Peter's granddaughter Emmy - lives next door to him - had a white cat run off to the woods last fall. That's usually it - coyotes, fox, bobcat - something gets 'em. But last month it came back. Started following her around and staring at her, nothing like a normal cat. Looked like it had some eye disease. The other animals didn't like it, and one day their biggest dog took it by the neck. It just went limp without even a squall.

"Over the summer Emmy was out swimming in the pond and a goat came in from the yard and kept her from getting out. Followed her around everywhere and kept pushing her back in with its teeth and horns. Had eyes like her cat. She'd a like to drowned. Curly, actually it was, came up and hauled her out. The goat started acting normal as soon as her brothers showed up, but the oldest one gave it a kick. It dropped like it was dead already, just waiting a reminder.

"Now the spooky animals have started coming to Uncle Peter's house. Maybe they been coming for a long time, but until Uncle Peter needed some taking care of, nobody knew about it. They been coming closer to the house and yard."

"Curly said he saw one there this afternoon."

"See? Well, I don't know what to make of it. But I think Uncle Peter's got his ways of dealing with this, and if you knew what he knew they would make sense."

V

My faith in the literal reality of an occult war of assassination - whose combatants were demonically possessed animals - was, as you would guess, faint; but my tendency has always been to regard paranormal claims, no matter how wild, on their evidence. Since physical evidence is seldom complete or consistent, the best test of an idea's claim to utility is how it squares with other, known circumstances to make a theory, a point I revisit many a time. I seemed to have entered a system of logic in which the theory was ready at hand. We know from the studies of faith healing and voodoo that people who believe they're going to thrive or die can make either happen, and my Iroquois friends believed. The possibility that I might lose one of them because of it was something I never doubted. What did I care about the logic? I cared about a dear, inspiring old teacher.

In March 1984 I met Eric Reynard at a coffee house in East Aurora and laid it out. "We have to do something," I said. "Get Mad Bear, get Hilda White, get help, get... anybody you know. We can't leave Uncle Peter alone like that."

"Mad Bear's not doing too good, either," said Rick. "He's out west trying to get over his own complaints. Uncle Peter seems all right with things as they are. Why don't you let him make his own decisions?"

"What's wrong with you?" I said. "If somebody sent something after him we have to do what we can to turn it off."

"Like Mad Bear said last fall, I'm not so sure you can turn it off. These things get in motion and take on a life of their own. Can you call back an avalanche?"

"You don't have to stand in the way of it!" I said. "I don't believe what I'm hearing."

"Let me try it another way," he said. "Can you stop an echo? You can yell back, but you can't stop the echoes of the first shout, and if the noise is the problem, you just make things worse."

"Let *me* try it another way," I said. "If you get jumped in an alley, do you expect me to just stand and watch?"

"In situations you understand, I'd expect you to do what's natural for you," said Rick. "In ones that are new, I'd expect you to take advice."

"I care about your Uncle Peter," I said. "You at least owe me some answers."

"I accept that," said Rick. "Meantime, you gotta be patient. If Uncle Peter wants you to know something about this, he'll see that you do someday, and you just have to trust that. There might be a few steps ahead of you before you settle down enough to get it, and for his sake and for you I'll try to help you be ready. There's nothing wrong with you spending time with Uncle Peter when you're in the neighborhood. Stay out of this in other respects, though. Everybody wants you to."

VI

If your only tool is a hammer, they say, every problem looks like a nail. Through indirect methods I finally got something I could pound. I couldn't think of the situation as anything but a war, but it was still the funniest one I had ever heard of.

My first step into any Native American question was to consult Native American sources, which, for me, started with Eric Reynard. I'd already done that, and what he'd told me about echoes and avalanches had registered no clearer than New Age-Native American goulash - and he was my confidante. Other Native Americans wouldn't talk to me past a certain point which I had already crossed. I was sure some of them were less guarded with Whites who were less actively out to piece the puzzle together, and I shook the grapevine in those quarters and sifted the results.

I learned quickly that Uncle Peter had a mortal enemy, but his refusal to fight Lester "Big" Green - the man I'd encountered with Alvin - had me totally puzzled. Apparently Big Green and some of his folk had been opposed to Uncle Peter's vision for the Six Nations; there was similar dispute over the use of Reservation land. This had been a bitter quarrel, developing across decades and allegedly entering even occult realms. Most of the old guard on either side was gone by the time I got involved, and during this inquiry word came to me that Hilda White's life had recently collapsed. Her daughter and granddaughter had been killed in a suspicious accident near Salamanca, and she had moved to Colorado to live with other children. I doubted I would ever see her again. Uncle Peter was the last of his crew, and it appeared that Big Green - the youngest of the opposing camp - would be the only one left vertical. The whole thing looked like a done deal. I called Rick in April of 1984.

"You've been busy," he said. "You may get to the bottom of this after all."

"Rick, we have to stop this. Why does Big Green think he can get away with it? Why can't we do something? Why can't we get after him?"

"And do what?" laughed Rick.

"Threaten him, pull a gun on him, whatever. Let him know that if Uncle Peter goes, he goes. Can't we do that?"

"That doesn't sound like you talking. No one on either side would support you bringing that into things. That's what we had to get away from. Besides, even if you got rid of Green, the process would go on. He stands to gain by it, and he helped put it in motion, but nobody can call it back now. I tried telling you that once before. It looks like you've gotten a little closer to it on your own, but when it comes to putting the facts together you still don't get the picture. By the time you do it won't matter. You said you wanted to stay out. Do it. Let it go."

VII

Ten years under Headmaster David Gow had taught me that some of the best decisions we ever make are decisions to accept advice. Whenever I went against his it was a mistake; but he always let me make it, if it wasn't too outrageous, because that way I would grow from it. So I took a step back from the situation at hand; but I kept trying to understand it.

It was obvious that something was going on at the Reservation, but when I cooled off I had no reason to get worked up about a paranormal cause for it. There was no objective reason to doubt that the animals everybody was reporting were just part of the rumor mill, and that Peter Arvidson's complications were due to age. He was about seventy, but very hale until this recent bout, and seemingly due another twenty years. He was doubtless getting medical treatment from Western and Native American healers, and if there was a curse at work, its effects were clearly slow-acting. I had to figure out what was behind all the talk about those animals. It took a bit of time and digging.

The Iroquois had many legends of supernatural beasts, talking, walking upright, and displaying other human behaviors. There were also shape-shifters - human wizards transforming into animals - in abundance; but I was never able to identify any metaphysical beastie of the Northeast Woodlands that met the description of those rumored of Uncle Peter's ridge.

I studied Native American tradition, thinking to find something to fill in the blanks. You can't presume similarities between old societies just because they shared a continent, but you can't rule out a link, either. There were some general features in common to native North American groups - as there are worldwide among preindustrial peoples - and I came across something very interesting in the lore of the American Southwest.

The *chindi* are assassins from the other world who take over the bodies of animals, and can appear in any natural form. Killing the animal will only kill the host, and the spook will show up in a nastier version soon enough. They usually kill through simple bad fortune, however: accidents, sickness, and the like. Occasionally they walk on their hind legs like humans, and it's not a good sign if you see that. The only sure way to tell them, though, is by the eyes: flat, unreflective, like those of dead fish.

I came across the story of a rich Apache clan that had offended a shaman, asking a heavy favor from him and refusing payment. He set this sort of demon on them. At first it was only the old and sick who died. Then accidents and ailments struck the middle-aged. The young ones interceded with the shaman, who was almost a century old. He talked to them, even though it was the second offense, but before he had a chance to undo his work, he died. Most members of the once very large family were gone by the time the story was recorded. I wondered if there was an Iroquois legend like this that had never been written.

They could be dispatched for personal reasons, but I got the feeling that the Southwestern *chindi*, however sinister they might be to their targets, were fairly impersonal beings. They went where they were sent; they addressed questions of natural justice, and they had in some sense the force of nature behind them. It only made sense if the Iroquois had bogeys like them. There was something like this - some force or custom - in the traditions of many preindustrial cultures worldwide.

I felt certain I'd at least identified the agent in the Western New York reservations quarrels, and I didn't care that I hadn't read about it in any acknowledged sources. There are Iroquois traditions that have never been exposed. I don't know them, but I know that. At a full moon gathering in February 1985 I felt ready to approach Rick with some heavier questions. I told him all I have told you about Native American tradition, the Iroquois, and my speculations related to the *chindi*. I asked him if he'd ever heard of anything like it.

"Something like that," he said as if he knew a world more. Now that I had him talking to me I didn't know where to begin.

"So how do you get one of these things after you?" I said.

"A medicine man or woman can send one, probably at will. I can't go into that."

"I'd figure," I said. "Wouldn't a .38 be easier?"

"Are you kidding?" said Rick. "They're the perfect hit-men. No White court of law would convict you. Keeps it all among the people of the Nation. Some hotheads that were out of the loop were shooting at each other in recent memory, but parties behind the scenes on 'the Res' decided a long time ago to settle things in the old way. Justice would always fall out, though it might take some time."

I was stunned. It made so much sense. "What can we do about it?"

"The good news is that the cycle of 'you got one of mine, I'm gonna get one of yours' is pretty near its end. Uncle Peter got involved in that indirectly, and he's accepting of the thing. He is an old man."

"With years ahead," I said. "Years of good, years of teaching. He hasn't given the world half of what he's got."

"The bad news is that the quarrel has one more stroke in it."

"Can't he fight it?" I said. "If anyone can, I'd expect it to be him."

"Well there's rules we've all got to play by," said Rick. "But I'm sure he could fight it. Maybe he was when he saw other people getting hurt. Maybe he quit, and that's when he started to get sick. Suppose the arrow slips off his shield. It's gonna hit somebody. Who would you pick? Emmy? Curly?"

VIII

By the fall of 1984 Mad Bear couldn't help anybody with anything. He'd been the victim of a series of his own ailments, as well as erratic behavior that few of his White friends understood. They often called Eric Reynard with some new alarm. "Mad Bear's got the air conditioner on at one end of his house, the heat cranked up in the other, and the windows in the middle wide open. You gotta do something!"

"At least he'll always have some part of the house where he can be comfortable," said Rick.

"Mad Bear's been in and out of spirit all his life," said other Native Americans. "What you're seeing now is just the signs of him starting to go all the way over." They seemed to feel that it would be best to simply step aside. Maybe it's my Anglo mindset, but this depressed me. I just couldn't see it their way.

The way he finally went was certainly peculiar, and his medicine pouch may have been involved. This was a bag of indescribables legendary for its powers, including protection from psychic assault such as he knew was constant during that period. Taking off this item one afternoon near Niagara Falls may have been the opening some parties needed. The bite of a non-native, purple-colored ant became fearfully infected, seeming to send his health over the edge. If a good man as powerful as he could fall that way, what hope was there for anything but chaos?

Mad Bear died too young in the fall of 1985. I didn't hear about it until weeks later. I hadn't seen him for at least half a year at that point. I had the feeling that the little energy he had left was best spent with people who had been more significant in his life. That was my respect for the man, that I would never presume.

IX

It may have been a testament to Peter Arvidson's spiritual vitality that he could hang on that long, but in the winter of 1986 I heard that his chapter was coming to a close. The feeling that I couldn't do anything about it was gnawing me almost as badly as the fact that I couldn't figure it out. I had a lot of trouble with the idea that he wouldn't fight whatever was killing him, but I had more deciding what he could have done to bring it on. It was part of my understanding that to be tormented by a demon like the *chindi* one had to transgress against the natural balance. What could he have ever done like that? He was one of the most saintly men I have ever known. How had he fallen afoul of a just force? Preindustrial religion and magic had been interests of mine for quite awhile, and I studied with even more focus for months. I brought up all I'd ever learned in these areas and thought about it hard.

Some analogous force had been extant in the philosophy of many ancient cultures. There are many words for it - *ch'i, kaa, prana, pneuma* - and though they all carry the idea of "the force of life," they're all unique enough to make them nearly indefinable to someone not deeply within the culture from which they arise.

Asian societies have gone far to try to explain and harness their concept of *ch'i*. The Chinese may have even captured this force on film inside a human body, in the lower back right where the mystics always said it was. This is most likely the force by which martial arts masters perform their apparent miracles. It could also be the power through which human shamans project their wishes into action, like launching demons.

The Iroquois word for something like this life-force was *orenda*. I get the sense that, though it was very much a telluric force, of earth and landscape, it was carried about personally within all individuals. Beings of great development - old shamans, spiritual beasts, Iroquois deities - were so conspicuous for it that they could recognize it in each other through any disguise. One sensed that *orenda*, or some more precise variant of it whose term no White has ever heard, flowed through those devil-beasts on Uncle Peter's ridge, through whoever could put them into motion.

It made sense to me to think that whatever the Iroquois considered their *chindi* was not only the tool of their mystical elite, but a metaphysical "customer service agent" that might be available in extreme circumstances to any truly wronged member of Longhouse society. Not only was it fair, but it suited what I had come to suspect about traditional Iroquois religion. The old White authorities presumed there was no such thing as an Iroquois "priest" or "priestess." This may have meant simply that they were unable to identify one; but even so, it seemed to imply that Iroquois spirituality was something so collective that all members of the group - and none to the exclusion of others - could speak for it. Thus "the force" - the spirit in general - flowed through them all.

This force was more directly concerned with natural elements and the balance of the world than with human virtue, though they all probably come together in the long run. The fact that they don't in the short run is probably the reason a shaman could invoke one of these *chindi* willfully, and possibly capriciously.

It was never a wise thing to get far to the bad side of this force, but anyone who had mastered it enough to channel it knew the troughs between the wakes, the still areas between the currents of aspiration, justice, and revenge. The fact that parties on both sides had been lost in this war among the reservation Iroquois (which I'd given up trying to sort out) seemed objective evidence that not only the "good" could employ it. It looked like Big Green had navigated those currents successfully and even come out on top. Ah, that made sense, too. There were "bad," or shall I say "selfish," druids among the ancient Celts.

On a late March afternoon in 1986 Eric Reynard and I caught a word at the stone fence outside my cottage. Even the snow seemed aged, low and condensed, and a little mist rose up to greet coming twilight. To the backdrop of a faint sunset I presented these speculations to Rick, mostly as a concordance, more to air my own feelings and maybe get a little counsel, an adage or something of the like to make me feel better. I had the sense of something inexorably fading away, something still in existence, still possible to touch, but just as surely gone as if it were a century in the past. It was an odd, melancholy feeling.

When I was through, Rick just looked at me as if I'd finally come to the bottom of things. He even seemed to be pleased, in a funny way, with all I'd turned up, though it was touchy territory. After all, he couldn't forbid me to keep learning, and he respected that. It was a funny anticlimax, though, to all my work and worry, and I found myself wondering about it at the time. He advised me that, now that I'd found my own answers, I should be ready to let the whole thing go.

"Let it go?" I said. I looked away into the creamsicle light seaming sky and earth. "You mean this whole thing is going to happen and I won't even get to know why? At least tell me what Uncle Peter did."

Rick thought for a few breaths. "You just talked to me for ten minutes about ancient spiritual forces. I thought you had this. It's not just a human dispute. It's a process, involving natural cycles, religion, everything, even politics. There's a balance here. There's been a lot of give and take, a lot of losses on both sides, but it's coming to an end. There's one more shoe left to drop, and then it's over. Nobody else has to die, at least over this."

"Why does he have to die over it?"

"Uncle Peter has lived a good life. It's his time, and he understands the process. Listen, one way or the other, it's his choice. Maybe he did something willingly years ago that he thought would be for the greater good, but that he knew would lead to this, and now that it's his time he recognizes it. Maybe he knew it all along from the moment he became one of our teachers. Maybe this was the choice Mad Bear made, too. Whatever. It's part of the plan, and if you respect him, you should respect that. With your head you seem to get more of it than I ever thought you would on your own. Now put it in your heart."

"Maybe I can't get it out," I said without thinking. I was floored, I was just desolate. It was hitting me as if I had just heard that it had happened. "So. Mad Bear, gone, Uncle Peter, gone. Big Green wins," I said. "You know, that's an apt nickname. Whoever's holding the cookies at the end of the game wins, doesn't he? I hardly thought the Reservation would reconfirm the nastiest bottom line of Western business."

"That's not what it says," said Rick.

After a long pause I said, "Are you going to see him?"

"He's not doing too good. It might be better for both you guys to remember each other the way you do now. He said something about you, though, the other day. He wishes you luck, 'Mason writer-guy.' He thinks you'll get what you want someday."

"Could you tell him..." I blinked, looking away. "Tell him..."

"He knows," said Rick.

X

I didn't put the picture together till years after its events were over. It fell into place in this sequence: Peter Arvidson died in May 1986. Ed Jamison died that July. I was driving near Salamanca at the end of the summer and saw an animal so strange that the possibility of it being paranormal was not out of my mind. That fall there was a final suspicious death among the Iroquois I knew - it was 'Big' Green. In 1997 I drove past the same spot at the same time of year, remembered the curious animal and all these details, and fell into an almost visionary state in which the pattern fell into place. It went like this.

On a gorgeous August twilight in September 1986 I was driving down the road to Salamanca from the trails at Allegany State Park. The canteloupe gleam of the western sky filled me with a content and an inspiration I could hardly describe. It was the end of another long summer, and the school year was set to begin. I liked that cyclical aspect to the work, always turning a new page. Even that day had been another good one, ending with a ride to end all. I felt that I was growing.

With me as well, as always in this region, were thoughts of the Iroquois mysteries packed into the woods, creeks, and hills, and of the supernatural events I'd encountered over the years. Looking up to the sky, I thought of my Iroquois friends, Mad Bear and Peter Arvidson and others about whom I haven't written, lost, evidently, in the occult wars I still didn't understand. I wondered if, with Peter Arvidson, the cycle had played itself out. I saw a strange animal.

It was as I was curving downhill and to the right, just before the narrow road throws open the river valley and lays the city of Salamanca before you. On my left between the road and treeline was a critter about the size of an adult groundhog. I gave it a hard look in the clear twilight. It seemed to have the features of many other animals, and its eyes were drilled at some spot on my side of the road.

It stood comfortably on its hind legs like a bear, and its ears, eyes, and snout were bearlike. It was too small, though, for even a cub. Its dangling front paws were like those of a dog or rabbit. Its chest and face were flat like a badger's, with pert bearlike ears. A West Valley woodchuck was my best guess. Its gaze was the giveaway, fixed with human intent across the road and right through the mountain. I'd never seen a stare like that, and through its laser-gaze I drove as if I didn't exist to it. I even looked at the relatively bare section of hill on my right to see what it was watching.

No matter how seriously I took my Iroquois friends or how much I'd seen with them - healings, visions, extra-sensory communications - I'd never become convinced of the objective reality of all of their ideas. I knew there was a war going on in which people died under circumstances with occult implications but, I presumed, psychosomatic causes. It was only as I looked away from the little animal and remembered the legendary demon-beasts that it occurred to me I might ever see one. I thought hard. I considered stopping the car and turning back up the hill, but saw in my mirrors that it was already gone. Even a natural animal could have disappeared quickly, and I filed it as a simple curiosity.

It was an almost identical evening eleven years later when I was again driving the same road down from the State Park, again after a crisp off-road ride, again curving down the hill and brooding on my life and the tangerine sky to my left, the dazzling lights of the valley city below where it was already night. How my life had changed between the two eves.

The years between had been sweet and bitter. I'd lost my father. I couldn't cry until that event, and then I couldn't avoid it. The internal change that may have represented mystified me, but the world looked different, and my attitude to people was. I'd left a school I really cared about and gone into an uncertain freelance career. It took a few years, but I'd become recognized, at least regionally, as a researcher and writer. My first book was only weeks from publication, and I felt like I'd finally accomplished something. Some things were too much the same. I was still single, and had come to suspect myself more dedicated to my work than I could be to any woman, to the possibility of family. This was out of the pattern I would have predicted for myself, and I was afraid I'd gone a step too far. I'd always looked for love to be a fire; now that I recognized it as a building, it seemed too late to lay any foundations, which was sad, because I'd always felt that children and a lasting trust were part of the good we can do here.

As if the visual effect of passing the same stretch of road on a similar night, though, in the fall of 1997 were an alarm, a sound almost audible and musical - the stroke of a supernal harp whose plectrum fell as I crossed the fated spot - I recalled something constant: the oddity, the strange animal I'd seen there years before, and a picture fell into place for the first time.

I recalled hearing of the death of Ernest "Ol' Ed" Jamison shortly after that of Peter Arvidson. I had blessed him sadly, but thought little more of it. He was ill, drunk, and sometimes hardly aware he was alive. One of the few respected Iroquois who showed him full respect had been his inspirational Uncle Peter, who always reminded everyone that the poor drunk was the bearer of a famous name. I presumed that "Ol' Ed" was so dispirited by this loss that he sank into a liquid oblivion from which he could forget old failures and new sadness. Soon after his death I saw the strange animal.

I recalled reading the *Buffalo News'* obituary of Lester "Big" Green not long after that. The morning was too busy for me to wonder what took him; 'unexpectedly' was the term used in the article. Green had been glowing with life and triumph, and I'd even heard people at a party discussing his curious death; but I made no connections before that 1997 twilight and passing the spot of my earlier vision of the curious animal, on an identical night. My mind soared to the copper-berry sky above, and, driving down that long winding hill and trying to make meaning out of the picture, it all came back.

As I crossed the spot, I remembered the animal with the odd gaze. If the little beast possessed X-ray vision with pointer-focus, I realized, it could have been looking right through the mountain at something in Salamanca. There was no likelihood of it, but it could have been tracking someone who lived there that fall night in 1986. If so, it would have to have planted itself there just for me to see. Was that a message?

I recalled the sequence of factors: Peter Arvidson died, in the last stroke of a war of wizardry and natural forces; Big Green, unopposed, begins to consolidate his financial empire; Ed Jamison dies, with pathetically little notice; I see an impossible animal in the Allegany Hills; Big Green dies 'unexpectedly,' months later.

My mind whirled as I drove that sunset eve in 1997, and a new mood came upon me, as if I'd entered the psychic state so many people I interview claim to frequent. I could reach forward, as I steered on the twilight road, to the call I would make to Eric Reynard late that very night as if it were happening that moment; I could live it vividly as if the two experiences were simultaneous. In memory, of course, they are; I'm convinced they were at the time.

As I calculated the events, my mind soared into the tangerine twilight and tracked possibilities on pipistrelle wings out above the smoky valley, set with its blinking lights like a mine shining forth its diamonds. I saw the night to come, through to that phone conversation with Eric Reynard that I knew would wait till near dawn.

As if it were a long, minutely-detailed prophecy - or the night ahead one huge deja vu - I knew I would brood as I drove, that I would sit with my thoughts and write and try to understand with consciousness until the Ellicottville coffee house closed; that I'd get roaring hammered in one of the pubs and walk the streets of the town shouting at myself for hours; that I'd be standing in a shadowy street at four in the morning with a phone in my hand, and that nothing of that talk would at the heart of my being surprise me.

"This better be good," he answered thickly.

"Rick, who got him?" I said. "Who got Big Green?"

"Who said he got got?"

"Rick, Big Green is gone. It was Ed Jamison, wasn't it?"

"People die all the time. They also talk all the time. Can it wait?"

"Rick, I have to understand it." I must have been stammering. "It was Ed Jamison. I know it. The war was over, and Big Green had won, and nothing else should have been able to happen. Because of balance, because things were even. But Ed Jamison got him. He stood up and answered the bell. He sent one of those *things*. Maybe I even saw it. But why? How? Rick, you told me that a medicine man or woman might be able to call up one of these curses, these animal *things*. Ed Jamison was no medicine man."

"How would you know?"

"Rick, answer my question."

He waited. "There's a thought that any Iroquois can do it."

"But what does that do to the balance?" I said. "I thought that's what this was all about. That was why things were even with Uncle Peter's death. That was why he was cool with them. That was why we had to back off. Why could Ed Jamison get in one more shot?"

"Because something in the deal he made kept things even." He waited for me to think about it, but I was already babbling.

"But he's *dead*, Rick. He was dead before Big Green..." And as if I could hear his mind saying, 'Precisely,' I got it. It landed on me.

A life for a life. I didn't know if it would be enough to tip the scales of the Nation's destiny, but this had been the trade. I'd never heard of it in Iroquois magic, but it was no stretch of imagination to think that someone who wanted to take a life in a single occult stroke might be able to do it with the instant trade of his own. It was only fair; it was one more way that an offended party could get some justice against all the odds. It made metaphysical sense, and it was one more of the equalizing factors I'd often noted in Iroquois thought. There was always an out, a joker in the deck. The moment of its realization was made no lighter.

I could imagine the ceremony whose details I was sure I would never know. Possibly it was guided, surely solitary at the climactic moment in which the old Seneca had given his life. Gun, noose, or knife? Had he simply willed himself to go over? Or did the unimaginable ritual know what was asked and suck his life away for him? What images came to him by the fire, by himself in the deep woods, alone in his cabin? Were they his ancestors? His ancestors' demons? Their angels? Did he wish he had done better with his life? Did the shadows soar over him, behind him?

As the enormity of the situation came over me, the human side of it settled in. I felt an immediate, overwhelming pity for the poor sot, of a famous Iroquois family, living as a clown to the bottle, who had given his life in a stroke to avenge his friend and mentor in the traditional way. I'd thought my tears were dry for all Iroquois friends, and that the few I had left were for losses in my own family, but they welled again. "'No greater love,' I guess they say."

"That was the kind of feeling my Uncle Peter could inspire," said

Rick. "He was a man of power. You forget he tutored Mad Bear."

But my mind was working again. "Ed Jamison was no 'man of power.'"

"How would you know?"

"He was a walking still. He would have been lucky to live another year. That's a faint life to trade for Big Green."

"How would you know?"

"This was all supposed to be about balance, Rick. How is that balance? A harmless lush trading himself for a man of power? A sick life over in months balanced against a bold one in its prime? That's a jalopy swapped for a new 'Vette. Couldn't pull that off anyplace else."

"It could be more balanced than you know," said Rick. He knew I was hurt and just trying to understand, but he sounded mad in a way I'd never heard before. We argue about history and politics all the time and I'd never gotten the sense that our friendship was in the balance; but I'd never pushed with anything before when I was told to stay out, and as I heard him reflecting, drawing his breath, I could feel it all - with any chance of my understanding - on the scales. Then he spoke.

"You know, the categories we humans put each other into don't matter very much in the big picture. Sooner or later it all gets stripped away. Maybe there's something about any human life, even one that isn't lived the way you think it ought to be, that is respected at all the levels of power-making; and the decision to give a life, to cut off even one single moment of it and jump into an uncertain forever, may be a trump card where the real judging gets done. There could also be something in this that you were supposed to learn. The sooner you let it start settling in the better. Now let me get some sleep. One of us works at eight."

All that I would hear in hours to come and remember to this day like it was this morning; but all that I would live in imagination as I drove that melon twilight, staring into the smoky trees and the sunset sky. Into the tangerine horizon on pipistrelle wings my mind would soar, out above the charcoal valley with its winking lights like diamonds on a felt display. I would think of all the bright and the strange, the inspiration and misery, the humanity and livid horror I had encountered in my years within the twilight of my small depressed region; I'd think of my own sadness and loss, and almost cry for the shortness of human life and the tragedies in the world; and a message of hope, of meaning, would come to me, almost as if the last bolt of sunlight, the drop of sun past horizon, the snap of parallax, were something musical, a stroke of tone rich and final, the gaudy conclusion to a symphony of renewal, of music that sunset hue.

That was the message of the low-sky-gold, a final assertion of the light and life against the reality of this day's certain end, and a promise of its continued dwelling apart and rebirth into another in spite. That was untouchable glory, but so is every stroke of this world around us. Sometimes it's so hard to see: the wonder that exists in our glorious earth, in all life, in each human life; the subtle, lasting, individual light that holds inside each one of us, I have come to believe.

CREDITS:

The point of this book has been to represent paranormal cases but to cloud circumstances so that neither the individuals involved nor those who have helped me with the "hot" material can be identified. Tributing them by name would hardly serve that purpose. They know who they are, and I thank them again. The following is an incomplete list of those who have helped with other nuts and bolts of the work. I thank:

Donata Ahern
Michael Bastine
Dr. Patricia Bell
George Besch
Dr. Anna Bloomer
Mike Brown
Tony and Liane Browning
Kathy Maher Burgin
Cassandra Butler
Sue Conklin
Tom Cratsley
Dr. Michael Galang
Paul Gromosiak

Daniel Harms
Sabrina and Rob Kane
Jerry Kegler
Steve Krastev
Larry Laprell
Franklin Lavoie
Martin Leal
Mike and Sherry Lesner
Sig Lonegren
Vince Martonis
Rebecca Murphy
Bill Nye
Natalie Price

Sallie Randolph
Ron Robertson
Robert Rust
Dr. F. Fero Sadeghian
Jenny Schneider
Kelly Schutrum
Solutions Plus
Rodger Sweetland
Elizabeth Thrasher
Edythe Turgeon
Robert and Ruth Wells
and
Frances Ward Winfield

and especially the artists, without whom this book... etc.:

FRONT COVER: DRAWING: SUSAN CARROLL
                PHOTOGRAPHY: KEN CAREW, PAUL CUMBO
The Twelfth Medallion: DRAWING: SUSAN CARROLL
                PHOTOGRAPHY: PAUL CUMBO
The Little People: PHOTOGRAPHY: KEN CAREW
Medicated Goo: DRAWING: SUSAN CARROLL
                PHOTOGRAPHY: PAUL CUMBO
The Voice from the Woods: PHOTOGRAPHY: KEN CAREW
Pickle-worms: PHOTOGRAPHY: KEN CAREW, PAUL CUMBO
A Sitting for Isabel: PHOTOGRAPHY: KEN CAREW, PAUL CUMBO
The Heart of a Black Bird: "IROQUOIS WITCHES" DRAWING: LAURA WILDER
"My Vengeance Lurks": DRAWING: SUSAN CARROLL
The Ho-ho Killers: "JACK THE RIPPER" DRAWING: LAURA WILDER;
                ADDITIONAL IMAGE: SUSAN CARROLL
The Whistlers: DRAWING: SUSAN CARROLL
                PHOTOGRAPHY: KEN CAREW, PAUL CUMBO
Soul out of My Soul: PHOTOGRAPHY: PAUL CUMBO
Bigfoot at Black Creek: DRAWING: SUSAN CARROLL
                PHOTOGRAPHY: KEN CAREW, PAUL CUMBO
A Question of Levels: DRAWING: SUSAN CARROLL
                PHOTOGRAPHY: KEN CAREW
BACK COVER: ALL ARTISTS

COMPUTER IMAGING: KEN CAREW AND ICE MOON STUDIOS' REGINA BARRY
'THE FINISHING TOUCH': TIM BAILEY, S & G PRESS

PHOTOGRAPH: PAUL CUMBO

THE AUTHOR:

Teacher and writer Mason Winfield studied English and Classics at Denison University and earned a master's degree in British literature at Boston College. For thirteen years he taught at the Gow School (South Wales, NY), an independent boarding school for dyslexic boys. While at Gow he served as English Department chairman, coached three sports, was ranked several times among the Buffalo area's top ten tennis players, and won a 50K cross-country ski marathon. His first book *Shadows of the Western Door* ("Haunted Sites and Ancient Mysteries of Upstate New York") was published by Western New York Wares in October 1997. He plans others inspired by Celtic tradition, East Aurora's Roycroft community, and the lore of the Six Nations. A sequel to *Shadows* is likely early in the new millennium, and cases of the sort that have made *Ghosthunter* are still developing.

Birth of a Publishing Company

The Buffalo area's most innovative publishing company will celebrate its 20th anniversary in 2004 by hitting a benchmark that few regional publishing houses achieve. By that time, Western New York Wares Inc. will have moved more than 175,000 books and other regional products into homes, schools and libraries around the world.

If all these books were laid cover-to-cover starting at the foot of Main Street near HSBC Center, the trail would stretch past the UB South Campus, snake through Williamsville, Clarence, Akron Falls Park and end somewhere around Batavia! Putting it a different way, we've printed and distributed about 21 million pages of information about our region. An impressive path for a company that sprouted its roots in trivial turf!

The year was 1984. The trivia craze was taking the nation by storm. Buffalo journalist Brian Meyer played a popular trivia game with friends in his North Buffalo living room, he envisioned a game that tests players' knowledge about people and events in their hometown. Western New York Trivia Quotient sold out its first edition in six weeks and established Meyer as an up-and-coming young entrepreneur.

A year later, he compiled a book of quotations that chronicled the feisty reign of Mayor Jimmy Griffin. Meyer refuses to disclose how many six-packs were consumed while sifting through hundreds of "Griffinisms."

A City Hall reporter for the *Buffalo News*, Meyer spent 15 years at WBEN Radio where he served as managing editor. As founder and president of Western New York Wares Inc., Meyer has collaborated with dozens of authors, artists and photographers. By 2003, the region's premier publisher of local books had published, marketed, or distributed more than 100 regional products.

A Buffalo native and graduate of Marquette University, St. Joseph's Collegiate Institute and Buffalo Public School #56, Meyer teaches communications courses at Buffalo State and Medaille Colleges and is treasurer of the Greater Buffalo Society of Professional Journalists' Scholarship Fund.

Meyer is assisted by Michele Ratzel, the company's business manager, and Tom Connolly, manager of marketing and distribution. The trio has nearly 45 years of cumulative experience in regional publishing. Connolly works as a news anchor and producer at WBEN Radio and co-authored *Hometown Heroes: Western New Yorkers in Desert Storm*. Ratzel works at the Park School of Buffalo.

Other Regional Books

Visit our Web site at www.Buffalobooks.com for a complete list of titles distributed by Western New York Wares Inc.

Shadows of the Western Door: Haunted Sites and Ancient Mysteries of Upstate New York – A supernatural safari across Western New York. Guided by the insights of modern research, author Mason Winfield pens a colorful, provocative and electrifying study of the paranormal.
ISBN: 1-879201-22-4 $13.95

Spirits of the Great Hill: More Haunted Sites and Ancient Mysteries of Upstate New York – Does a historic curse linger over the Niagara Frontier? Was Buffalo designed by occult societies? From Mark Twain's Buffalo ghost, to Houdini's Halloween, Mason Winfield pens a riveting sequel to his supernatural survey of the region.
ISBN: 1-879201-35-6 $13.95

A Ghosthunter's Journal: Tales of the Supernatural and the Strange in Upstate New York - A delightfully diverse smorgasbord of strange encounters, all of them set in Western New York. The 13 fictional stories are inspired by the files of Mason Winfield.
ISBN: 1-879201-29-1 $12.95

Buffalo Memories: Gone But Not Forgotten -- Blessed with a phenomenal memory, the late George Kunz began chronicling his recollections of his Depression upbringing. His anecdotes on everything from Bisons' games at Offermann Stadium to rides on the Canadiana and shopping excursions to 998 Broadway graced the pages of the Buffalo News. This book is a collection of about 200 of these anecdotes.
ISBN: 0-9671480-9-X $15.00

Victorian Buffalo: Images From the Buffalo and Erie County Public Library – Visit Buffalo as it looked in the 19th century through steel engravings, woodcuts, lithography and other forms of nonphotographic art. Author Cynthia VanNess has selected scenes that showcase everyday life and views of historic structures created by luminaries like Frank Lloyd Wright, Louis Sullivan and E.B. Green.
ISBN: 1-879201-30-5 $13.95

The Erie Canal: The Ditch That Opened a Nation -- Despite its shallow depth, the Erie Canal carries an amazing legacy. In canal towns like Lockport and Tonawanda the doors to the American frontier were unlocked. Written by Daniel T. Murphy, including dozens of photos.
ISBN: 1-879201-34-8 $8.95

Erie Canal Legacy: Architectural Treasures of the Empire State -- Photographer Andy Olenick and author Richard O. Reisem take readers on a 363-mile journey along the canal route. This hardcover book is comprised of full-color photos and an enlightening text.
ISBN: 0-9641706-6-3 $39.95

National Landmarks of Western New York: Famous People and Historic Places -- Gracious mansions and thundering waterfalls. Battleships and nostalgic fireboats. Power plants and Indian longhouses. Author Jan Sheridan researched nearly 30 National Historic Landmarks in the Buffalo-Niagara and Finger Lakes regions. Dozens of photographs, maps and an index.
ISBN: 1-879201-36-4 $9.95

Beyond Buffalo: A Photographic Journey and Guide to the Secret Natural Wonders of our Region – Full color photographs and informative vignettes showcase 30 remarkable sites. Author David Reade also includes directions and tips for enjoying each site.
ISBN: 1-879201-19-4 $19.95
Western New York Weather Guide – Readers won't want any "winteruptions" as they breeze through this lively book written by former Channel 7 weather guru Tom Jolls. Co-authored by Brian Meyer and Joseph VanMeer, the book focuses on historic and humorous weather events over the past century.
ISBN: 1-879201-18-1 $7.95
White Death: Blizzard of '77 – This 356-page softcover book chronicles one of the region's most dramatic historical events. Written by Erno Rossi, the book includes more than 60 photographs.
ISBN: 0-920926-03-7 $16.95
Great Lake Effects: Buffalo Beyond Winter and Wings – A unique cookbook filled with intriguing historical facts about the region. The hardcover book has been compiled by the Junior League of Buffalo.
ISBN: 1-879201-18-1 $18.95
Buffalo Treasures: A Downtown Walking Guide – Take a fascinating tour of 25 major buildings. A user-friendly map, dozens of illustrations by Kenneth Sheridan, and an enlightening text by Jan Sheridan.
ISBN: 1-879201-15-1 $4.95
Church Tales of the Niagara Frontier: Legends, History & Architecture – A first-of-a-kind book tracing the rich history and folklore of the region through accounts of 60 area churches and sacred places. Written by the late Austin M. Fox. Illustrated by Lawrence McIntyre.
ISBN : 1-879201-13-5 $14.95
Symbol & Show: The Pan-American Exposition of 1901 -- A riveting look at the greatest event in Buffalo's history. Written by the late Austin M. Fox and illustrated by Lawrence McIntyre, this book offers a lively assessment of the Exposition, bringing to light many forgotten facts.
 ISBN: 1-879201-33-X $15.95
Frank Lloyd Wright's Darwin D. Martin House: Rescue of a Landmark -- The untold story of the abandonment and rescue of the region's most architecturally-significant home. In vivid detail by Marjorie L. Quinlan. Includes color photos and detailed architectural plans.
 ISBN: 1-879201-32-1 $13.95
Buffalo's Brush With the Arts: From Huck Finn to Murphy Brown – A fascinating adventure behind the manuscripts and million-dollar book deals, highlighting the Niagara Frontier's connection to many creative geniuses. Authored by Joe Marren, the book contains more than 20 photographs from the Courier-Express Collection.
ISBN: 1-879201-24-0 $7.95
Classic Buffalo: A Heritage of Distinguished Architecture -- A stunning hardcover book tributes the region's architectural heritage. Striking full-color photographs by Andy Olenick & an engaging text by Richard O. Reisem make this coffee-table book a keepsake for history buffs.
ISBN: 0-9671480-06 $39.95

Uncrowned Queens: African American Women Community Builders of Western New York. Historians Peggy Brooks-Bertram and Dr. Barbara Seals Nevergold celebrate the accomplishments of African American women. Some are well-known; others are newly recognized.
ISBN: 0-9722977-0-7 $11.95

Buffalo's Waterfront : A Guidebook – Edited by Tim Tielman. A user-friendly guide showcasing over 100 shoreline sites. Includes a handy fold-out map. Published by the Preservation Coalition of Erie County.
ISBN: 1-879201-00-3 $5.95

Tale of the Tape: A History of the Buffalo Bills From the Inside – Eddie "Abe" Abramoski reflects on scores on humorous, emotional and enlightening anecdotes that stretch back to the first Bills training camp in East Aurora. Many photos accompany the lively text.
ISBN: 1-879201-41-0 $10.95

Bodyslams in Buffalo: The Complete History of Pro Wrestling In Western New York – Author Dan Murphy traces the region's rich wrestling history, from Ilio DiPaolo and Dick "The Destroyer" Beyer to Adorable Adrian Adonis. Dozens of photos.
ISBN: 1-879201-42-9 $9.95

Game Night in Buffalo: A Town, Its Teams and Its Sporting Memories -- Sal Maiorana chronicles momentous events that have shaped Buffalo fandom. Includes the Bills, Sabres, Bisons, Braves, and college basketball. Dozens of vintage photos.
ISBN: 1-879201-44-5 $13.95

Goat Island: Niagara's Scenic Retreat – Historian Paul Gromosiak explores the people, attractions, animals and plants that makes the islands above Niagara Falls a fascinating destination. The book includes color photos and a detailed map.
ISBN: 1-879201-43-7 $9.95

Nature's Niagara: A Walk on the Wild Side – Learn more about the wildlife, plants and geology at Niagara Falls. Written by Paul Gromosiak, the book includes many full-color photographs and maps.
ISBN: 1-879201-31-3 $8.95

Daring Niagara: 50 Death-Defying Stunts at the Falls. Paul Gromosiak pens a heart-stopping adventure about those who barreled, boated, even bicycled to fame. The book includes vintage photos.
ISBN: 1-879201-23-2 $6.95

Niagara Falls Q&A: Answers to the 100 Most Common Questions About Niagara Falls. -- Author Paul Gromosiak spent four summers chatting with 40,000 Falls tourists. This invaluable guide answers 100 commonly-asked questions. Includes photos, many in color.
ISBN: 0-9620314-8-8 $4.50

Please include 8.25% sales tax for all orders in New York. Also include shipping charges: Orders under $25: $3; $25-$49: $4.00; $50-more: $5.00.
Visit our Web site at: www.Buffalobooks.com or write for a catalog:
Western New York Wares Inc.
P.O. Box 733
Ellicott Station
Buffalo, New York 14205